UNTAMED REAPER

AN URBAN FANTASY

ANN GIMPEL

CONTENTS

Untamed Reaper 1

Book Description, Untamed Reaper 3

Books in the Gatekeeper Series 5

Author's Note 7

1. Chapter One, Cait 9

2. Chapter Two, Liam 25

3. Chapter Three, Cait 37

4. Chapter Four, Liam 53

5. Chapter Five, Cait 67

6. Chapter Six, Liam 81

7. Chapter Seven, Cait 97

8. Chapter Eight, Liam 109

9. Chapter Nine, Cait 123

10. Chapter Ten, Liam 139

11. Chapter Eleven, Cait 155

12. Chapter Twelve, Liam 171

13. Chapter Thirteen, Cait 185

14. Chapter Fourteen, Liam 199

15. Chapter Fifteen, Cait 215

16. Chapter Sixteen, Liam 231

17. Chapter Seventeen, Cait 243

18. Chapter Eighteen, Liam 257

19. Chapter Nineteen, Cait 271

20. Chapter Twenty, Liam 287

21. Chapter Twenty-One, Cait 299

Epilogue 313

Book Description, Timespell 323

Timespell, Chapter One 325

About the Author   339
Also by Ann Gimpel   341

An Urban Fantasy

**By
Ann Gimpel**

Tumble off reality's edge into myth, magic, and Death

I did it! I'm free. Well sort of. Freedom isn't as cut and dried as the word implies. In this case, I'm at the top of Death's Worst Reaper Ever list. What it signifies remains to be seen.

I broke free from Death because there wasn't any other way out of Reaping Vampires. She refused to let me off the hook or consider other arrangements. I'd have been content leaving it at that, but word about my choice got out. Other Reapers clamored for independence too.

Death's fury expanded another notch with every defection until nowhere is far enough away for me to run to. If I was only fighting her, it might be manageable. Toss in Vampires who hate my guts, a phalanx of dark gods who want my hide, and a bunch of bigoted mortals who've decided magic is holding them back.

Pah. Humans are their own worst enemy, but they're the least of my problems.

It's been a rocky journey. Along the way I've uncovered allies and even a man who loves me. Will we be enough to slam the gates and send darkness packing?

We have to be.

No prisoners.

No choices.

BOOKS IN THE GATEKEEPER SERIES

Shadow Reaper, Book One
Rebel Reaper, Book Two
Untamed Reaper, Book Three

AUTHOR'S NOTE

After a million dragon books, I'm branching out. Good to cross-train that muse of mine. The concept of the Grim Reaper has fascinated me for years. I used to work for a residency program where I taught bedside manners to newly minted doctors. A few of them were quite sensitive to supernatural phenomena, and they'd come into my office and talk with me about sensing Death's presence before a patient passed.

They'd also talk with me about the numinous aspect of both birth and death.

Fast forward the clock a few years to *Supernatural*. Sam and Dean dealt with both Death and Reapers—until Dean killed off Death in I believe season ten. Then it's mostly Reapers.

A Reaper tale has been running around in my mind for quite a while. I hope you enjoy the Gatekeeper Series.

CHAPTER ONE, CAIT

The Cessna 172 dipped and banked to counteract a stiff wind. I sat in the right seat keeping a close eye on Liam. He'd asked for flight lessons, and he had real aptitude, but only because he cheated.

"Uh-uh." I resisted shaking a finger at him.

He turned his arresting hazel gaze my way and asked, "Uh-uh, what?" as if he was the soul of innocence. White-blond hair streamed down his back, secured by a length of leather at the nape of his neck.

I stifled a snort. "You're using magic to keep the plane straight and level. An infusion of air beneath the right wing, to put a finer point on it."

His lips parted in a "so sue me" smile. Damn, it was hard to be angry with him when he looked like that. "Does it truly matter how I master this?" He furled his blond brows and cast a sidelong glance my way.

I lacked a ready reply, so I said, "Turn sixty degrees left and take us up another thousand feet."

The little plane responded so readily to him, it almost made me jealous. I have magic of my own, but it had never occurred to me to employ it while I was learning to fly. Now, sure, but not a hundred years ago.

I fell in love with the concept of flight not long after the Wright brothers' historic trip above Kitty Hawk, and I've been hanging around one airstrip or another ever since.

Liam trimmed the plane up and asked, "What's next?"

"Stall it," I said.

He frowned. "You have to say more than that."

"Tip the nose up until the plane starts to shudder then return to straight-and-level flight."

"Like this?" He tugged the yoke toward him, and the nose floated upward. Soon the stall horn blared a warning. "Handy," he muttered and tapped the yoke.

"Indeed. The plane lets you know before you fall out of the sky."

"Would that really happen?"

"What do you think?" I countered.

He scrunched his forehead. "Seems like at some point the wings would work as airfoils again."

"You guessed right."

He made a rather male sound that reminded me of a grunt. "Why do you suppose it was a guess?"

Rather than answering, I grinned and asked, "Ready for your first landing?" At his nod, I outlined the mechanics of flying a pattern. "Once you get better," I said, "you'll be able to set a flight path and come in straight, but it's simpler to judge speed and height when you fly downwind, crosswind, and final legs."

I stopped talking and left it to him to figure things out. We were a little lower than I'd have liked on our final approach, but he added a cushion of air to fix things.

"You did really well." Enthusiasm lined my words.

"Coming from you, I bet that's high praise." He taxied the plane off the runway and headed for the hangar.

"I thought about what you said," I murmured as we buttoned up the aircraft. It needed fuel before its next flight, but I could take care of that later. Who knew when I'd have this plane in the air again. For that fact, who knew when I'd get back to Seattle and *Carrick Sky Sports*.

"Which thing?" Liam stepped close and wrapped his arms around me.

"You addle my brain when you're that close." I dipped from beneath his embrace. "I've been thinking about employing magic to help you control the plane. There's nothing wrong with it, except it kind of feels like cheating."

"How so?"

I clasped my hands together. "What if something really went wrong?"

"If I couldn't fix it, I'd teleport out of there."

"How hard would you try to fix it?" I pressed.

He nodded, his smile fading. "Point taken," he rumbled in his deep, rich voice.

"Don't get me wrong," I went on. "Not much that magic can't repair, at least temporarily. Air provides float, and water will cool an overheated engine. What it won't do is tell you precisely what's wrong. If you don't know—because you never bothered to learn the mechanics of flight and how each part of the airplane keeps it airborne—the magic you apply will be a Band-Aid. It might get you on the ground, but then you won't have the first idea how to fix your bird."

He curled a hand around my forearm. His touch felt amazing. That's the thing about brand-new lovers, everything about them is intoxicating. I could look at him forever, breathe in his sandalwood-and-damp-greenery scent, listen to the music of his voice.

And hunger for more.

"How about if I do both?" he suggested. "Learn the traditional way but keep the door open to filling in with magic."

"Perfect. It's exactly what I do." I angled my head and regarded him. "Do you want to get licensed?"

"Is it like getting a license to drive a car?"

"More or less," I replied. "There's a written test and an in-the-air test and a few tasks in between like a flight physical and getting a student pilot certificate."

"How long would it take?"

"Minimum is forty hours," I told him. "At least twenty with an instructor and ten solo hours."

"Looks like I have my first hour. Do I get credit for when we flew to Canada?"

"It might be arranged. As I recall, I did a bit of teaching on that flight too."

His forehead crinkled in what I'd come to recognize as his thoughtful expression. "Sure. I'll give it my best shot, but it might not happen for a while."

This time it was me who tossed my arms around him. He laughed and stroked a lock of hair back from my face. "Most women want gemstones and flowers."

"Airplanes all the way for me," I murmured from where my face was buried in the crook of his neck.

"I'll keep it in mind."

Almost as if it had heard me and was jealous, my scythe clattered to the floor next to me. I picked it up and propped it over my shoulder. Up until recently, I hadn't seen the Reaper tool for months. Something about me claiming the full spectrum of my power had encouraged the silver-gray implement to not only become visible, but to follow me around.

"I noticed it behind the rear bank of seats," Liam said.

I had too, even though I hadn't carried it aboard.

We strolled out of the hangar, arm in arm; I locked it behind us. "Have you heard from anyone?"

He shook his head. "It worries me a little. This is our second day here, and I have checked my email a couple of times. Unless there's anything else pressing you want to attend to, we should head back to Scotland."

I'd been surprised we hadn't seen Death, but I kept my thoughts buried. Saying her name out loud might encourage her to appear.

"Taking the plane up wasn't urgent. It was an indulgence," I murmured.

"Maybe not."

Something about his tone caught my attention. "You've been expecting Vamps to show up, haven't you?"

He nodded. "It's a reasonable expectation, since they've swarmed your office every other time we've been here. Humans Rule knows about you too."

I winced. After a plane got into trouble, I'd engaged in a very public display of magic to ensure no one got hurt. A few people thanked me, well, more than a few, but shortly afterward delegates from HR—a bunch of bigots who badmouth magic by day and practice it by night—visited my office accompanied by Vamps and one of the dark gods.

Probably hadn't helped I'd outed myself, announcing I was a Reaper to whoever might be on the field that day. "Surely someone has figured out we're here," I muttered.

"My assessment as well," Liam said. "Not sure what it means they've let us be."

I sent a jolt of magic to open the door of the Quonset hut I use for an office, intent on grabbing my bag so we could leave. "Do you want to teleport from inside?" I kept my voice low.

"Better than vanishing in plain sight," he agreed.

The sound of footsteps slapping against asphalt sent me spinning to see who was running straight toward us.

Kiko Tanaka, one of my closest friends, ran as if demons dogged her heels. Slight, with mounds of dark, straight hair, she's a pharmacist who loves to fly. I met her years ago at a mixer for pilots and the various businesses peppering the airstrip. Usually, she wore jeans and sweaters, but today she hadn't taken the time to change out of her scrubs from the pharmacy.

The scythe winked out of sight.

"Thank God you're here," she panted and skidded to a stop in front of Liam and me. "I've tried and tried to call you. Must've left you twenty messages."

I took one look at her and grabbed an arm, dragging her inside the Quonset hut. Liam followed us and shut the door. I felt the bite of his magic as he erected a hasty ward and sound screen.

"Sorry," I said. "First I was away, and recently I haven't

been checking my phone. I closed my business for two weeks, so it didn't seem as important."

The harsh rasp of her breathing pounded against me. I've known Kiko for years, and she's not the excitable type. Like most pilots, she's normally stoic and unflappable. I waited until she stopped gasping for breath before I asked, "What happened?"

Her pupils were so dilated, I wondered if she'd sampled some of her own wares. More likely, she was just frightened.

"This is going to sound nuts," she said in a high, thin voice that didn't sound much like her, "but someone's been following me, watching me."

Breath hissed from my lungs. Crap. Fuck. Were Vampires —or Humans Rule—going to start targeting everyone who knew me? So much for my flight school. One of my concerns had been putting my students at risk.

"Tell us more," Liam urged, clearly not worried about *Carrick Sky Sports*. Why would he be? Good thing one of us was rational.

Kiko blew out a long, noisy breath. "Maybe a week ago I got a creeped-out feeling when I went from my car into the pharmacy. I was working the late shift, so it was just getting dark. I tried to tell myself I was being foolish, that nothing was out there, but"—she trained her dark eyes on me—"you've taught me magic is real."

"Why'd you think it was something magical?" I asked. "And not some pervert stalking you?"

"Same thing I asked myself all through my eight-hour shift. Never did come up with anything definitive. It was past midnight when I got off, and I requested one of the security guards to walk me to my car."

"Good call," I murmured.

"Yeah, except I felt like a total wimp." She shut her eyes for a moment. When she opened them, she kept talking. "Driving home was okay, but once I'd parked near my unit I had the same feeling, a sense I was being stalked. My apartment complex has security too, so I called and waited for one of the guys to escort me into the building. Told him I was worried about being shaken down for drugs."

Kiko straightened her back until she stood as tall as her five-feet-two-inch frame allowed. "Every day, it's gotten worse until I have to psych myself up to leave my house. Whatever it is doesn't feel human. There's a smell..."

I battled a sinking sensation and leaned closer. "Describe it."

She crinkled her nose. "It's horrible. Fetid. Rotten."

"Vampires," Liam growled. "Has to be."

Kiko's eyes widened. "Erm, they're real? They're not on the list with witches and druids and the rest of them."

I still had hold of her arm. "It's not a them," I reminded her. "It's an us."

She blinked and looked at Liam. "Figures you'd be something too. What are you?" She made a face. "Sorry, that didn't come out quite like I wanted."

"Stop worrying about being politically correct," I said. "Liam is a Sidhe."

"Like a faery?" She directed her gaze at her feet. "Don't you guys have wings?"

"That would be the Fae and only a few varieties of them," he told her with only the slightest hint of humor riding beneath his words.

"Not important," she said. "I've been drugging myself to

sleep. By earlier today, I almost had myself convinced I'd hallucinated the whole thing."

Oh-oh.

"What happened?" Liam and I blurted almost in unison.

Kiko swept a hank of hair to one side displaying obvious fang marks over one of her jugular veins. "These were there when I woke up. Freaked the fuck out of me. When you said Vampires, everything clicked. One of them came into my house. While I was asleep. And I didn't even wake up. Don't locks keep them out? Christ, Cait. Am I going to turn into one of them?" Her dark eyes sheened with tears.

"No to both questions." Liam kept his voice soothing. "Locks aren't much of a deterrent to anything magical, and you won't turn into a Vampire. That's a two-stage process. They'd have to drain you to the point of death—and you wouldn't sleep through that. Then you'd have to drink their blood. Right now, the biggest problem is they've marked you."

"Ewww." Tears spilled over. "Why me? What did I ever do?"

I felt like crying too. "Nothing. You did nothing. Your only crime was associating with me," I told her. "It's me they want."

"Can I get rid of this mark thing?" She turned toward Liam. I did as well since I didn't have an answer for her.

"Maybe. The question is where we should go to finesse eradicating it. It will be dark soon, and Vampires know about this spot."

They knew about my houseboat too. And obviously, Kiko's apartment. "Why do we need a spot they haven't discovered?" I looked Liam's way.

"To give us time to undo their actions. They put a ball into play. They won't take kindly to me dismantling it."

"Even if you do," Kiko wailed, "what's to stop them from sneaking into my house again?" She dropped her head into her hands. "I can't stay there anymore. I don't feel safe."

"What will we need to fix Kiko?" I glanced at Liam. "And how long will it take? Hey. Would that deserted storefront work?"

He snapped his fingers. "I'd forgotten about it. Aye, 'twould be perfect. I'll require an hour, more or less."

"Death knows about that spot," I reminded him.

"Aye, but she doesn't have a pony in this race," he replied.

"What deserted shop?" Kiko asked in a strangled-sounding voice. If she was freaked out now, things weren't going to get better for her over the next hour or two.

I bent so we were closer to eye level. "It's an empty shop maybe half a mile from my houseboat. We need a spot the Vampires don't know about, which rules out my home, your home, and this place." I swung an arm wide.

Before she could say anything else, I continued. "We will use a magical spell to move us from here to there. The moment we arrive, Liam and I will ward—er, protect—the place and shield it from prying eyes and ears. Then he will use magic to hopefully undo what the Vampires did last night."

"As in plural?" Kiko shrilled. "There was more than one of them?"

"We don't know." Liam added a dash of a calming spell to his words. "If we're fortunate, I can shield you from future attacks, but I'm not as certain of that."

Kiko's eyes had grown big. "I don't have to do any of this, right?"

I nodded. "It's your choice, but if you don't let us help you, what will you do instead?"

"Run away," she said in a small voice.

"Vampires are everywhere," I told her, wanting to make certain she understood. "They have a way of communicating with one another."

"Damned if I do, damned if I don't, huh?"

"About the size of it. I'm sorry," I told her.

"I know you are. You were honest with me, and being friends was my choice. I could have walked after you told me you were a Reaper."

"If we're going to leave, we have to go now." Liam's voice was uncharacteristically sharp.

"Why?" Kiko asked.

My nostrils twitched, picking up the roadkill stench of Vamps. They were closing on us. "Because Vampires aren't far away."

Her head swung from side to side. "But I don't see any."

"They're traveling through channels not accessible to mortals," Liam said. Magic crackled around him as he called a teleport spell.

I grabbed my shoulder bag and snatched my silver-and-iron-infused Vampire killing blade from my locker. A stifled gasp from Kiko said more than words would have. She was about to plummet headfirst into a world she'd had no idea existed.

Apologies died on my lips. We had to get out of here. I cracked my magical center open, offering Liam assistance, and the Quonset hut dropped away, replaced by the dusty deserted shopfront where he and I had taken refuge one night. We'd been spying on Humans Rule and had needed a spot to regroup.

"Why do Vampires hate you?" Kiko asked, keeping her

voice low as she turned in a circle and examined the empty store.

"Because part of my job is sealing them behind the veil separating Earth from the realm of the dead. They might be dead, but they like it here and have no intention of leaving. Not under their own steam."

"Sorry I asked," she muttered. "Geez. What else don't I know about?"

"Lots," Liam said succinctly. He moved next to Kiko, but didn't touch her. "Do you request my magical intervention of your own free will?"

"What is this?" She came as close to smiling as she had since she'd run up to us. "A disclaimer in case shit goes awry?"

"Nay. Working magic on mortals is forbidden unless they specifically request us to do so."

"Got it," she said, followed by, "Yes, I want your help. Please."

"Good enough." He placed one hand on her shoulder, the other on her head. "This won't hurt, and you shouldn't remember anything."

"I don't like the not remembering part," she mumbled just before she sagged against him.

He laid her on the floor and knelt next to her. Power flowed from his fingertips, and a numinous shroud took shape, encasing her from head to toe.

"Tell me what you need from me," I murmured.

"Keep your magic accessible."

I wanted to ask what he was doing but was afraid to interrupt his concentration. Minutes clicked by. A lot of them. I felt a tug on my power from time to time. The shroud changed colors. Sometimes Liam chanted, sometimes not. I kept tabs on

Kiko's soul. It looked healthy to me, and firmly tethered to her body. Somewhere along the way, my scythe made an appearance, leaning against a wall where it glowed softly.

Gradually, the fang marks vanished, replaced by smooth, ivory skin.

Liam rocked back on his heels, and the shroud dissipated into blue and violet streamers. Kiko opened her eyes with a start. "Was it successful?"

"You're no longer marked," Liam said.

Kiko reached for her neck, trailing fingertips over the spot the indentations had been. She struggled to sit. "Thank you so much."

"You're welcome," Liam replied and helped her to her feet. "It wasn't too bad. Healing isn't one of my natural talents, but I had a fallback position."

"Dena?" I furled my brows.

He nodded.

"Who's she?" Kiko glanced at me.

"A Sidhe in the Scottish Highlands. Fortunately, we don't need to travel there."

"Not sure how fortunate it is. I've always wanted to see Scotland." Kiko tried to joke, but she sounded tapped out.

Liam scooped up a chunk of what looked like quartz from a spot where the shroud had been. He handed it to Kiko. "I'm not certain how well this will perform, but I've matched it to your energy. Keep it with you at all times, and it should offer protection against Vampires."

"Will this make it okay for me to return home?" She took the stone from Liam and zipped it into her jacket.

"How about if you stay in hotels for a week or two?" I jumped in, not wanting anything else to happen to her.

"I can do that," she said. "I'd been considering it anyway. Um, guess I can take a taxi back to my car."

"Where exactly did you park?" I asked.

"Down by *The Tailwind*." She named the small restaurant at the far end of the airfield.

"I'll take you back to your car," I told her.

"And then meet me at the houseboat," Liam said. "We'll leave from there. I'll transport the blade."

"Leave for where?" Kiko's dark eyes skipped from him to me. She was a proud woman, but I could tell she was wondering what would happen if she needed us again.

"We'll be gone for a while," I told her. "If you run into problems, text me or email me."

"Neither works where we're going." Liam reminded me.

"Not right away," I corrected him, "but I'll be checking messages every day or two."

"Good enough," Kiko said. "I sure won't be talking with anyone else about any of this. They'd commit me."

I didn't know what to tell her. Apologies were inadequate, and shy of dragging her across the Atlantic, we'd done all we could. I draped an arm around her and visualized the airfield. My spell spit us out between two buildings not far from *The Tailwind*. I swathed us in invisibility and walked her to her car.

When we got there, she threw her arms around me. "Thanks, Cait. Don't blame yourself, please."

I hugged her back and smiled and said the right words while I made certain she got into her car and drove off without incident. No one was around to see her step beyond the boundaries of my spell as she entered her vehicle. When you cut to the chase, her run-in with Vampires was my fault. All my fault. Only my fault.

I shook my head and slid behind a hangar. My scythe took up its customary spot hooked over one shoulder. I wasn't competent enough to teleport from behind an invisibility casting. Not yet, so I dismantled it.

Kiko was safe for the moment, but any of the remaining dark mages could undo Liam's good work.

Fuck. What had happened to Kiko was unacceptable, and also beyond my control.

Who else would I put at risk before this was done?

CHAPTER TWO, LIAM

I straightened things up at the houseboat while I waited for Cait to return. We were close enough for her to employ telepathy if she ran into difficulties. The blade hadn't taken kindly to my touch, but it hadn't fought me, either. I'd dropped it in the mudroom and made myself a promise to wrap the hilt in something that offered more protection from the metals it had been forged with.

The development with Kiko was worrisome. We'd defeated two of the dark mages, Perrikus and D'Chel, a few days ago. Presumably they were locked in one of Hell's basements for the long haul. But the four who remained had turned up the heat. They assumed—and rightly—Cait would do damn near anything to keep someone like Kiko safe.

Lucky for us, we'd had a chance to intervene before the Vamps got their claws so deep into Kiko's soul, she'd have been seduced by their unholy beauty. Finished with cleaning the small living room and bedroom, I moved into the kitchen and splashed magic around to clear away the dirty dishes.

Neither Cait nor I had wanted to waste even one of the moments we'd stolen to be together. In between some of the most inspired sex in my long life, we'd raided her cupboards, her freezer, and resorted to ordering food in. Memories of almost nonstop lovemaking brought a grin to my face and stiffened my cock. The house was rich with Cait's heather-and-wildflower scent, and it took very little to imagine her in my arms, writhing with passion.

We were new as lovers. Very new. Still solidly within the phase where each time we were together unlocked more secrets. I was developing lists of things I wanted us to experiment with, and ways we'd been together that were so erotic, I couldn't wait to try them again.

Done flirting with getting hard, my cock made a commitment to a full-blown erection. I rearranged myself so my trousers weren't quite so uncomfortable and finished the kitchen chores. Losing myself in lustful imagery of a naked Cait, breasts splotched with patches of rose as desire spiraled out of control, was delightful, but not productive.

I forced my thoughts back to Kiko. What had the Vampires been thinking? That she wouldn't notice two fresh fang marks? They weren't the type of thing anyone could chalk up to insect bites. Eh, well maybe some people, but Kiko was a pilot—and a pharmacist. Two vocations where lack of attention to detail either put your life at risk, or someone else's.

I did a quick tally. Cait had shuttered *Carrick Sky Sports* for two weeks roughly six days ago. It gave us a small window where no one was likely to stop by her Quonset hut.

Aye, but that wasn't where Vampires had found Kiko. From

the sound of her story, they'd been tracking her for days before they finally struck. Who else did Cait know well enough to merit up close-and-personal Vampire attention?

I'd have to ask once she returned. Just because their attempt to nab Kiko had failed didn't mean they'd quit trying. Even if the magical talisman I made for her didn't offer complete protection, it would serve as an early warning device and alert her if she was in danger.

I made a note to text her with that bit of information. All I needed was Cait's phone and Kiko's number.

I moved to Cait's computer, set up in a corner of the living room, and brought up my primary email account. Ways existed to shield telepathy, but no one's magic was strong enough to use mind speech from two continents away. Any type of electronic communication was eminently hackable, maybe not by Vampires who weren't all that smart, but they had a variety of humans under fang control.

Wouldn't surprise me at all if they kept more than one computer hacker at their beck and call.

Unlike the machine in Cait's office, this one was older and took its sweet time booting up. By the time I was done with her personal identification code and all my credentials, a few more minutes had ticked past. I resisted rolling my eyes. All the fancy-schmancy username-and-password combos didn't really offer much protection at all.

They'd grown harder to navigate, though. Many sites required cell phone verification. Another reason I'd have to break down and get one of the blasted things one of these days.

Finally. My email scrolled down the screen. Amidst the junk, two looked interesting. I clicked open the first one, which turned out to be from Padhraic. Who would have guessed

JunkYardDog would be him? His missive was short and troublesome.

Time to return. Problems from within and without. Paddy

I told him I'd be back very soon and offered an estimate roughly ten hours from now. That gave Cait and me an hour of travel time and took the nine-hour time difference into consideration. Basically, we'd be in Scotland very early tomorrow morning.

Once I hit *Send,* I moved on to the next email. It turned out to be from Dena. Her screen name was Everyday_Goddess. She said much the same thing with a few more details.

D dropped in. Again. Wreaking havoc with the Rs. A & H just arrived. Not sure if it will help or hinder. Get back here. Dena

Interesting. Apparently, Death couldn't stay away. It would be very like her to slather guilt, hot and thick, over Reapers she assumed belonged to her. Except they didn't. A & H had to be Arawn and Hades, two of the gods of the dead. I wondered if Cerebrus, Hades' three-headed dog, had come with them.

The ungainly canine and Cait had a thing going. I suspected Cerebrus didn't allow too many people to fuss over him, but he welcomed Cait's touch.

I sensed her before she shimmered into corporeality a meter away, scythe slung over one shoulder next to her ever-present brown leather shoulder bag. After getting to my feet, I moved to her side and gathered her close. "Everything go all right?" I asked.

She nodded. "I'm worried about Kiko. This is deucedly unfair."

After one more lush moment where I reveled in the feel of

Cait in my arms, I let go. "I need your phone and Kiko's number."

"Sure. Why?" Cait tugged her phone out of a pocket and scrolled through her contact list, tapping the display. "There. Just type whatever you want to say here." She pointed. "Or tell me, and I can do it."

"Thanks. Those things look like they'd be hard to manage. My fingers are too big."

"No. They're not, but go ahead."

I thought about what to say that wouldn't frighten her half to death. "Tell her this. The stone also provides a warning. If it vibrates or grows warm, pay close attention."

Cait nodded and sent the message. Her phone chimed almost instantly.

What do I do then? Showed on its display.

"What should we tell her?" Two vertical lines formed between Cait's dark brows. "It's not like we're going to be here."

I took the phone and typed, *Lose yourself in the biggest crowd you can find. Remain until the stone is quiescent.*

"No wonder you've never taken to texting," Cait mumbled. "Too many big words."

Got it, flared across the tiny screen, and I gave the phone back to Cait.

She set the scythe in a corner and glanced around. "Thanks for cleaning up. It's never been one of my, erm, strong points."

"We need to go," I told her. "Death is back at Scourie Castle, and she's creating problems among the Reapers. Hades and Arawn just materialized, but it's too soon to tell what impact they'll have. Or what their motivation is for being there."

"I see. I'll change into something clean, and we can leave."

"Mind if I watch?"

She snorted laughter. "Yeah. I do. If you're anywhere near me when I'm naked, we'll never get out of here."

"True enough, wench." The enticing swing of her hips as she vanished down the hall was tough to resist. I returned to the computer and scanned the remainder of my emails. Nothing else critical, so I sent Dena essentially the same message I'd sent to Padhraic, and then I shut the machine off.

Cait strode back into the living room garbed in black pants, a colorful sweater in blues, greens, and purples, and a black jacket. The study, practical boots she favored graced her feet. More clothes were draped across one arm. Her leather flight jacket was still in my living room in Malin.

"Not sure when we'll be back here," she said. "While I appreciate your wardrobe selection, my own things fit better."

The scythe, apparently intuiting we were leaving, floated to where Cait stood and settled around her shoulders. She eyed it before shifting it to the other side to accommodate her leather bag and extra clothing.

I gathered the sword she'd taken from her locker and joined her in the living room. "Where'd this come from?" I tapped the blade.

"I had to hunt for it. Even harder was coming up with lessons in how to use it. I'm still not very adept."

I avoided commenting, In truth, I hoped she never got enough practice to develop that particular skillset.

"Some Sidhe must be good swordsmen," she persisted. "Maybe you?"

"We can work in a few lessons. Would you like to manage the journey spell?"

"I'd love to. Thrusting and parrying aren't the only skills I need practice with."

I kept a close eye on the progression of her magic as she built her spell. She was careful, which told me some of her earlier efforts had given her grief. When the casting was almost done, I motioned her to follow me out the door and onto her large, shadowy porch. Shielded from other houseboats and the street by awnings and its rounded architecture, it was a good spot to leave from.

While she put the finishing touches on the teleport spell, I patched up the warding around her houseboat. It wasn't absolute. No ward was. But it would tell me if anyone had attempted to breach it in our absence.

"This is getting easier," Cait murmured as the porch vanished, replaced by the unending black of journey spells.

"Everything will."

"The sickle seems to help. It concentrates my power, so I don't have to work as hard."

I didn't know much about Reapers and their scythes. "Handy. Plus it doubles as a weapon." The length of silvery-gray whatever-it-was glowed brighter. Maybe my words had pleased it. "What's it made of? Not metal, certainly."

Cait ran her fingertips down part of the handle. "I don't know. It's not wood. It can't be metal, except maybe aluminum, and that's quite a recent invention."

I focused a small amount of power at the blade, trying to sort it out.

"Any answers?" Cait asked.

"Nay. 'Tisn't wood, or metal, or stone. It might be a specialized type of tempered glass."

"Or perhaps the same magic that made Death's scythe

created all the rest of them. If she hadn't turned into Helga the Horrible, I'd ask her. There was a time when she would have told me, but those days are behind us."

I put an arm around Cait. The tip of the sickle's blade grazed my neck. It was warm, and I felt a flicker of intelligence as it assessed me, maybe making certain I had honorable intentions toward its mistress.

"You took a little longer than I expected with Kiko," I said.

"Eh, that part went fast. I was ready to leave, but then I decided to run past the Quonset hut."

"Any particular reason?" I kept my question as bland as I could manage. Stopping by *Carrick Sky Sports* was not a good idea after dark, given it had all but turned into a Vampire nest.

She twisted and shot a penetrating look my way. "I know that tone. Give me credit for being cautious. I swapped power out of the teleport spell I'd begun and resurrected my warding. It's been quite the day, and walking felt good. Helped clear my head."

"What'd you find at the Quonset hut?"

"Didn't exactly get that far."

Frustration vied with worry. "Cait. Don't make me drag this out of you. What happened?"

"Shades happened. Bunches of them. The scythe moved from my shoulder to my hand, which is always a clue. It was certain I'd need it, and I've come to trust its instincts."

She leaned against me. "Hang on. Need to double-check my destination."

I was quiet until she made certain we'd end up at Scourie Castle. "Did the ghosts give you any problems?"

"Not really. Doug was there."

"Who was he again?"

"The dude who foisted a broken plane off on me in hopes of sticking it to me for repairs. Anyway, he appears to have amassed a cadre of shades. They can't hurt me—so long as I don't open a gateway for them. And I didn't. Doug had a few choice words.

"I told him to find another Reaper if he wanted to cross so bad. Not like I'm the only one."

"There's more," I said, certain she'd omitted some important details.

Cait nodded. "He sneered and said my problems hadn't even begun yet. I told him if that was true, why the hell would I want to build a gateway for him? When he didn't answer, I asked him pointblank if he was working with the Vampires."

"And?" We were nearing Scotland. The edges of Cait's spell had developed a pearlescent aspect that meant we were nearly there.

"Shades can't lie. They can not answer, and he didn't, but one of the ghosts behind him shouted the Vamps had promised to bring Doug back if he delivered me to them.

"Doug hit him, which was a joke since his fist passed right through the other guy. Somewhere in the ensuing tussle, they all vanished."

"Is that even possible?" I asked. "Not the vanishing part, but the other. I thought Vamps needed living flesh to effect their transformation."

"Same thing I believed," she said as Scourie Castle's courtyard formed around us. It was just past dawn. This far north so late in the year, that meant it was pushing nine in the morning.

"Nicely done," I told her as she swathed us in a cushion of air, and we touched down lightly.

"Thank you. Anyway, according to one of the mechanics who works the airfield, Doug was highly placed in Humans Rule. If he was one of the members mucking about with magic, who's to say he didn't alter something that would make it possible for him to turn into a Vamp, even after death?"

"We'll worry about him later." I was in a hurry to get inside and see what was happening.

"Not much point worrying about him at all," Cait muttered. "Nothing we can do about it."

"Why do you suppose the one shade talked with you?" I asked as we hurried across the puddled courtyard for the broad stone stairs.

"Because I have power over them. Far more than Doug does. The only reason Vamps control the ones they do is because they used them for blood. It changes people when they're alive, rots their souls if it happens enough."

"So they don't act like they should after they die?" I tugged one of the heavy front doors open.

"Something like that. Can I drop all this stuff in your room?"

"Certainly." I set a quick pace for the small chamber I'd selected after leaving Malin. At the time, I'd wanted something where the fireplace had a prayer of warming the space. Several corridors and stairs later, I pushed a door open. As soon as we were inside, I laid the saber down. Even my brief tenure hanging onto it had raised blisters along my palm. Delivering it to the armory could wait.

Cait walked inside and draped her spare clothes over the room's single chair. She set her leather bag on the floor. "It's really different from your flat in Malin," she said.

"What a tactful way of describing it." I tried but failed to suppress a wry grin. "This castle was a dump in its heyday. Not much has changed. You will notice it's warm in here, though. Unlike the rest of the castle outside the kitchens."

"Your other place is cozy, homey. It feels like you. That's more what I meant."

"I knew what you were getting at. No one would ever accuse the castle of being cozy. Ready to dive into the fray?"

She shrugged. "Not really. I'm sick of Death and her manipulations."

"Maybe by now Arawn and Hades have talked her into leaving."

"Ha. Hope springs eternal." She transferred the scythe until it sat beneath one arm. Probably if she left it in my chamber, it would just follow us. "Say. Do you suppose Cerebrus will be here?"

"Maybe. Have you had dogs?"

She nodded enthusiastically. "Oh my, yes. Lots of them but not for a long while. Once I started Reaping Vampires, I wasn't around enough. Do the Sidhe keep pets?"

"Some of us have kept birds and the occasional cat, but it's not common."

"I guessed as much since I didn't see a single animal in your compound in Malin."

I led the way back along hallways and staircases until we drew close to the castle's main room. The hum of voices reached us. They didn't sound happy, and I placed a hand on Cait's arm.

"No matter what's going on in there, we take sufficient time to get the lay of the land," I cautioned her.

"Don't just jump in slugging?" The corners of her mouth twitched downward.

I borrowed her phrase from a few minutes before and murmured, "Something like that."

We stopped just beneath the lintel of one of the rear doors. So far, no one had noticed us yet. Death was in the middle of what had clearly been a "look at everything I've done for you" lecture. Reapers were bunched to one side. Sidhe stood on the other.

Whenever Death stopped to take a breath, either Arawn or Hades tossed out a suggestion about now being a good time to leave. Death ignored them. Cerebrus was indeed present and clinging to his master's side until he raised one of his three heads and scented the air.

Giving a happy little yip—very out of character for such a gruesome appearing beast—he ran full tilt for where we stood.

"We've been discovered," I murmured.

Even before I said anything, Cait was on her knees, arms spread as the dog ran right into them, licking her face with abandon.

"Cait. Cait. Cait," rose from every Reaper present as they surged toward where she crouched, arms around Cerebrus.

I didn't even have to look at Death's expression. Fury and outrage turned the very air electric with her wrath. I'd told her what would happen if she didn't soften her stance. She hadn't listened to me, and now the chickens had come home to roost.

Or in her case, they'd fled the coop for more tolerant pastures.

CHAPTER THREE, CAIT

I have no idea what it was about Cerebrus that sang to my soul. Maybe because we both dealt with the dead. I'd never met a dog I liked more than the three-headed beast nuzzling my neck and slobbering all over me. Short, thick black fur covered his body. I hoped his affinity for me wouldn't piss Hades off, but when I sought out the god, he wore an indulgent expression.

Reapers surged toward Liam and me from all directions, chanting my name. I'd warned them about transferring the same blind allegiance they'd harbored for Death to me—or anyone else. It was why we'd formed a Reaper council. Constructed similarly to the Sidhe ruling body, it gave everyone an equal voice.

I let go of the dog reluctantly and got my feet under me. Sticking two fingers in my mouth, I whistled. The shrill notes had the desired effect; everyone stopped shouting my name as if I were some kind of savior.

I fully expected Death to plant herself right in front of me, but she took the opposite path, ignoring me completely. Frankly, I liked that approach better. But it had to be a sneaky end run on her part. Death hadn't been piloting Reapers this long to give up the helm now.

Her motivation didn't make any difference. Not really.

I grabbed my advantage, however bogus it might be, and made my way to her. My timing. My terms. "We've formed a governing body," I told her. "Currently half a dozen of us sit on it. If you'd like to be part of our council, we'd welcome you."

Hisses and boos from the Reapers buffeted me from all sides. I whistled once more and amplified my voice with magic. "I invited her to be one voice on the council, not to run it."

Liam materialized next to me, watchful and waiting. He'd tried to talk Death into a more egalitarian structure, and she'd spat on his idea. Had things changed enough to make a difference?

"See?" Arawn's deep voice rose above the din. "They're still willing to include you."

"'Tis a kind gesture." Hades snapped his fingers; Cerebrus ambled over to him. The god reminded me of paintings of Odin. Burly with substantial shoulders, he had silver hair gathered into a queue low on his neck. Well-worn, stained leather covered him along with a mail hauberk and vambraces. A battle axe was slung across his back. Sky-blue eyes stared out above a full black-and-silver beard.

I smothered a wince, anticipating what would happen next. Death would view the other gods' words as patronizing. She didn't disappoint me.

"Kind?" she shrieked. "I don't require pity or condescension. Or *kindness*." She turned in a full circle, black robes swirling in an unseen wind, no doubt ginned up by her fury.

"All of you are mine." Her voice was so loud, my ears rang. "Mine. I made you, and I can unmake you."

"Not anymore," Pavel called; anger sparked from his dark eyes. "The magical bits that linked us are gone." Brown braids trailed down his chest. Tattered jeans encased his long legs, and he wore a tan button-down shirt with a gray wool jacket over it.

"Aye, and not a moment too soon," Stacia yelled. Her words spawned a volley of cries from the Reapers, all repeating variations on the same theme. She'd sought me out a while back, worried about the Vampire problem—and Death's unpredictable moods. Short with bright-red hair, blue eyes, and freckles, she sported gray trousers and an oversized purple sweater.

"We need Reapers," Arawn reminded Death.

"Unless you wish to return to taking care of all the dead," Hades added.

While grateful for their support, I wished they'd shut up. The two of them were making things worse by reminding Death she'd lost her spot at the top of the heap.

I didn't think I'd get through to her, either. I tried anyway. "Inclusion in our council might not look appealing now," I began, "but maybe after you've calmed down and given it some thought—"

"Shut up," she screeched.

I've never been good at following directions, and I'd have just kept on talking, except she'd quit listening to anything except the sound of her own voice.

With her arms raised to the sides, silver hair spilling almost to the floor, eerie eyes moving so quickly the imagery in them was a blur, she cut an imperious figure. "I offer you one last chance to return to my side."

Silence stretched through the room. Not a single Reaper responded to her call.

"One last chance, or what?" I asked.

"You'll find out."

Something about those three words chilled me. She'd quit raging and retreated to a calm, cold place I knew well. It was the same demeanor she'd worn slicing through hordes who'd died of plague. Or the Black Death. She'd do what she believed was right, no matter how many of us she took down.

A memory battered me.

Back in Reaper school, a fellow had been unsure of his role herding souls. Perhaps Death had chosen badly with him, but the touch of the newly dead made him cringe. Rather than working with him, helping him through his ambivalence, she'd dragged him outside one night, wiped his memories, and left him to wander in the Arctic until he froze.

The only reason I knew about it was because I'd snuck out to take in an unusually brilliant display of Northern Lights. I'd heard the Reaper crying, begging, pleading, and hidden behind a ward. I wasn't proud of myself, but at the time I was convinced I'd wait until Death retreated within. Then I'd locate the Reaper and help him find his way home.

He was clearly finished as an acolyte.

Except Death hadn't left for hours. By the time she was finally gone, so was the Reaper. I'd hunted and hunted, tried to follow his tracks in the snow and ended up back where I'd begun. Several nights later, his shade accosted me. He still had no idea who he was, but he was done with Earth and desperate to move on.

I'd hustled him through a gateway and kept my mouth shut. The lessons I'd learned that night had stuck with me. Death was ruthless, and my best bet was not to cross her. I'd managed to walk on the good side of the line—until she decided I was the best choice to help out with her Vampire problem.

My eyes widened. It was indeed "her" problem. The question was why she'd ended up burdened with it.

Lots I didn't know, but before I could craft a cunning question—one where she might slip up and actually answer me —it was too late. Hades had moved to one side of her, Arawn the other. Power flowed around the trio. When it quieted, she was gone.

"She'll rethink things," Hades said.

"I wouldn't be so sure of that," I told him. "Being busted from queen back to rank and file won't sit any better tomorrow than it did a few moments ago."

The dog pushed between Liam and me. Snuffling breath from his three mouths was warm and comforting.

"Good riddance," Stacia huffed.

"Nice pipe dream. She is far from gone," Liam spoke up.

"Aye." Krin detached himself from the group of Sidhe. "She's declared herself your enemy. I feared that outcome when she dropped into our midst."

"How long was she here?" I asked.

"Perhaps a couple of hours," Krin said. His red-gold hair had developed a shaggy appearance, and his dark eyes were somber. Broad-shouldered like Liam, he was maybe an inch or two shorter. He'd traded his usual leather garments for black canvas pants, a green plaid flannel shirt, and a tan fuzzy jacket. The part that didn't change was his feet, which were perennially bare.

"At first, she was pleasant enough," Dena spoke up. Her black hair was arranged in many small braids, plaited close to her skull. Leather trousers covered her long legs, topped by a colorful linen top and a buff-colored shearling vest. Ebony skin set off her deep-brown eyes.

"She was," Krin agreed.

"I feared she was about to rebuke me for my role freeing Reapers from her control," Dena went on. "It almost appeared she'd forgotten all about my confession."

"She didn't seem anything like herself," Arawn said in a thoughtful tone.

"I disagree," I tossed out. "She seemed precisely like she's been ever since she saddled me with Vampires."

"Aye, child. But she is very different from who she has been in times past," the Celtic god of the dead persisted. Arawn always looked the same. Tall and thin to the point of emaciation, he favored black robes sashed in black. Dark hair hung loose past waist level. A set of shrewd midnight eyes was framed by a sharp-boned face with a hawk's beak of a nose and a square chin.

"None of that matters," Liam said. "She has something in mind. We'll have to wait to find out what it is. Meanwhile, what happened while Cait and I were gone? Padhraic's note said you were beset from within and without. Death takes care of the within part, except Paddy couldn't have known she'd visit when he emailed me."

Padhraic detached himself from the rear of the group of Sidhe. Until recently, he'd been a Leanan Sidhe. In other words, the Sidhe version of a Vampire. The rest of his kind were moldering in a pit that would hopefully hold them for a few hundred years. Padhraic had begged to be cured, a task the other Sidhe had reluctantly agreed to.

I hadn't been present for the healing, but apparently it was long and arduous and came close to ending Padhraic forever. I was glad it hadn't. His magic was strong, and he and Liam had been fast friends before his foray into Vampirism. Garbed in an old-fashioned tartan layered over an undyed shirt with full sleeves, he looked more Scottish than Irish. Abundant dark hair was trimmed to shoulder level, and his silver eyes held a worried aspect. When we'd rescued him from being a Leanan, he'd been painfully thin. In the weeks since then, he'd begun to fill out courtesy of his new diet of something other than blood.

"I didn't predict Death's precise arrival," Padhraic agreed, "but I knew she'd materialize. Much of her life is wrapped up in her Reapers. She won't walk quietly away from something she's spent the last thousand years building."

"We're no longer 'her' Reapers," Stacia pointed out.

"True enough," Padhraic agreed. "Poor choice of words. The beset from without part involves Scourie Castle. It's mounted its defenses. We were discussing what steps to take when Hades and Arawn showed up with Death on their heels."

"Huh?" I leveled my gaze at him. "What defenses? We just came through the courtyard, and it looked the same to me."

"We wouldn't have noticed," Liam murmured. "I am Sidhe, and the castle recognizes me as such."

"Remember the mists surrounding our compound in Malin?" Krin asked. At my nod, he continued. "The castle sits behind a similar veil. It didn't when we first took up residence, but it does now."

I thought about it. We'd teleported into the courtyard, so we must have missed the barrier.

"The castle is far stronger magically than our domicile in Malin," Padhraic said. "Last evening at dusk I went out for a stroll and walked to the village before I turned back around. I'm still sensitive to Vampires, and I felt them the whole way. Not in this world, but rustling along one of the corridors spanning Earth. It was why I stopped at that little teashop to email you."

"You should have teleported," Liam snapped. "The moment you sensed them."

Padhraic shrugged. "Not much they can do to me. They view me as a traitor, but my magic outstrips theirs. It did when I was a Leanan, and that's triply true now." He stopped long enough to take a measured breath. "I was more curious than anything. There were a lot of Vamps, and more were joining them every few minutes. They reminded me of rats scurrying inside the walls of a building."

"Probably part of the next salvo from the dark gods," Hades suggested. Cerebrus growled in agreement.

"My thoughts too." Padhraic frowned, drawing his black brows together. "And one more reason I held my ground. I didn't hurry, but neither did I tarry. Vamps can't do much to me, but I'm not so sure about Adva, Tokkhots, and Majestron Zelia. Slototh has never been a threat to anyone."

"Well?" Liam spun one hand in a circle.

"Nothing dramatic happened," Padhraic replied. "Except when I drew near Scourie Castle, it was buried in layers of mist. They parted to allow me entrance."

"Has it defended itself from Vampires before?" Arawn asked, followed by, "Didn't there used to be hundreds of them roaming the northern reaches of Scotland?"

"Maybe not hundreds, but you raise a good point," Liam

said. "We've always had Vampires, but the castle ignored them."

It was as good a lead-in as I was likely to get. "I had kind of an epiphany before Death left," I told the group.

"Aye?" Dena raised a dark brow as she regarded me.

"Arawn is correct. Vampires have been around forever. We didn't pay much attention to them. Reapers never worried about making special efforts to hustle them across the veil."

As an aside, we'd never made a point of forcing anyone to cross who didn't want to go, either.

"There are more Vampires," I went on, "but why did Death suddenly become fixated on them. Do either of you know what happened?" I shifted my gaze from Hades to Arawn and back again.

Something about the quality of their silence told me they knew something. Whether they had the whole story remained to be seen. As did whether they'd be willing to reveal anything to us.

To fill in a silence that was stretching longer than I liked, and hopefully to siphon off some of the pressure my question had created, I started talking again. "I'm not sure why this came to me, but Vampires are Death's problem. They never were a Reaper concern. We're trained not to force anyone across the gateway. Lots of shades don't want to go. We let them be until they're ready."

A bevy of *yesses* and *it's how we've always done things* rose from the Reapers. Stacia stepped to my side. "That was exactly what Jake said. And why he was so uncomfortable when Death told him he had to corral Vampires and figure out a way to compel them to cross over. He told me he couldn't do it. When a Vampire hissed and snarled and snapped and tried to glom onto his neck, he ran."

Poor Jake. I hadn't known him except by sight, but why the hell had Death pinned so much responsibility on him? Surely she'd known he wasn't up to the task.

"She must have been desperate," I said slowly, testing out my words.

"What do you mean?" Liam asked.

"Well, it pains me to admit this, but Death knows us pretty well after all this time. She must have realized Jake wasn't up to the task, but she assigned it to him, anyway."

"Do you suppose he was some kind of test case?" Stacia asked.

"As in, finding out if we could even deal with Vampires?" I mumbled.

"Something like that," she said. "When it didn't work out very well with Jake—"

"Not very well?" I sputtered. "Hell, she banished him." Another thought blasted me. I didn't want to sidetrack us, but I blurted, "Can you free him?"

"Was that a question for me?" Hades asked.

"Or Arawn," I replied.

"Maybe," Hades said.

"What aren't you saying?" Stacia tossed her head back and sent a pointed look at the two gods.

"He was a broken man when Death dumped him in with the Vampires," Hades said. "We didn't agree with her approach, but neither did we intervene."

"Why not?" Liam spoke up.

"Her minions. Her decisions," Arawn said flatly.

My temper has always been my worst enemy, and I made a

grab for it before I said something I regretted, something that might alienate the gods. We needed their help. It was more important than however I felt about Jake and his fate.

"We might have made a different choice today," Hades said.

"Mayhap," Arawn agreed. "We know more than we did then. Regardless. Jake has lost what little was left of his mind. 'Twould be a kindness to move him to a spot by himself. That we can do."

"I would very much appreciate any consideration." Stacia's words held a formal note, and I wondered what Jake had been to her.

"Understood," Hades said.

"We will do what we can," Arawn added. "Now about the Vampire problem. We do not know as much as you hope we do, but this conundrum has been centuries in the making."

"It came to our attention about the time D'Chel freed the Leanan from the *Dreaming*," Hades growled and pinned his blue-eyed gaze on Padhraic. "You should know this part."

"What part?" Padhraic turned his hands palms up. "I remember D'Chel showing up and making a lot of promises, but he wanted things in return."

"Usually the way of it," Liam muttered under his breath.

"We'd always avoided Earth-bound Vampires," Padhraic went on. "Part of the deal was we had to join forces with them. Teach them tricks to walk in daylight and enter houses without being invited."

He paused for a beat, perhaps organizing his thoughts. "The *Dreaming* saps your will to do much more than exist, and we'd been there for a long while before D'Chel showed up. It took many visits before most of us decided being free was worth any price tag. I wasn't one of them, but I missed the warmth of mortal women. When the gate opened, I left with everyone else."

"There's more," Hades pressed.

"Sorry. That's all I know," Padhraic said. "I went back to my old haunts, found a woman who would remain with me for one year. Once the time was up, I located another. Mortals who stay longer turn into monsters."

I nodded, remembering that part.

Magic flared around Hades and Arawn, clearly a private conversation. I tried to imagine what they were saying but gave it up for a lost cause.

"The condensed version," Arawn said at length, "is Death took up with several Leanan, trading one for another as she tired of their company."

"Took up with as in had sex with them?" I was so shocked—and disgusted—I almost couldn't get the words out.

"No wonder she was so helpful when we went after them," Liam said. "She had a big secret to conceal." He stared at Padhraic. "How is it you didn't know?"

Padhraic shrugged. "I've always been one to mind my own affairs. Besides, we weren't into bandying our partners' names about. Unlike Earth-bound Vamps, we'd settle in with a partner for a year. During that time, we didn't look elsewhere."

"We lack proof of this next," Hades said in an even rougher voice than usual, "but we suspect the other Vampires threatened to reveal Death's dalliances. We already knew, but she didn't realize it."

"So that was when she decided the only good Vampire was one who'd crossed the veil?" Liam summarized what I'd been thinking.

Both gods said, "Aye," in unison.

"Damn." I felt like punching something. "She roped us into a war of her own making."

"Roped you," Stacia corrected me.

"It was only a matter of time before some of the rest of you ended up conscripted," I told her.

"With the Leanan out of the way—except for Padhraic—" Arawn said, "Death only had to worry about a stray Vampire spilling the beans about her poor choices."

"Gah. I'm surprised she hasn't tried to end me," Padhraic muttered.

"No need," Liam said. "She probably scanned your mind and knew you didn't pose any kind of risk."

"Why would we give a fuck who she slept with?" I asked. "Seems like a really Draconian approach to an almost non-existent problem."

"If I'd found out, I'd have broken ranks with her," Pavel said.

"As would I," Stacia seconded.

Mmph. Not so inconsequential as all that. Maybe I was the only one who could have cared less about Death's choice of bed partners.

"Did she ever find out you knew her secret?" Liam asked the gods.

"We don't believe so," Hades said.

"Subject never came up." Arawn made a sour face. "We hoped the topic would vanish."

I chewed my lower lip. They'd known she'd sicced her Reaper workforce on Vampires and said nothing. It wasn't my place to rebuke them, but their lack of concern for those like me grated. And I kept coming back to a hunch sex was only part of the bargain.

Suck it up, my inner voice ordered sharply. It was good advice.

The gods were being who they'd always been. Their lack of attention to those outside their immediate circle was nothing new.

"What's our next move," I asked too brightly. Liam looked askance at me but didn't mine for details.

Cerebrus barked. Another head bayed. Hades cursed in Gaelic as a gash tore from floor to ceiling at the far end of the room, and shades swarmed through.

"What the fuck?" Pavel shouted.

Reaper power shimmered through the chamber.

"Save your magic," Hades yelled. "They've already been Reaped. Someone opened the gates to Hell."

I was pretty sure exactly who that someone was, but I could get even later. In direct contradiction to Hades' order, I unlocked the floodgates and welcomed my Reaper magic. The gray, chill world of the dead took shape around me as I shuffled through plans to move all these unholy fuckers back to where they belonged.

They'd been Reaped, but part of my power is herding the dead, bending them to my will. Didn't work very well with the Vampire minions, but these were garden-variety dead. I cupped my hands around my mouth and shouted a set of instructions. None of us used necromancy enough to be very practiced, but there were plenty of us here.

Hades and Cerebrus leapt to my side. "What are you doing?" the god growled.

Arawn joined us. "Let her work," he told Hades. "It

appears Death not only withheld vital information from the Reapers about their skills, she didn't bother to tell us, either."

They were doing fine figuring things out, so I plowed into the mass of shades. "If you want to do something," I called over one shoulder, "close the hole."

"But they require a route back," Hades said.

I started to remind him we built gateways, but Arawn beat me to it.

CHAPTER FOUR, LIAM

As attacks went, we'd certainly dealt with worse. When the dog yowled a warning, I scented the air fully expecting the sickly-sweet rot of Vampires. Smells buffeted me —variations of decay and decomposition—but they were clean, natural.

Vamps smell wrong, used, perverse. Not unlike the dark power they dabbled in that traded their humanity for an existence where they transitioned into Undead creatures.

Cait didn't seem to have a plan, but it had never stopped her before. The woman is quick on her feet. She and the Reapers waded into the writhing mass of dead shouting suggestions back and forth as they tried one thing after another. Shades floated, slithered, and passed over, under, and through one another in unending clumps where it was impossible to tell where bodies ended or began.

It didn't take much imagination to fit the puzzle pieces into a coherent whole. Death had left here, stopped in Hell, and booted shades across Earth's veil. I hadn't exactly known she could do that. I'd viewed the barrier as a one-way track. If it weren't, all the Vampires Cait had chivied across would have just popped back at will.

That line of reasoning disturbed me. We did not need any more Vampires to deal with. Where this batch of shades were annoying and an inconvenience, they couldn't do any harm.

Padhraic bounded to my side. "Remember that thing we did near Prague?"

I did, indeed. We needed a gateway, but once we had one, we could scoop bunches of ghosts into groups and send entire batches packing. At least Hades and Arawn had managed to eradicate the rough entryway that had disgorged the ones roaming through Scourie Castle's great room.

My bet was the castle had helped seal the breach. I was linked to the ancient stones, and their fury and outrage reverberated in my soul.

"Build a gateway," I told Cait in mind speech to avoid screeching over the din filling the room. I'd always believed the dead to be a rather silent bunch, but they were yowling and hooting and screaming. Maybe they were outraged to have been disturbed, turned into pawns in Death's war against the Reapers.

Don't forget the Sidhe, my inner voice said sourly. *She's none too fond of us, either.*

The Reapers had split into several groups with perhaps a dozen in each. Working together, they surrounded shades with shimmery magic. Their characteristic scent of heather and wildflowers thickened until it filled my nostrils every time I took a breath. Soothing and enticing by turns, it diverted me from my task.

Padhraic elbowed me in a "let's get this show on the road" gesture that had a sobering effect. No wonder Reapers could control the dead. Hell, this many in one spot had made inroads into controlling me.

We pushed around Reaper circles as I used telepathy to talk with Krin, Dena, and the other Sidhe in the room, describing how Padhraic and I had shunted shades back across the veil.

Cait and Pavel had just opened a gateway when Padhraic and I drew close enough to loose magic we'd prepared. Scooping up part of the thrashing mass of dead protoplasm, we kicked it through and went back for the next section. Meanwhile, the Reapers herded their charges closer to the portal.

"This is too easy," Padhraic muttered.

I was beginning to harbor the same suspicion, but we'd begun something. We'd finish it and pick up the pieces later.

Somewhere between the third and fourth bunch of shades leaving, fresh ones leapt through the hole.

"Fuck!" Cait screamed.

She and Pavel withdrew the power holding the gateway; it winked shut. We'd only gained maybe four ghosts, but it was four too many. I was breathing hard, heart thumping against my chest. I'd been running wide open, and magic was a harsh mistress.

"Requires a different strategy," I ground out around working to catch my breath.

"Yeah." Fury had turned Cait's green eyes a darker mossy shade. "Pavel. Stacia. Abby. We'll work fast, open a gateway, the Sidhe will boot shades through. Then we'll shut it and start over."

"It's going to burn through a whole lot of magic," Stacia panted.

"Tell me something I don't know. If you have a better suggestion, let's hear it," Cait said.

I assessed the shades. Maybe we could finish this in three more rounds. It would tax all of us. And nothing said Death wouldn't open another passageway, and then the round robin would begin anew until we were all prostrate on the floor waiting for our magic to recover.

"Let's do this," Pavel growled. "I like my shades compliant. This collection has something wrong with them."

I'd suspected as much, but hearing it corroborated by a Reaper added fuel to my theory about the shades being hopping mad. Death had disturbed their eternal rest, and they resented being used.

I raised my mind voice and started to outline our latest plan to the other Sidhe. Krin cut me off after the first few words, telling me they'd already begun using a variation of our scheme. Cerebrus bayed from somewhere behind me. I hoped it boded well and wasn't yet one more warning.

The next part went fast because none of us held back. Four Reapers built and dismantled gateways, Padhraic and I did our part. One gateway came down, replaced by the next. The other Reapers cut the remaining shades into groups and herded them in front of Padhraic and me and the other Sidhe.

Gasping as if we'd just run a race, my small group stood looking at each other after shooing the last shade across the veil. No one celebrated. We were all waiting for the next catastrophe to develop. All around us, clusters of Reapers and Sidhe were doing the same thing.

Regrouping.

Cerebrus headed for Cait. She buried a hand in one of his three necks as he rubbed the nearest head against her side.

"Reapers!" Hades' voice boomed in stark counterpart to the silence. "What other skills do you have? Death had us convinced you only built gateways. It was why I told you to save your magic. We didn't need any other portals until we established control over the one the shades used to enter Scourie Castle."

Cait straightened her back and faced him. "We're not totally certain. Until Liam showed me some old scrolls, I thought my magic began and ended with gateways. I've always known I could influence shades, but we were told not to pressure them in any way."

Stacia moved to Cait's other side. "So far, we've found we can teleport, use telepathy, launch a reasonable defense, and engage in necromancy on more than a cursory level."

"Deploying the magic Death never told us about also allows us to remain on your side of the veil for more than a few minutes," Pavel told Hades.

"About the original breach," I spoke up, aiming my question at the gods of the dead. "Is it truly gone?"

Arawn nodded. "The castle helped with that."

"It did, indeed," Krin concurred. "I felt its power being activated. Once it recognizes an enemy, it will mount a defense right away the next time."

"Does that mean it won't allow any more incursions from Hell's halls?" Hades asked.

"Maybe," Krin replied. "It's been a long while since the castle has done aught but stand empty. It may take a few incidents before it's back to its former strength."

I remembered the three Reapers Death had made off with.

Since I wouldn't recognize them by sight, I asked, "Are Gregor, Rolf, and Anya here?"

"Good question," Cait muttered. "With all that's happened, I didn't exactly forget about them, but—"

"We're here," A medium-height man with salt-and-pepper curls and blue eyes detached himself from one of the groups. A moment later, he was flanked by a petite woman with auburn hair and a brown-eyed, dark-haired man.

"I'm Rolf," the first man said. Tan pants encased his legs, and he wore a wool sports coat over a pale-blue oxford shirt. Scuffed black loafers covered his feet.

The other man had to be Gregor, and the woman Anya.

Cait hurried to where they stood. Cerebrus hugged her side like a shadow. "I'm so relieved you're all right. What happened? Why'd Death let you go?"

"She took us to that place in the Arctic. I have no idea why she released us." Anya raked a hand through her hair, pushing it out of her face. Her eyes were a clear violet shade, and a smattering of freckles dusted her nose. A long blue woolen cape was wrapped around her body. Black slacks and tennis shoes peeked from beneath it.

"All of us remembered the compound from Reaper school," Gregor said. "When Death snapped us up in a teleport spell, I was worried we'd come out in some parallel universe where we'd never find our way back." Tall with a rangy build, he wore jeans and a black T-shirt emblazoned with "Reapers Rock" in gold letters beneath an image of a sickle.

"Lucky for us, we'd just learned to teleport," Rolf said.

"Aye, Death has never had a very long attention span," Gregor added. "I figured we could wait her out and leave."

"Did she say anything while you were there?" Cait

persisted. "Something that would shed light on why she abducted you in the first place?"

"She would take offence to the term abducted." Anya made a snorting noise.

"She said she was extending us an honor." Rolf set his lips in a thin line.

"How about one of you tell this in order?" I suggested and covered the distance to where they stood.

"Fair enough," Rolf agreed. "And a time-saver. If I miss something"—he tapped first Gregor and then Anya on the shoulder—"wait till I'm done to jump in."

"Sure," Anya said.

"We were finishing up Reaping," Rolf began, "when Death plummeted out of nowhere. You know how she does. You don't see her for months, and all of a sudden, she's just there. I figured she was going to rebuke us for the number of shades who'd piled up in our brief absence."

He frowned, maybe selecting his next words. "She didn't say one word about Reaping or dereliction of duties. Instead, she dropped this spell over us. By the time I understood she meant to take us somewhere, it was too late to fight her."

"Aye, we got to the Arctic in record time," Gregor piped up, followed by, "Sorry. But it did happen unusually fast."

"It did," Rolf agreed. "Between the space of two breaths, we traded the Australian Outback for her compound in the Arctic. She plopped us down in the study, the one with a fireplace powered by magic. It was the first hopeful sign. That building complex has far less pleasant portions, and a couple of underground cells."

"What?" Cait's eyes widened. "I'm the original Ms. Snoop, and I never located them."

"She might have built them after you left," Rolf said. "We're younger than you. Regardless, she poured us tea. None of us drank it. Figured it might be poisoned."

"She was trying to be considerate," I said.

Rolf nodded. "And it was so out of character, it totally creeped me out."

"I know you said to be quiet," Anya broke in, "but I assumed she wanted something, and badly enough to pretend to care about us."

"She did want something," Rolf went on. "She launched into this speech about how much Reapers meant to her, how she'd created us, and how much of her own magic we'd absorbed. Like we were a bunch of mini-mes, and as such we owed her absolute allegiance."

"No doubt about it," Gregor rumbled in his deep, rough voice. "She out and said the allegiance part before she was done."

"Aye, and then she asked how we felt about remaining with her in the Arctic," Rolf continued. "None of us said a word. I was afraid if I said no, I'd set her off, but if I'd said yes, I'd have been lying, and she'd have known."

"So she trapped you." Cait pursed her mouth into a sour moue.

"Not necessarily. She'd have taken a yes, even if it was a lie," I said, certain I was on solid ground.

"It pains me to admit it, but you're right," Arawn muttered. "The worst part about the lot of you"—he swung his arms wide —"walking out on her was it injured her pride."

Cait frowned. "Sort of what I figured. Losing me was one thing—and a more or less acceptable loss. But when it spread throughout the Reaper ranks, she took it personally."

"And blamed you," Arawn said.

"Yup. About the size of it," Cait agreed. "Even with everything that's happened, I wouldn't change anything. If I'd kept on herding Vampires, sooner or later, I'd have ended up turned."

"Gah. That's worse than dead," Stacia said.

It was, and I had no idea if a ritual cleansing, like we'd done for Padhraic, would have worked on a Reaper. We'd nearly ended Padhraic, and his power was more robust than Reaper magic.

"Let me finish this tale," Rolf said. "We all stood around in the library-slash-study, mostly staring at our shoes. By then I'd set my teacup down so the fact I wasn't drinking from it wouldn't be quite so obvious. Death had developed that thousand-yard stare of hers. The one where she might be standing in front of you, but the rest of her is a long way away.

"I had no idea what would happen next. Would she smite us on the spot? Could she even manage it now that our linkage to her had been severed? I wanted to confer with Anya and Gregor, but anything private was out of the question, so we just exchanged glances, waiting."

"Why not teleport out of there?" Cait asked.

He shrugged. "We're not very swift with the new magic yet. By the time I'd gotten a spell together, Death could have cut me off at the knees. All in a rush, she was back in the room with us—all of her, not just her body. She scrunched up her face like she does and said, 'So that's how it is.'

"None of us uttered a word. There weren't any palatable answers. The same magic she'd used to transport us to her compound dropped over us. I was certain we were heading for

Pluto, but when her casting cleared, we were right back here in Scourie Castle."

"Still can't quite believe it," Anya said. "I was certain we were doomed."

"Killing you wouldn't gain her anything," Hades said.

"Far from it. In truth, she'd lose quite a bit because eventually we'd have found out, and she'd have owed us a major explanation," Arawn added. "Creating acolytes is one thing, destroying them quite another. We have regulations governing such things."

It was news to me, and I would have liked to know more, but the gods didn't owe the Sidhe any explanations about their inner workings.

"Will she try again with different Reapers?" Pavel asked Arawn.

He exchanged a long, pointed look with Hades before answering, "Seems unlikely. She's probably figured out the result would be the same no matter which Reapers she shanghaied."

Something had been banging around in my head ever since he and Hades had revealed the bit about Death dallying with Vampires. "I may be way off course with this," I said, "but it's been a long while—centuries—since Death created any new Reapers. The process requires magic from her, and I'm guessing each existing Reaper also drains a bit of power."

"They did," Dena spoke up, "until I clipped the ties that bound them. After that, Reaper power stood on its own feet."

I absorbed that bit of information. "Does it mean Death will be a whole lot stronger all of a sudden?"

"Probably," Hades answered before Dena could formulate a reply.

I was getting sidetracked. Reapers' magical independence was brand new. "Is it possible sex wasn't Death's only motivation to spend time with Vampires?"

"That's an open-ended question," Arawn growled.

"Aye, be clear, Sidhe. Say what you mean," Hades tossed out.

I nodded and plowed forward. "The Leanan were also Sidhe, and their Sidhe magic predated them becoming Vampires. The transformation altered their power but didn't weaken it. If Death was feeling the pull of too many Reapers—and I'm guessing she was because she'd quit making more—wouldn't she be on the prowl for adding to her magic any way she could?"

"Damn. I'd thought exactly the same," Cait said. "That there had to be something more than sex. She could have gotten laid anywhere."

Hades made a face. Two of Cerebrus's heads growled. Cait cooed to the big dog, soothing him.

"'Tis possible," Arawn said, "but I'm not about to ask her. Besides, the Leanan are gone." He dusted his long-fingered hands together as if to say, problem solved.

I wasn't so sure dumping the Leanan in a pit had solved much of anything. After all, plenty of Vamps remained of the non-Leanan variety. Their magic wasn't anything to write home about, but still.

As time had passed with no new rips in the ether, I was feeling more confident that maybe the shade incursion had been a one-time event. They weren't dangerous in and of themselves, but enough of them on the wrong side of the veil would skew the balance of magic badly.

It wouldn't take long for wicked manifestations to get the

memo they could break through Earth's boundaries and feast on the spoils. In this case, mortals. I ground my teeth. No more collateral damage. Not if I could help it.

"We're all here." I projected my voice so it would reach the farthest corner of the big, chilly room. "The gods have honored us with their presence and their magic. Shall we make good use of their generosity?"

I went on without waiting for answers. "Follow me to the dining rooms. We have two. They're warmer than here. We can eat and replenish our magic as we plan our next moves."

"Your focus must be the remaining dark gods," Hades said.

"Only reason we're here," Arawn concurred.

I nodded and smiled and hustled everyone out of the great room before Krin or someone spouted off about this being a Sidhe stronghold and mentioned we voted on all major decisions. Democratic process was one thing, but I felt certain the gods wouldn't stick around for us to figure out what to do about Earth-bound Vamps or Humans Rule.

My theory about Death drawing power from the Leanan hadn't sat well, yet neither god denied it. I glanced at Padhraic striding along beside me. The castle's corridors were wide enough to accommodate six men walking abreast.

"Why do I have a feeling you know something about Death and the Leanan?" I asked him in deeply shielded mind speech.

"Because you know me, but the rest of the Leanan are gone. What difference does it make what she did with them?"

"Know your enemy," I reminded him. *"The better we understand how Death thinks, the more ammunition we'll have to deal with her the next time she shows up."*

And there would be a next time. She wasn't about to waltz

into oblivion. Not without her Reaper taskforce by her side. Even now, she had to be plotting her next move, and she wouldn't rest until she'd won. Bending the Reapers to her will wouldn't be enough—or she'd have hung onto Gregor, Rolf, and Anya. No. She wanted adulation, for them to love and revere her.

Not that they'd done much of that before—except in her imagination. After Cait's defection kicked open the possibility for others to bolt for the gates, reality had intruded, and Death didn't much care for it.

I felt certain she wouldn't give up until the other gods ganged up on her and meted out their version of punishment. It would have to be pretty brutal, though, to cut the legs out from under her dreams of establishing dominion over her subordinates once again.

I tried to tell myself it was the other gods' problem, not mine, but didn't get very far. Death had declared herself, and joined the list of problems we had to address. I didn't expect help from Hades or Arawn. They had a soft spot where she was concerned, but once we'd dealt with the dark mages, Death had to be our next target.

Presuming nothing else intervened. Once I'd told Cait to fight what was in front of her. We'd do the same. Death might end up not being next on the hit parade, but we'd get around to her sooner or later.

I turned hard right into the nearest dining room.

"Meet you in the kitchens in a bit," Padhraic said. "We can talk there."

"What was that about?" Cait caught up with me.

"Food. Magic will help, but we need to turn out a meal. Everyone blew through scads of magic."

"I'd offer to help," she said, "but you know what an abysmal failure I am in the kitchen."

"How about if you come along anyway?" I started to mention Padhraic might know some juicy bits about Death and the Leanan but held my tongue. His comment about talking in the kitchen might not have had anything to do with the other topic. One he'd slammed the door on as soon as I brought it up.

"Sure. See you there in a bit." Sickle slung over one shoulder, she walked into the dining room and made certain everyone was comfortable.

Hades and Arawn swept past me and into the dining chamber. Low-ceilinged, compared with other spots in the castle, it remained reasonably warm. Talking quietly, the gods took up chairs near the hearth. Cerebrus padded after them. I interpreted their presence as a positive omen. I'd been worried they'd leave. They owed us nothing, and we needed their magic to have any hopes of success against the four remaining dark gods.

At least D'Chel was out of the way. It had been stupid of me to let him get a taste of my blood. I hoped to hell he hadn't passed it to one of the others. The possibility sent a chill down my spine.

I'd find out one way or the other soon enough. No point worrying about something I had no control over.

Curious what Padhraic had to say, I announced I'd return with food before striding along one of the castle's many back hallways toward the kitchen.

CHAPTER FIVE, CAIT

I milled around the dining room until all the Reapers were settled. The topic of every side conversation was Gregor, Rolf, and Anya's miraculous return from the Canadian Arctic. If I was a conspiracy theorist, I'd have placed bets Death had scribed the Reapers with some sort of magical markers, not unlike tracking devices, to replace her original beacons.

I'd have to ask Liam if there was a way to detect such a thing. My own hasty scans had been subtle, but I hadn't picked up anything amiss. The three Reapers had been through enough. I decided not to give voice to my suspicions unless there was a surefire way to assess if they were accurate.

Cerebrus was curled at Hades' feet, enjoying the hearth's meager warmth, and I'd stooped to nuzzle his three snouts. It offered convenient cover while I examined the shanghaied Reapers. I'd have to be more careful what I said around the god of the dead. My casual comment about Death getting laid whenever she felt like it clearly hadn't pleased him. He'd had a similar reaction to something I'd said earlier about Death having sex.

Was he besotted with her? It could be why the idea of her sharing her body with anyone else bothered him. The other explanation might simply be he was a prude. Open talk about sexual matters was a relatively recent innovation. Up until maybe thirty years back, discussions about sex happened behind closed doors.

Anyway, his reasons didn't matter. I'd do well to watch the content of my verbalizations. After a last doggie ear scratch, I stood and walked out of the dining room. I wasn't paying attention to where I was going and overshot the corridor leading to the kitchens. Scourie Castle was huge, and the various passageways seemed to move about. Had the castle herded me back into the great room for a reason?

I didn't stick around long enough to find out. I'd be damned if I'd let a building dictate my destinations. My scythe vibrated slightly. When I moved it so the blade was in front of me, it was glowing.

"What? So now you and the castle are buds?"

It glowed brighter. I took it as a yes. To be on the safe side, I patted the nearest stone wall, surprised to find it warm. The sound of footsteps brought me spinning around in time to see Krin and Dena striding purposefully along the corridor.

"We were just talking about you." Krin nodded my way.

I leaned the sickle against a wall. "Was that why I ended up waltzing through one of the arched entries into the great room?"

"Maybe." Dena turned her hands palms up. "The castle is

sentient, and becoming more so with each day we bide here. I'd forgotten how helpful it could be."

I smiled. "What were you were saying about me? Before we get into that, is there any possibility Death sent the Reapers back as some type of latter day spies?"

"What do you mean?" Krin asked.

Dena got it because she was nodding. "After I mucked around with their magic, Death lost her ability to zero in on each Reaper's location. What Cait just asked is if Death did something to restore that connection."

"Exactly. I was going to pick Liam's brain but ran into you first. Is there some way you can check?" I pressed, and then added, "I tried to examine them myself, but nothing looked out of place."

"I can try," Dena replied, "but if Death did something, it will be a whole lot harder to unearth and dismantle than before."

Krin turned the full force of his dark eyes on me. "Many difficulties lie ahead. Is there any chance you could, um, pretend to establish détente with Death? At least until we have the other issues under control."

I fell back a pace, mouth agape. Shutting it, I just stared at him before I managed to get a few words out. "Is that what you were talking about relating to me?"

Krin nodded. "Aye. Sometimes 'tis best to simplify matters where we can."

"Won't work," I said flatly. "She doesn't know the meaning of compromise. And if I say a bunch of mea culpas, she'll make certain her next binding is bulletproof."

"Have you ever made a good faith effort to find some

middle ground?" Krin persisted. "Something more egalitarian, where you work under her but she's not queen of the world?"

"Liam suggested something similar. She spat on it."

"Did she say why?" Dena drew her brows together.

I nodded. "She has a system. She built it from the ground up, tweaked it, perfected it, and isn't willing to alter a thing."

"But it just crashed around her," Krin pointed out.

I shook my head. "I'm not the one you have to convince." Holding up a hand I ticked things off on my fingers. "One. She lied about the scope of our magic. Two. She laid down a set of rules. If we didn't follow them, she knew right away and showed up to rebuke us. Three. Some of her punishments—like dumping Jake in with Vampires—were uncalled for and harsh."

"Hades and Arawn said she wasn't always like this." Dena managed to infuse hope into her words along with a calming spell.

I curled my fingers around the handle of my scythe. It vibrated, layering calm over my ragged edges. Dena and Krin weren't being callous. They'd obviously taken an impartial look at how we'd deal with the dark gods, a proliferation of Vampires, and Humans Rule.

Balanced against the rest of the slate, Death was an inconvenience, but one that could sabotage our other efforts. If she'd shown up in the middle of something like our last battle with Perrikus and D'Chel and Adva, she could have tipped the scales.

And not in our favor.

"I see what you're getting at," I murmured, doing my best to adopt their worldview. It was hard. I wanted to launch into a litany of all the shit Death had shoveled in front of me. Every indignity and humiliation.

But she'd been kind too—when she wasn't intent on annihilating me.

Nothing was as black and white as I'd have liked.

"When we're all in the same room, Krin or I will float how to best derail Death. Not forever, but for long enough for us to accomplish our other tasks." Dena dropped a hand onto my shoulder for a moment. My scythe glowed brighter, soaking up the proximity of her magic.

"Neither of us wanted you to feel we weren't sensitive to your situation," Krin said.

"I understand. Determining what's best for everyone isn't simple." I closed my teeth over my lower lip, opting for honesty. Better here than in the midst of all the Reapers. "Death won't be inclined to believe anything I say at this point. I was the vanguard, the leading edge of the Reapers' rebellion."

"Which is precisely why you are well-positioned to be a spokesperson for your kinsmen," Krin said. "You don't have to lie."

"She can't," Dena spoke up. "Death would know right off."

I looked from one to the other of them. "But the truth won't fly, either. I can tell her it's in everyone's best interests to be batting on the same team. She'll agree in theory, but she'll expect 'her' Reapers to go back to being the good little minions we've always been. Seen and not heard."

"There you are," Liam's voice called from beyond one of the corridor's many twists and turns. He hustled to my side. "Food's ready. Nothing fancy..." He must have picked up on the tension bouncing about like an out-of-control Ping-Pong ball.

"We were just telling Cait the Reapers need to find a way of mollycoddling Death. At least for a while," Krin said.

"What?" Liam sounded thunderstruck. "We just freed them, and you were instrumental in that effort." He stared at Dena. "Why would you want to undo all that good work?"

"Because Death has declared war on us, and it's one more layer we don't need right now." Krin raked a hand through his shaggy hair.

Liam sliced an arm downward. A ward formed around us. If I'd dug deeper, I felt certain I'd have found a sound shield. "That is an extremely bad idea," he said in clipped tones.

"Why?" Krin folded his arms across his chest.

"I just had a very interesting conversation with Padhraic." Liam's forehead crinkled into a mass of lines. "It took a little prodding on my part, but my instincts have always been solid."

"What instincts?" Dena muttered.

"Aye, so far you've said less than naught," Krin growled.

His tone offered me insight. At the heart of things, maybe he wasn't much more flexible than Death. He'd been civil to me —because I'd agreed with him. If I'd gone to the mat, argued with his pronouncement about the Reapers and Death, I might have seen the side he'd just let seep through.

"True enough," Liam conceded. "We already know Death was fucking the Leanan. I felt certain it had to run deeper than that. For one thing, unlike many deities, she didn't have a reputation as a slut. To suddenly jump off the abstinence wagon into debauchery was out of character."

"And?" Dena spun one hand in a circle in a get-on-with-it motion.

"Turns out she was draining magic from the Leanan Sidhe. Sex was a front, a vehicle to allow her to get close enough to them to siphon power. She was enticing enough, no one figured it out for a long while. But eventually, a couple of Leanan compared notes. One thing led to another, and soon no one welcomed her into their bed."

I whistled long and low. "Wow. Bet that pissed her off."

"You have no idea." Liam nodded. "Her rejection had to be a driving force behind how the Sidhe suddenly discovered the Leanan had escaped. She was who suggested I check on them in the *Dreaming*."

"And then, she was conveniently oh-so-helpful taking them down," Dena muttered, her words laced with sarcasm and her even features screwed into a disgusted mask.

"Mmph. That does put a new spin on things," Krin said in a thoughtful tone.

"For you maybe." I rolled my shoulders back and stood straight. "Those of us who've worked closely with her in recent years don't have any trouble seeing her as a cold-hearted, self-serving bitch."

"New plan," Dena said. "We bring this intel to the group."

"In hopes of?" Krin asked.

"Encouraging Arawn and Hades to do something."

I shook my head. Both Sidhe glared at me, but Liam intervened. "Let's hear what she's thinking," he told them.

"Both times I mentioned Death and sex in the same sentence, Hades shut me out, and Arawn looked like he wished the floor would open up and swallow him." I took a measured breath. "She's one of them. They're not going to lift one finger to rein her in, not without hard evidence."

"But she was bleeding magic from Sidhe Vampires. How much worse does it have to get?" Krin's tone was strained.

I swallowed hard. "They didn't catch her at it. All we have is Padhraic's word. We believe him, because we know him, but the gods might see things differently. Was he one of her victims?"

Liam shook his head. "Death wasn't his type. Beyond that, the Leanan enter into a twelve-month pact with their prey. During that time, they're not supposed to step outside the bonds of that agreement."

"I recall something like you described," Dena muttered. "So, Padhraic was honorable, but many of his fellows weren't."

"It will make him less credible," Krin mumbled. "More like a snitch passing on thirdhand information."

Standing around second-guessing deities wasn't productive. I banged the bottom of my scythe on the stone floor to get everyone's attention and said, "We're not going to figure this out in a vacuum. I say we join everyone, let Padhraic say whatever he's willing to, and see which way the wind blows.

"Our first priority has to be Adva, Tokkhots, and the other two. We can plan that offensive. If Death throws a clod in the churn and derails things, I bet Hades and Arawn will be more motivated to deal with her."

"Maybe they'll get some of the other gods involved," Liam said.

Krin's head snapped around as if he were listening to something. He placed a hand on one wall. Dena did the same.

"I'll take care of it," Liam said and took off at a run in the general direction of where I thought the front door was.

I sprinted after him. "Take care of what?"

"Someone's knocking at the gates," he told me.

I felt mystified. "Why is that a problem? Don't you get UPS out here? Or Fed Ex? Or a mail service?"

"No to all of the above. The locals believe this place is haunted. They're superstitious enough to offer it a wide berth.

It was why Scourie Castle was such a solid choice when we were forced to leave Malin."

While I was wrapping my mind around any twenty-first century population in a first-world country not only believing in spirits but also shaping their activities around those beliefs, we reached the front door.

It opened without any help from us, and we pelted down the front steps into a punishing deluge. Whoever stood on the far side of the gates had to be drenched. My scythe had switched to invisible mode. I felt its weight but couldn't see it.

Magic flowed from Liam's outstretched hand, and the large front gate constructed of wood banded in iron creaked open on rusty hinges. Water sheeted down my face, neck, and back. I directed a thin thread of power to keep myself warm.

A small, black car sat on the other side of the gate, motor humming, windshield wipers slapping rain from side to side. The driver's window rolled down, and a rounded woman with steel-gray hair and bright-blue eyes poked her head out.

"Deidre!" Liam exclaimed. "What brings you to Scourie Castle?"

She didn't return his warm smile. "I drew the black ball," she said in a sour tone. "We have Vampires in the village. Leastaways, it appears so."

"That's horrible." I crouched so I was closer to eye level with her. "I'm Cait Carrick. I'm a Reaper, and I'll do what I can to chase those unholy fuckers out of your village."

"Eh. Too bad you didn't get to it before they killed Tommy and Lia and Nigel."

Breath hissed from Liam as he said, "Damn it. I am so sorry. We'll fix this."

"See you do," she said. "We didn't have a problem until you

showed up. Doesn't take a genius to see the connection." She rolled the window up, cutting off Liam's string of apologies. The car backed up, spun in a circle, and drove off, spattering wet gravel in its wake.

My scythe had come out of hiding. I cracked my grave vision, and the half-light of the world of the dead formed around me. I sensed Liam next to me. "What are we doing?" he asked.

"Seeing who we find," I told him.

Shades ebbed and flowed. So far, they'd all been here for hundreds of years. Part of the recalcitrant group who weren't interested in leaving. They skittered around me, not too close.

"I'm not here to Reap you," I reassured them. "Only if you want to leave."

"Why are you here then?" a woman with tangled white hair garbed in a rotting-away gown that had gone out of style in the 1700s asked me.

"I'm hunting Vampires."

"Aye. A passel of them passed through," a man who might have been a buccaneer spoke up.

"Does it mean they're gone?" I sought clarification.

"Nay. They're still around. Just not in this spot," the man said.

"Do they have a nest?"

The woman nodded. By now, we'd garnered quite the group of ghosts huddled in a rough circle around Liam and me, but not too close. They didn't trust I wasn't planning to pull a fast one and turn my Reaper compulsion on them.

"Do you know where the nest is?" Liam asked.

I offered him points. The thing about dealing with shades is they've lost most of their mental acuity. So the only way to glean information is by playing twenty questions.

"They move around," another shade said, "but they prefer the graveyard. The old one behind the livery stable."

"It's an automobile place now," the woman corrected him.

"Thank you." I bobbed my head. "If you ever change your mind about crossing over—"

Amid boos, hisses, and cursing, the shades dispersed fast. I cut the flow of Reaper magic, and Scourie Castle's gates came back into view. I blinked rainwater out of my eyes, certain I couldn't get any wetter.

"We have to go into town," I told Liam.

"Same conclusion I'd come to," he said. "But we should take a few folk with us."

"Yeah. Maybe two or three more Reapers and at least one other Sidhe."

"And props." Liam made a face. "Dead man's blood, silver stakes, and a blade or two. We should have asked how many Vampires."

"They wouldn't have known," I said. "They lose the ability to count much beyond the fingers of one hand."

He wound an arm around my waist and guided us back inside the castle. "Even knowing if it's more or less than five would have been useful."

"Want me to ask?"

"Nah. We'll plan for more. That way, we'll be prepared." He shook himself and water flew every which way as we tromped to the dining room. The smell of food hit me like a sledgehammer. It had been hours—days?—since I'd last eaten.

I crammed meat and cheese between two halves of a biscuit and ate it in a few bites while Liam put out a call for volunteers.

"This is just another of Death's smokescreens," Stacia protested.

"Doesn't matter," Liam said. "We can't ignore it."

"Vamps have already killed three mortals," I said.

"Have they turned any?" Krin asked.

"We don't know," Liam replied.

Hades stood and surveyed the group. "If you react to every single diversion, you will never rid yourselves of your primary problem. Adva. Tokkhots. Majestron Zelia. Slothoth. Remember them?"

He had a point. I inclined my head. "You're absolutely correct. Apologies for bothering you. I'll just run into town and take care of the Vampires. Back as soon as I'm done."

Liam clamped a hand around my arm. "You are not going alone. And we are not leaving without tools."

Dena hustled to us. "Stop by my workshop. What you need is in the lower cabinet beneath the windows."

"Thanks." Maintaining what felt like a death grip on my arm, Liam steered us out of the room.

Somewhere between Dena's workshop and the armory, Stacia shimmered into view. "I was in the back. No one noticed me leave. Let's do this."

"You don't have to—" I began.

"Not up for negotiation," she cut in. "You came after me when I was in trouble."

Liam handed Stacia a few vials of blood and two silver stakes. "Do you want blades?" he asked us.

"The scythes are enough," I said.

"At least they don't cut our hands to shit," Stacia agreed.

"Have you ever used one to behead a Vampire?" Liam asked.

As if my sickle knew we were talking about it, it buzzed near my ear. I snorted and patted the handle. "It says it will be more than adequate."

Stacia chuckled. "Funny, but mine just inferred the same thing."

Power shimmered around Liam, and a long blade took shape, attached to his hips by a sword belt. The hilt was ornate, clearly handcrafted, and from a much earlier era.

I waited for a journey spell to sweep us up. Instead, Liam ran lightly toward the front door. Anticipating my question, he said, "We're driving. That way we can sneak up on the bastards without magic giving us away."

"It's still daytime," Stacia said. "Can we bank on some of them being asleep."

"Nope, not even close," I said.

"Wait here," Liam told us. "I'll bring the car round."

Stacia and I huddled beneath the eaves watching an icy sleet fall. "Thank you," I told her.

"Don't thank me yet. We have no idea what we're walking into."

"We're stronger than them, and we hold the element of surprise." It wasn't just talk. I believed my own hype.

A battered BMW sedan slewed through the mud in the courtyard. "After you," I told Stacia. "Our chariot has arrived."

CHAPTER SIX, LIAM

I could cheerfully have shot Hades when he threw down an obvious gauntlet. What he didn't exactly say, but was abundantly clear, was either we did things his way or he was leaving. That, in a nutshell, was one of many reasons Sidhe have steered clear of the gods.

They'd never been interested in our issues before, and probably wouldn't be now if the dark mages didn't pose a threat. I understood why Death had been so helpful when we fought the Leanan. Dead men tell no tales. Or, in this instance, as good as dead. What I didn't know was exactly why Hades and Arawn were willing to help.

We'd all been so grateful for crumbs from their table, none of us had thought to ask. I ducked through the carriage house door and noted it was damn near as wet inside as out thanks to the roof falling to ruin. If we remained at Scourie Castle, I'd have to see about repairing it.

I grabbed the petrol can, undid the fuel filler, and tipped a few liters of gas into the car. It had been nearly empty when I last drove it. Satisfied we'd have enough to make it to the village and back, I dropped the can back in a corner and tugged my door open.

"What took you so long?" Padhraic asked before I even got inside.

"A better question is what the hell do you think you're doing?"

"Coming with you. Isn't it obvious?"

I tapped the ignition, and the car rolled out of the decrepit building that had once housed carts and wagons. "Not sure it's such a good idea," I told him. "Hades didn't want any of us leaving."

"I was near one of the doors, and I masked my exit with magic. Special magic that provides the illusion I'm still there. No one ever talks to me, or questions me, so it seemed safe enough."

"You'll have to teach me that one."

"Happy to. Look, Liam, we won't be gone very long, and I understand Vampires far better than you."

Hard to argue with him on that point. Impossible, actually. I stopped the car as close to the castle steps as I could manage. Cait and Stacia made a run for it.

"Want me to get in the back?" Padhraic asked.

"Nay. Not worth it," I replied.

Cait opened the passenger door on the heels of his question, shut it after she saw Paddy, and dove into the back with Stacia right behind her.

"What are you doing here?" Cait asked Padhraic.

"Liam asked me the same thing. I'm the closest thing you have to a Vampire expert. Beyond that, I want to see the damage close up. It seems odd to me that Vamps have suddenly targeted Scourie village. There aren't that many people here, for one thing. For another, Vamps pack up, and this has to be a long way from their seethe."

"Speaking of which," I said, "we never did address the seethe Maxwell revealed."

"What seethe?" Stacia asked. "If there's a Vampire lair nearby, I want to hear about it."

"When I made a gateway for Maxwell," Cait replied, "he told me the location of a major seethe. He was reluctant, said they hated me, but I can be persuasive, and I had him in thrall since he was at the stage where he was blending with me to pass through."

"That explains how you knew but not where it is," Stacia said.

"It's located in crypts associated with an old castle on the outskirts of Dublin."

"Kind of like this one?" Stacia pointed out the back window at Sourie's retreating bulk.

"The British Isles are full of moldering castles," Padhraic said. "Why didn't you mention the seethe?"

"I did," Cait replied, "but no one thought it important enough for more than a few moments of consideration. Vampire seethes have been around as long as they have, and we've never troubled ourselves with them before."

"Mmph. Must have been one of the times I was helping Dena clear magic from her workshop between batches of Reapers," Padhraic murmured. "No matter, but I'm fairly certain I know the castle. There are only two with intact crypts, and one is in the center of the city."

"Aye. I know where it is as well," I said, "but they're not our immediate problem."

"They could be," Cait said, "if any of the ones we run up against today hustle back to Vampire Central to sound the alarm."

"Why would you assume they're associated with that seethe?" I asked. The question may as well have come with flashing neon announcing how little I knew about Vamps and their ways. And that was after devoting a month to reading everything I could find in the Sidhe library.

Padhraic waited, perhaps to see if anyone else wanted to weigh in. When no one did, he said, "Vampires have a rather rigid social structure. It didn't apply to the Leanan, but we were Sidhe before we became Vampires, so we retained most of our original ways of interrelating.

"Earth-bound Vampires have masters, meaning the Vampire who turned them. After a Vampire has created a number of minions, he—or she—starts thinking about developing their own empire. Existing master Vampires don't take kindly to interlopers, though. If an upstart becomes too much of a problem, a master Vampire will do away with them and absorb their followers."

"Internecine warfare," I muttered.

"About the size of it," Padhraic agreed. "Seethes do best when they're spread out. There is one in the British Isles, one in Europe, and two or three in the States. Others are scattered widely, but they're not our concern."

"Eventually, they will be," Stacia said in a tone that inferred the only good Vampire was a doubly dead one who could never rise again.

"If Deidre was correct about Vampires being responsible

for deaths in the village," Padhraic went on, "they were dispatched from the seethe in Dublin. My thoughts were we would verify her story and then proceed from there."

Suddenly, Padhraic's presence took on a deeper meaning. "You weren't planning to stop after we did away with any Vampires we found in Scourie, were you?"

"You know me too well," Padhraic told me. "They all talk with one another. Telepathy is one of their magics."

"By that token," Cait spoke up, "maybe we should start with the seethe. There's no way we'll mow through a pack of Vamps without at least one sounding the alarm back at the mother ship."

"We need more of us," Padhraic said. "While our numbers are sufficient to deal with whoever we find in the town, they are woefully inadequate to address a seethe. And its master."

"Or mistress," Cait mumbled.

"Whatever," Padhraic said. "Master Vampires are unbelievably strong. They've been feeding their power for centuries on blood from other Vampires, not mortals."

"For all we know, the dark gods could be aiding them," I said.

"Of course they are," Padhraic corrected me. "It throws a monkey wrench into what kind of power we're fighting."

"And is a solid argument to assemble a larger contingent to annihilate the seethe," Cait said.

We were on the outskirts of Scourie. The sleet had turned to ice mixed with snowflakes, but the unrelenting misty gray offered protection from immediate discovery. We'd appear as ghostly as the shades Cait and Stacia herded to the other side.

"Let's get moving," I suggested. "Since there's no way to avoid having the seethe alerted, I say we seek out and destroy whatever Vampires are here—except for one. We bring him back to the castle where he can be...interrogated."

"You mean tortured," Padhraic said.

"Does it matter what we call it?" I shot back.

"Nay. I'd love to extract my own pound of flesh from those bastards."

It was a bloodthirsty thing to say. I parked between two buildings and murmured, "Once, you were part of them."

"Pfft. You know how Sidhe are. We always see ourselves as a cut above. The only reason we had anything to do with the other breed of Vampire was because it was part of the quid pro quo we agreed to with the dark gods."

"They freed you, and you taught the other Vampires shit like daywalking," Cait said.

"Aye. And not a day passes I don't regret my part in that. We should pair up and fan out," he said, and then turned to Stacia. "Would you hunt with me?"

"Thank you for asking and not just assuming," she replied. "Yes. I will work with you. I have dead man's blood and silver stakes. Will we need a blade beyond my scythe?"

"I brought one," Padhraic said and exited the BMW, dragging a longsword in a sheath after him. He buckled the belt into place.

I hadn't noticed the blade, but he'd been in the car before me and had tucked it between his body and the door. The rest of us piled out. Our first task was to confirm the dead had died by Vampire hands—or fangs.

"Bodies should be laid out in the church." I kept my voice low and took the shortest path to the simple white clapboard structure's back door, crafting a ward as I went.

"I'm assuming Deidre was correct," Padhraic said. "Stacia and I will check the east side of town."

"Wait until you hear from me before you strike," I told him.

"Understood." He paused to take a breath. "If Deidre was wrong, and the deaths were spawned by some other supernatural creature..."

"We'll need a different approach," I finished his thought.

He and Stacia faded into the worsening weather. A wind had blown up from the Irish Sea, howling and screeching. The only good part about the beastly conditions was they'd keep mortals from wandering about in the storm.

I twisted the latch on the church's rear door and found it locked. Nothing I couldn't solve with a shot of magic. I tightened the weave around Cait and me to ensure we'd be invisible—to mortals—and we walked into the church.

It smelled of incense and stale wine. Someone was chanting in Latin. I assumed it had to be the priest, but he'd never notice us. We crossed cracked red linoleum, passing doors to bathrooms and a kitchen, before we came out behind the altar.

I've never cared much for churches, mostly because mortals have demonstrated an unerring instinct to pray to the wrong deities, but this house of worship was pleasantly simple. No garish statues. No stained glass. Just an altar and rows of wooden benches. A wooden cross adorned one wall, but it didn't have a dying Jesus nailed to its boards.

The corpses were indeed laid out on raised tables along the transept. The priest's prayer focused on safe passage to the kingdom of heaven as he worked to purge evil from their souls. My plan had been a quick in and out. I hadn't counted on Cait.

She took on the glowing aspect I associated with her Reaper magic.

Her heather and wildflower scent bloomed around us, spicy and alluring. The shades had been milling around the church, and they made a beeline right for her.

"Release the ward." She resorted to telepathy so the priest wouldn't hear. *"I can't work through it."*

No time to argue the priest would see her. He'd already noticed the scent wafting through the transept and had been glancing around. I rearranged the warding until Cait was free, and then I joined her in the realm of the dead.

I could still see the priest, but his outline was fuzzy. Perhaps my concern about Cait popping out of nowhere and scaring the crap out of the padre had been based on incorrect assumptions. Reapers managed to ply their trade in plain view without sending mortals screaming for the exits.

Cait had raised her arms. A glowing silver gateway took shape just behind where she stood. "Tommy. Lia. Nigel," she crooned. "Come to me. I offer passage."

The shades glided closer. All three had fang marks in their necks, but we had to be certain. Many things could mimic the look of death-by-Vampire.

I didn't need my ward, not here in the gray, crumbling half-light of the realm of the dead, so I released it.

The shades stopped in their tracks. "Who's he?" a man with short brown hair asked.

"A Sidhe and my mate. He will not harm you." Cait's voice was musical, soothing.

So long as they were staring at me, I inclined my head. "We would avenge your deaths. What manner of being killed you?"

The woman, not yet twenty by the looks of her, brushed

blonde hair away from her neck and pointed at multiple puncture wounds. "Horrible things. At first, they pretended to be human, but they did something. We couldn't get away, and then they weren't human any longer."

"Aye," the other man concurred. He was as fair as the woman, and they might have been related. "They developed an incredible stench, rot like I've never smelled afore. And then fangs shot out, and they jumped us."

"How many?" Cait asked.

"Four," the first man said. "Two attacked Lia as if they couldn't get enough of her."

Tears tracked down Lia's cheeks. I hadn't known the dead could cry. Fury ran through me, hot and feral. "We will find the Vampires and end them. I offer my word, which binds me. I will not rest until the deed is done."

"Your time here is over," Cait said. "Pass through my gates. Relief from pain and worry lies beyond them." Behind her, the portal shone even brighter. One by one, the shades walked into her arms, through her, and then past the gateway.

Cait's eyes glistened with unshed tears; she lowered her arms, and the portal disappeared. "I'm going to release my magic. When I do, we'll be back inside the church."

"I can teleport us out of here. Might be cleaner."

She shook her head, wearing a resolute expression I'd come to know. "I want to reassure the priest their souls have found rest."

I extended a hand. She took it. "If he has any spiritual depth, he already knows. We have Vampires to hunt."

Cait drew her dark brows together. I'd have done this any way she wanted, but I was relieved when she finally nodded and said, "You're right, of course. Besides, the priest has probably had a bellyful of supernatural creatures. He might not appreciate I'm one of the good ones."

The priest was still chanting and pivoting around the three biers when I moved us outside into the sleety rain. His prayers had been answered, but not in the way he might have envisioned. The weather in the realm of the dead was always the same. Still, gray, quiet. Too bad we couldn't transport it back across the veil.

"*Find anything?*" I raised my mind voice, aiming it at Padhraic.

"*Aye. Where have you been?*"

"*Dealing with shades,*" Cait answered.

"*I thought as much,*" Stacia's sending was garbled. She hadn't yet mastered telepathy, but it wasn't as critical as other magical skills.

"Did you expect the ghosts would want to cross?" I nudged Cait.

She trained her green-eyed gaze on me, a haunted expression in her eyes. "No. And I should have. At first, I was worried they might be Vampire minions."

"How did you determine they weren't?"

Her gaze skittered to one side. "Trial and error. When the first one passed through me and didn't cause me pain, I figured it would be all right."

I opened my mouth to tell her she'd taken a ridiculous risk, but before I got any words out—because I was hunting for a combination that didn't berate her for sketchy judgment—she squeezed my hand tighter.

"I'm a Reaper. It's what I do. I'm not going to quit offering passage because I'm worried about my safety. What kind of person would that make me?"

Shame swamped me, making my skin feel two sizes too small. My main worry had been for her, but she hadn't lost sight of her calling. What she'd done for the shades had been critical. They'd been through hell, and it wasn't fair to make them search for a Reaper before they could leave.

I wrapped my arms around her. "It makes you a whole bunch better than me. I love you."

She leaned into me. "Not sure about the 'better' part."

"Meet us partway up the hill behind the village," Padhraic said. *"Hurry."*

My teleport spell still fluttered around us. I reset it to take us to a spot close to Padhraic and Stacia's location.

"We should walk," Cait said. "Vampires are sensitive to expended power. We don't want to tip them off any more than we already have. My gateway packs quite a wallop. Besides, we can't get any wetter than we already are."

I let go of her and led the way around back streets until I reached an old sheep track leading to where I thought Padhraic was. Soon, the faint glow of his power told me I'd guessed right.

Stacia ran to us and hugged Cait. "Nice work. I felt them cross."

"Thanks. I hadn't planned on them being there. If it were me, I'd have run as far from my Vampire-contaminated body as I could get. But when they approached me, I couldn't have refused them. Not after probably being the reason they were killed."

"Best we can tell," Padhraic said, "the Vampires are holed up inside a cottage on top of this hillock."

"Aye. I ken the place well enough. No one's lived there for a long while. It used to be a shepherd's hut."

"They'll be lethargic, having just fed," Padhraic went on.

"Means we should be able to bust in, hit them with dead man's blood, and then stake them."

"What about saving one to drag back to the castle?" I asked.

"I thought about it," Padhraic said. "I'm still in favor of the idea, but we need to pick carefully."

"Find the weakest link, if there is one. If it's not obvious, they're all dead." I skinned my lips back from my teeth. I hated Vampires. Dealing with them offended me because they were such an affront to nature.

We'd begun trudging uphill. The noise of the storm muffled our approach. Almost as if the weather was trying to help, lightning and thunder rolled through, adding to the fog and sleet. Vampires had keen senses, but they were more likely to smell us than hear us. That particular observation cut both ways. The characteristic sweetish rotten stench of Vampire reached me before we crested the hill.

The hut, a long-since-abandoned single-room affair came into view. No light shone from within, but I hadn't expected any. No electricity up here, and Vampires didn't have the type of magic to fuel mage lights. All that research I'd done hadn't totally been for naught.

Looking inside would have been helpful, but like many structures built hundreds of years ago, this one lacked windows. Back in the day, it made it simpler to heat. No smoke curled from the stone chimney, but since Vamps were already dead, being cold didn't bother them.

I handed Cait a syringe with dead man's blood.

Padhraic focused magic at the door. It burst inward with us right behind its shattered remains. Vampires shot to their feet from where they'd been crouched in a circle on the floor.

Damn it. Way more than four. I tugged my blade free, shouted, "Plan B," and lopped off two heads.

I saw Padhraic's sword swinging out of the corners of my eyes. Cries of, "It's the traitor. Get him," filled the cold, dank air.

"In your dreams," Padhraic shouted in Gaelic.

I happened to be watching when Cait hefted her sickle and sliced it through flesh, sinew, and vertebrae. The Vamp's head rolled to the floor, but didn't turn to riddled bones. The body remained intact too—with the severed head lurching toward it. I kicked the head so hard it shattered when it came into contact with the wall of the hut.

Even reduced to bloody pulp, it crept back toward the body it had once been attached to. My hands ached from the touch of the metal in my sword, but I brought the flat side down on the neck stump to finish the macabre display playing out in front of me.

After that, Cait and Stacia worked as a team with dead man's blood and silver stakes. The reek of Vampire was thick in my nostrils, twisting my stomach into a hard, painful, nauseated knot.

In the back of my mind, I wondered why they weren't fighting back harder. Or leaving. Surely, they could teleport back to the seethe.

Cait screamed, an outraged shriek filled with anger and fear. I spun to help and saw a Vampire clinging to her, mouth poised over her neck.

Stacia plucked a stake from a downed stack of moldering bones and drove it into the Vamp's back. It crumpled, and Cait shook off its remains. "Thanks," she shouted.

"No thanks required. I owed you."

We were down to two Vampires, out of the twenty we'd faced, when I felt a wave of electric, ozone-saturated power bearing down on us. Only the dark mages felt like this. "Ward yourselves," I yelled.

A ripping, tearing noise was so loud my ears protested. It felt like something had slashed the world asunder. A portal eviscerated one side of the hut, followed by two more. Almost quicker than my eyes could follow, Adva leapt through one, caught Padhraic in a wrestler's tie-up, and lunged through another gateway.

With an unholy shriek, Stacia swooped after them, managing to grab one of Adva's legs. He tried to shake her off, but she hung on like a rabid dog. As quickly as they'd formed, the gateways frittered to nothing.

The Vampires looked as shocked as we were. We had to go after Padhraic and Stacia. Right now before the trail grew cold, but I wasn't about to let any Vampire walk free.

They were still staring at where Adva had vanished when I sliced cleanly through both their necks. Ichor spurted from one, black and stinking. I didn't bother wiping my sword before I sheathed it. My hands were bleeding from gripping the damn thing for so long, and I was done.

"Come on," Cait urged. "We need to find them."

"Aye, we're leaving, but I have to let Krin and Dena know." I raised my mind voice, keeping the channel one-way. They could hear me, but I didn't care what they had to say. For all I knew, Hades would announce to everyone that Padhraic was damaged goods, and we had to keep our eye on more important balls.

I didn't have anything of Padhraic's so I ginned up the feel of his energy, set a tracking spell in motion, and loosed it. "No matter what," I told Cait, "do not leave my side."

She didn't answer. When I glanced at her, her face could have been etched in marble. "We'll find them." I tried for reassurance but didn't hear it in my voice. Adva was the god of fucking portals. He could lead us a merry chase, and we'd end up back at our starting point.

Or lost in some psychic black hole.

CHAPTER SEVEN, CAIT

I'd thought only Death could kindle my rage. Not true. Anger burned a vicious track through me. Fear wasn't far behind. Had this whole thing with the Vamps been a setup? A trap? I'd wondered why they hadn't fought back harder. Even the one whose mouth had been poised over my jugular had hesitated long enough for Stacia to stake him. She had her sickle, but it wasn't much good ending Vampires.

As soon as I'd used my own, I understood the magic was incompatible. My blade concentrated my power, and Reapers weren't usually killers. We harvested the dead. What happened to them on the far side of the gateway wasn't our concern. I used to joke it was above my paygrade.

Today taught me I should have schlepped my sword along. The one tipped against a wall back in Liam's chamber at Scourie Castle. I hadn't wanted the bother. It was clunky and awkward—and it tore holes in my hands—but it would have helped. A lot.

I gave voice to my worries. "Do you think it was a trap?"

Liam nodded. "The leading edge of one. I suspect their targets were you and me, but Padhraic had the bad luck to be closest. Adva would have had to go around him to get to me, and Padhraic would have cleaved him from crown to arsehole. He'd have recovered, but it would have taken time."

Bands of color flashed by as we moved farther away from Earth. At least, that's what it seemed like we were doing. My scythe had taken on a soft glow where I held it tucked beneath one arm.

"Any idea why Stacia jumped after Padhraic?" Liam asked.

"Not really. She's brave and all. Maybe she was worried he'd be alone." I shook off a sense of impending hopelessness. "At least she knows where he is. We may not find them."

"Uh-uh. None of that."

I clamped my jaws tight. I knew the drill. Magic required belief, so I chased my doubts off to one side and focused on feeding power into Liam's seeking spell. "Uh, do you know where we are?"

"Roughly. We've traversed most of the bands—corridors—circling Earth. Only one or two remain. Beyond them, there's nothing. No place the dark gods could have established an outpost."

I homed in on the bit of Paddy's energy Liam had set as our signpost. It hadn't changed. It pulsed as robustly as it had when we'd left the falling-down shepherd's cottage. The only good thing about where we were now was it wasn't raining. Tracking has never been one of my magics, unless I counted luring and herding the dead. I had built-in procedures for that.

Liam had an arm looped around my waist. The hand pressed against my hip was a wreck from wielding the sword, but it seemed to have quit seeping blood. Worry sheeted from him, turning his aura red-gray. I tiptoed around what I wanted to ask. "Tracking isn't one of my skills, but is it usual for Padhraic's energy signature to remain static?"

"What do you mean?"

"When I lure the dead, the feel of them changes as they come closer to me."

"I've been worried about that," he admitted. "I've never crafted a glob of my memories of a person and used it as a focal point. I've always had something like clothing or hair or a weapon."

"If we returned to the castle, you could get something of his. Or of Stacia's. Maybe it would make our search shorter."

"Damn good idea. I'm embarrassed I didn't think of it."

The pitch and cadence of Liam's Sidhe power that had been humming in my ears changed dramatically. When it cleared, the walls of his chamber formed around us.

"Where's Padhraic's room? Do we need something of Stacia's too?" I asked, still feeling edgy. Time was short, and may well have run out for Padhraic and Stacia.

"This way to Paddy's chamber." His voice was low. "We'll be quick. In and out and gone again. All we need is something from one of them."

I'd wondered if we were going to rustle up help. If we were running headlong into a nest of the four dark gods, the two of us would barely be enough to make a dent. In a fairytale world, Padhraic and Stacia could help, but they might be imprisoned, slapped behind iron that eroded their magic and their strength.

The Sidhe were immortal. I wasn't sure about just how far my enhanced magical spectrum reached, but I had a feeling it stopped shy of conferring eternal life. Worry for Stacia ate at me.

"Cait. Let's go."

I hurried out the door after Liam, scooping up my sword and buckling it into place. It might come in handy, even if we didn't end up facing off against a Vampire horde. I felt the bite of the metal through its fancy hilt. Too bad it wasn't made of the same stuff as the scythe.

Where had the Reaper blades come from originally? Had they been Death's doing? After all, she had one, but I'd never known her to do any blacksmith work.

"Hold up!" Krin's unmistakable tenor reverberated off the stone walls.

Liam pushed past him. "Not now, mate. I'm in a hurry."

I tried to slither around Krin, but he clamped a hand over my lower arm. "What happened?"

"Adva has Padhraic and Stacia. We're tracking them." I yanked on my arm, but I may as well have been chained to the castle itself.

"There's more," Krin said.

"Yeah, but I told you the important part."

"Let go of her," Liam thundered. He'd circled back to where Krin held me in place.

"When you left, it was just the two of you going to demolish some Vampires," Krin pressed, but he did let go of my arm.

"We did that too," Liam growled. "Then Adva popped out of nowhere, grabbed Paddy, and vanished through another of his infernal portals. Stacia dove after them."

Krin scrunched his face into a grim expression. "What tipped me off first was Padhraic created a doppelgänger, but it was fading, so I knew it was illusion. After you sent me that *one-way* telepathic message"—he emphasized one-way, turning it into an accusation—"I started scanning for your magic."

"Fine. We have to get moving." Liam headed back down the hallway and stopped at the top of a staircase. I trotted after him. So did Krin.

"It won't only be Adva," Krin muttered. "At least one of the others will be with him." His demeanor changed from channeling one of the Furies to something far more reasonable.

"Probably," Liam agreed. "So?"

"We haven't reported to anyone since Hollis revealed himself as a fraud," Krin said. "I'm not telling you what to do, but I'm asking you to stop by the dining room before you leave."

"Why?" Liam sounded as approachable as a female lion guarding a kill.

"Everyone is in agreement about going after the dark gods. This provides an exceptional opportunity. I feel certain we'll find them wherever Padhraic and Stacia are."

"I'll do it on one condition," Liam said.

"Name it." Krin spun one hand in a get-on-with-it gesture.

"No one attempts to stop me. I will retrieve something of Paddy's to make it possible to track him. Once I've done that, Cait and I will visit the dining room. Either you'll be ready to come with us, or we're leaving without you."

"I understand," Krin nodded briskly. "Timing is critical. While you're rooting around in Padhraic's things, select a few items."

Liam spun and raced down the stairs. I ran after him, catching up two floors below in an unadorned room similar to Liam's, but twice the size. He riffled through a scuffed armoire and withdrew a few shirts, settling on a cream-colored linen one I remembered Padhraic wearing.

"Let's go," Liam told me. I knew him well enough to practically taste the worry seeping through him.

"I thought Krin asked you to grab several things."

"He wasn't thinking clearly. We can cut this shirt in as many pieces as necessary. That way, we'll all be working off the same psychic energy. Assuming anyone is interested in accompanying us."

"Why wouldn't they be?"

"Padhraic was a Leanan. Many of the Sidhe still view him as damaged."

I chewed my lower lip. What Liam hadn't said was some of his kinsfolk wouldn't believe Padhraic was worthy of them risking themselves on his behalf. "What about Stacia?" I blurted. "She was never a Vampire."

He turned to look at me, his face scrunched into an uncomfortable expression marked by embarrassment and determination. "Aye, but neither is she a Sidhe."

Breath hissed from my mouth, making clouds in the chilly air as I hustled after Liam. I wanted to like the Sidhe, view them as allies, but Liam's assessment of his kinsmen painted them in an unflattering light. Much as I might want to, I couldn't discount his judgment. He'd known the Sidhe a whole lot longer than me.

No conclusions. No assumptions, I lectured myself as we covered the distance to the dining room and stood beneath the arched entryway.

Cerebrus gave a cheerful little yip and loped to where I stood. The dog might not show this side to many, but he may as well have been an overgrown puppy with me. I crouched in front of him and dipped my fingers in his thick, short, black fur.

Three tongues licked me.

Hades stalked behind his dog. "We shall launch an attack." He held out a hand. Liam ripped the shirt, hanging onto a piece for us. The god of the dead grabbed the remainder. Black-edged power flickered to life around him, and his blue eyes widened with surprise.

"Och, they dinna go far," he said in Gaelic.

"We traveled to almost the farthest corridor," Liam said, "and didn't find them."

"Adva tricked you. Big surprise," Arawn said. He'd glided to Hades' side.

"We suspected as much," Liam said. "I'd have kept looking, but Cait called us back, said we needed a more foolproof tracking method."

"Good woman." Approval in Hades' voice warmed me, but I didn't take it too much to heart. He could turn on me in a heartbeat if my wishes ran counter to his. I'd spent enough of my life kowtowing to Death to understand how things worked.

"Are you going to tell us where Padhraic is?" Liam rolled his shoulders back and met Hades' keen blue-eyed gaze.

"And Stacia," I spoke up. "She's not exactly immortal. At least I don't believe she is." A chill crept through me. Sensing my distress, the dog nuzzled me, breathing warm, doggy breath on my neck.

"She might be. We're not sure at this point," Arawn said. "Once Death comes to her senses and returns from her self-imposed exile, we'll find out more about the full extent of Reaper magic."

Death.

I hadn't thought about her for a while now, and it had been such a welcome respite. Never knowing when she was about to bounce in and read me the riot act had taken a toll.

Yeah. One that's far from over, a sour inner voice reminded me. I pushed to my feet and regarded the room. Sidhe and Reapers were all on their feet wearing worried expressions. It appeared they'd formed groups, perhaps the same ones we'd used when we captured Perrikus and D'Chel.

Good thing I wasn't in line to be a military commander. My attention to detail sucked.

"They're one corridor to the northeast from the place we encountered them last time," Arawn told Liam.

He turned to go, motioning for me to follow him.

"You might wish to wait for the rest of us," Hades said. Though couched as a suggestion, I recognized it as more of an order. What would the god of the dead do if Liam kept on walking?

Liam turned back. "Waiting is a very bad idea. We have to move now. Padhraic's been through enough. His magic has barely recovered from our surgery to cut out the Vampire parts."

"Stacia too," I said. "Reapers have never been warriors. Which reminds me"—I projected my voice with magic—"Reapers. Your scythes will not end Vampires. You can behead them, but it doesn't spell their doom."

"Already outfitted from the armory." Arawn turned his gimlet gaze right on me. I faced him squarely. Compared with Death, it was easy to look him straight in the eyes.

"Leave in your designated groups," Hades called out. "In the order I assigned."

Krin moved smoothly to Liam's side. "We're together, mate. You too," he addressed me.

"Does our merry band have a commander?" Liam asked.

Krin nodded. "You and me. Shall we?"

The sandalwood-and-wet-greenery smells of Sidhe magic thickened as groups prepared to depart. Heather and wildflowers from the Reaper side of things mingled with it, creating a pleasing mixture. If I breathed deep, I could easily delude myself about the gravity of our undertaking.

I remembered our last confrontation. Then the dark mages hadn't had hostages. This time, they did.

It could make a huge difference.

"Our first project has to be freeing Padhraic and Stacia," I said softly, keeping my mouth next to Liam's ear.

"Agreed," he said, not bothering to match my barely there voice volume. "No one is going to turn them into collateral damage to serve the greater good."

"We'll do everything we can to free them," Krin said.

Scourie Castle faded, replaced by the darkness of a journey spell. Except it wasn't very dark, not with all of us glowing in various shades. The scythes took on a silvery fairy dust aspect. I was glad to have mine propped across my shoulders. It made me feel complete, kind of like Liam did.

I hadn't allowed myself to think much about him since our stolen hours where we'd greedily inhaled one another. No matter how many times he kissed me or touched me, I wanted more. Hell, I could lose myself looking at the squared-off line of his jaw or the silken strands of his fair hair or his deliciously muscled body. Especially now that I'd had a sample of that body, of him touching me, kissing me, looking into my eyes and telling me how important I was to him.

Would we ever have more than the occasional few minutes to love one another?

I gave myself a swift kick in the backside. Mooning over the man I was rapidly falling in love with wasn't on today's menu. War held a starring role. It was the dish du jour, and would be for the foreseeable future.

Liam was worried about Padhraic. It came through loud and clear. Did he have weak spots from his time as a Leanan? Places he could be corrupted anew? In the brief time I'd know Padhraic, I'd developed a healthy respect for the Sidhe. He had an inner strength and resolve. I had faith they'd carry him through.

We were nearly at our destination. The spell was developing pearlescent edges. I tossed a ward together, not knowing what we'd face when the journey casting spit us out.

The last corridor we'd visited had been flat, barren. This one was full of cliffs and gullies, not unlike an illusory world I'd visited on the far side of a barrier in the realm of the dead. The sky was dirty white with a lemon-colored sun listing to one side, almost as if it was too heavy to remain in the air.

"Fuck." Liam spat the word.

"Aye. Those terrain features are handy for them. Not so good for us," Krin muttered.

Reapers and Sidhe popped into view all around us. I scanned the pock-marked terrain with magic, hoping something would jump out at me, but if anyone was here, they were well concealed. "You still have the shirt, right?" I nudged Liam.

He pulled a scrap of the linen garment from a pocket and knotted it before chanting a power word in Old Gaelic. The bit of fabric hovered in front of us before floating off to our right.

Liam took off after it with me on his heels. I expected Krin to summon us back, but he didn't.

Maybe he understood how pointless it would be. He did call after us that he'd deploy the remainder of our group hunting for a back way into wherever Paddy and Stacia were. Liam's pace slowed dramatically. It was rough going as we skittered to the bottom of deep ravines and then clambered up the other side.

Something about this place made my skin crawl. It felt wrong, as if it housed untold evil just beneath its surface. Was the corridor riddled with gateways into Adva's hall of mirrors?

The thing about mortals and their games is those games had their beginnings in a far darker reality. Every Halloween house of horrors could have been spawned from this place with its blind corners and indefensible gorges. Rock avalanches pounded against my ears, eerie and threatening since I couldn't actually see them.

I felt naked, exposed, like someone could pierce right through my warding.

My scythe vibrated a warning. I shouted at Liam to stop. Thank the gods he listened. A gaping chasm shot to life right in front of him, punctuated by still more rockfall. Damn, it was loud and ominous. Liam teetered on the edge of the gorge before regaining his balance and stepping back.

"It's a portal into Adva's realm," I said, not sure how I knew, but knowing all the same.

Arawn materialized between us, his dark eyes glittering with menace. "It is, indeed. I can smell him. Let's go. I've always wanted to corner that one on his own turf."

"I'm game." Liam pointed at the scrap of shirt floating below us. "Paddy's down there."

I said a quick hopeful prayer Stacia was still with him, wrapped myself in magic to cushion my fall, and jumped after Liam and Arawn.

What would we find?

Would three of us be enough?

Shut up! I tuned my inner critic out. I'd survived Death's manipulations—and Vampires. How much harder could this be?

Rhetorical questions are a bitch. They come back to bite you in the ass and shriek, "I told you so," so loud you wish you'd paid closer attention before leaping and hoping for the best.

Kind of like I'd just done.

CHAPTER EIGHT, LIAM

Wobbling on the edge of an abyss, I started to tell Cait to return to our regiment. She wouldn't have listened, though, and I'd have hurt her feelings. She'd just saved my ass by shouting a warning. I wanted to know why she'd sensed the crater before me, but we could sort it out later.

The bottom of the hole rose up to meet me, as jagged and uneven as the surface above it. Mirrors hung at crazy angles as if Adva's hall of malevolent glass had downed a psychedelic drug. Where before the mirrors had been lined up, now some lay on their sides. Others balanced precariously on edge. Still more floated above me, suspended by the god's power.

Caution had been my friend during my last sojourn; I bent and marked the spot I'd landed. The ground heaved beneath my feet, so I settled for scratching a deep gouge into the nearest mirror. I'd no sooner finished than it floated a few meters away.

"This way," Arawn's deep voice echoed in my head.

The tattered corner from Paddy's shirt floated near the god of the dead.

Above us, the convenient hole was knitting itself shut beginning with the upper portion. My mage light flared to life. "We have to leave a trail, or we'll never find our way out."

"Give me some credit." Arawn directed a pointed look my way.

A scritching sound brought my head around in time to see Cait dragging the pick of her scythe across the uneven ground. It left a path that burned with an inner light. "I've got this," she said.

Half a dozen Reapers and four Sidhe piled into the hole. "Figured we'd better get down here while we still could," Pavel said. Rolf, Anya, Gregor, and Abby were with him.

"Aye, the abyss has a damnably fluid aspect." Moire pursed her mouth into a thin line. Violet hair fluffed around her ageless face, adding highlights to her silvery eyes. One of the older Sidhe, she exuded a quiet competence.

"We noticed," I muttered.

Arawn was done waiting. He surged forward, surprisingly nimble with his bare feet and robes. Cait and I scrambled to keep up. The scrape of her sickle over dirt and glass was reassuring. Would its magic defeat Adva's? Or did the god have a way of perverting our Hansel-and-Gretel-breadcrumbs trail?

Arawn hadn't seemed worried about our egress. I hoped his optimism was based on something other than hubris. The sliver of light from above winked out as the earth rearranged itself.

"Do you suppose Adva can only manage that because of the proximity of his mirrors?" Cait asked.

"Are you referring to him shuffling the geography of this corridor?"

"Yeah. Pretty much. It wasn't illusion like that place near Prague. This excavation was real, but so's everything down here." She spread an arm to one side. "Commanding magic that can hollow out this much dirt is...impressive."

"Don't be too astonished. The stunt came with a price." I suddenly understood what had happened to the mirrors. And maybe the composition of the cave.

"Not sure what you mean." Cait scribed the scythe's blade around two fallen mirrors.

"I'm certain it didn't look like this down here before Adva—or whoever—created the cave-in."

"Mm-hm. I wondered about that."

The deeper we moved into what was obviously an extensive cave system, the edgier I became. We were playing right into the dark mage's hands. Adva had hung out the welcome sign, and we'd taken the bait.

The mirrors were thinning out, and the floor was smoother than it had been. I nodded to myself. Magic wasn't limitless—for anybody. We were already marching along like the children following the Pied Piper of Hamblin. No need to squander power on unnecessary impediments for us to trip over.

Some of the mirrors had been real enough, but probably not nearly as many of them as I'd assumed. A low, ominous whistling started from somewhere behind me, followed by a chilly wind carrying the acrid scents of decaying meat.

It took me a moment to connect the dots. Vampires. Newly turned ones smelled like that.

The jaws of the trap were about the spring shut.

Apparently, Arawn had come to the same conclusion. "Run," he shouted. "This way."

He stood in front of a rock wall. The stones glowed like a

bizarre symbol of hope in a world that had come loose from its moorings. Arawn made certain all of us were close enough to see him when he executed a leap where he twisted midair and pelted through what appeared to be solid granite.

Reapers and Sidhe followed him. I grabbed Cait's hand, and we formed the rear guard, not crossing until we were certain everyone else was safe. Behind us, boulders crashed down, and the air clotted with dust and particulate matter that made my throat and lungs burn.

The passageway was closing behind us, shutting off our exit route. At least twenty Vampires marched in the wake of all that destruction. Their stench had expanded to a nauseating miasma that made sweat break out on my forehead. Newly made Vamps had yet to be socialized. Drunk on their freshly discovered power, they gloried in flogging people with it.

Look at me! I can drink your blood. I can kill you. I can fuck you if I feel like it. While I'm drinking your blood.

"Now would be a good time to leave," Cait muttered.

"That's my darling. Understated as hell." I walked into the stone, expecting it to part around us like it had for everyone else. It didn't. My face clonked against the rock.

"What's wrong?" Cait pounded a fist on the wall, but it acted like rock was supposed to.

"The illusion moved," I said around my clenched teeth. "I suppose we should be flattered. It's a whole lot of trouble to go to for the two of us."

"We always knew we were Adva's target," Cait said. "We outfoxed him last time, and he's probably a sore loser."

"No probably about it. I'm going to try to get us out of here."

"I have a better idea." Turning, she raised her arms. The

silvery shimmer from her scythe encased the rest of her, and she began to sing in a high, clear voice. Her Reaper scent puffed out around her, filling the cavern with the promise of better things to come once a shade moved past the specter of their death.

All around us, ghosts hastened to her call. My vision bifurcated until the gray, crumbling world of the dead surrounded me with a glistening white gateway just coming into view.

"Mistress. You came for us," rose from dead throats.

I swallowed back surprise. These ghosts had been dead for a long while. Long enough to have resisted the call of many a Reaper. Cait's song swelled. The dusty air formed a vortex around her. Something about the combination of music and her magic drew the shades. One by one, they passed through her, cooing their pleasure.

From the corners of my eyes, I finally saw the Vampires. Their faces held rapt expressions, and I understood Cait had them in thrall as well. Being careful not to interrupt the flow of her hypnotic trance, I fed power into it, strengthening it until it should be irresistible to the Vampires.

One shambled toward her, joining the line of shades as he moved closer to Cait's outstretched arms. So new he still had fang marks in his own neck, he was low-hanging fruit.

Maybe.

He hung back at the last moment until Cait's music developed a multitoned aspect, as if it came from more than one Reaper. A very unvampirelike smile lit his face before he walked through Cait and the portal behind her.

Half a dozen more Vampires sashayed through her. The first one had given them courage, hope.

"What the fuck are you doing? Stop!" The shout came from our other side. I recognized Adva's singsong tones. Except they were far from dulcet today. Nothing like when he'd challenged us to run after him. The god of portals was furious.

Cait was lost in her Reaper power. Apparently, it didn't have a nice, neat on-off spigot. But the Vampires were in thrall as well. Two more passed through her before Adva bounded out of nowhere and planted himself in front of the remaining Vampires.

"Go back!" he screeched, magic pouring from him as he tossed up a wall between the Vampires and Cait.

Her song changed, developed menacing undernotes. Was she trying to pilot the Vampires? I drew magic, balancing the flow between my hands, ready for anything.

"Take Adva," Cait cried. "He stands between you and me." White light edged with blue glittered around her. The scythe glowed red.

I diverted more magic her way, surrounding each Vampire with the will to destroy Adva. If it had never occurred to them before, it would now. I painted pictures of Adva screaming for mercy as the Vampires trampled over him and into Cait's waiting arms.

A mirror clanged down in front of the Vamps. "Blood is that way," Adva shouted. "Willing mortals just for you."

Cait never quit singing, the music evocative of salvation, of hope. The Vampires hadn't chosen evil. It had been foisted upon them. They could recant, enter the afterlife with a clean slate. She, Cait Carrick, would see to it.

Or maybe it wasn't what she was promising at all. Her song had no words. My guess was everyone heard something different, and I'd tapped into one of the Vampires' interpretations.

What would they choose? Adva's mirror or Cait's otherworldly beauty and assurances of better things to come?

Adva wasn't taking any chances. He circled behind two of the Vampires and gave them a hefty shove with his fists and magic toward the mirror pulsing with a sickly nacre glow. At first, they appeared to follow like meek little sheep, but Adva hadn't counted on them being newly made.

Fresh Vamps are assholes. They have a lawless streak; it's why they're paired with older Vampires until they've become trustworthy, a process that can take fifty years or more.

"Take him," Cait shouted again, but this time it held a seductive edge. She wanted to bathe the Vampires in Reaper love. Adva stood in the way.

A rustling wail came from the rearmost Vampires, spreading through their mass until it turned into a mantra. "Reaper. Reaper. Reaper."

"Yessss. Come to me." Cait drew out the words and repeated them, punctuated by musical riffs and trills.

The Vampires streamed around the mirror, jostling for who could avail themselves of Cait and the gateway first. Because I was paying attention to her—and our shared power—I didn't notice Adva until magic walloped me from behind and pushed me to my knees.

Only two Vampires remained. Cait had them well in hand. I redirected my power at Adva. Before I could scramble to my feet, he launched himself on top of me. We rolled around in the dirt, landing punches where we could.

"What the fuck?" I snarled. "You've resorted to brute force?"

"Whatever works," he snarled back. "I should have ended you last time you sullied my hall of mirrors."

"My recollection is you tried and failed," I taunted him as I punched his nose. The satisfying crunch of bones and spurting blood reminded me I was wasting time, energy, and magic. Adva's face would heal faster than I could destroy it. I kneed him in the chest and used the rebound motion to get my feet under me.

He somersaulted through the air, landing in front of the mirror the Vampires had thumbed their noses at, barking words in what sounded like demonspeak. Harsh, guttural, they culled everything good and decent out of the world.

Glass shattered outward, showering the god with shards. Dots of blood formed where glass dug into his hands and face. He swiped a finger over the blood and painted a rune on the mirror's frame.

Cait's song had faded, along with her magic. She'd expended gobs, and she tottered on her feet. I had a bad feeling about the mirror. And Adva. Cait was right about him being a sore loser, and he'd lost pride and face when the Vamps had chosen Cait over him.

I hurried to her side and wrapped an arm around her waist, propping her up. "Nice work," I told her, "but we're not done."

"Yeah. Got it." Her words were slurred, testament to her exhaustion.

The rest of the mirror cracked, sounding like ice on a frozen pond. High-pitched shrieks pounded against me as winged fuckers flew through the ruined glass. About the size of turkeys, they had two pairs of wings, long reptilian snouts, and a combination of scales and feathers. The bitter stench of poison curdled my stomach and abraded the inside of my nose and mouth.

"Jesus. Are they real?" Cait muttered, seemingly shaking herself out of her lethargy.

"Aye, and poisonous too. Take care they don't bite you."

The whirr of wings and hoarse cries filled the still air of the cave. When I looked for Adva, he was gone. I'd thought he'd stick around to egg his army on, but maybe he'd gone to rustle up Tokkhots or check on Padhraic.

Or nurse his wounded pride.

A wing sliced through my cheek. Eh. Not feathers after all, but scales in the shape of feathers. Cait yelped as one of the abominations buried its talons in her hair. She reached for it, but I got there first, blade swinging as I sliced through the bird-thing.

Green ichor with black streaks spewed everywhere. I swatted its body with the flat of my sword; it let go of Cait and dropped to the ground. Her scythe was mowing through the bird things, working of its own volition.

I heard the swish as she pulled her blade from its scabbard. We'd both have major wounds on our hands, but it was tomorrow's problem. The sound of our breath rasped loud as we struck again and again. Blood dribbled from multiple wounds in my face, scalp, and hands. Cait's too.

The toxin oozing from the birds stung and made me lightheaded.

Every time one of the wings got close enough to touch us, it cleaved through flesh. "Why are they so fucking sharp?" Cait screeched and lopped the heads off two of the monsters.

More flew through the mirror. Adva had opened a gateway to somewhere south of Hell. I focused a blast of destructive power at the remains of the mirror, intent on closing off the passageway. That way, we'd have a fighting chance.

My power floated around the mirror as if getting too close burned it. Fuck that nonsense. I threw power words into the mix. So many my throat wanted to close, and my lungs were on fire from effort.

With a rending boom that left my ears throbbing, the mirror crackled to dust.

"No more birds," Cait panted, sounding as if remaining upright had turned into a chore.

"No new ones." My words were grim. At least twenty of the misshapen monsters cawed and hissed. I'd been hoping shutting the gate would have closed them off from whatever intelligence powered their flight.

I'd been wrong.

"Liam. Something's not r-right." Cait's words were garbled, but I understood her well enough. Before I could react, she crumpled to the floor.

The bird things piled on top of her. At least they were all in one spot. My right hand was trashed. Bone showed through, but I didn't care. I wrapped what was left of my palm around the hilt and killed every single bird, kicking them to one side to open a path to the ones beneath.

One left the flock and scribed uneven circles above me. Poison dribbled from its open jaws. Where it contacted my clothing, it smoldered and stank. Bitter orange and rotten meat and sulfur fumes.

"You're last," I told it and built a sloppy ward. My reserves were running dangerously low, but I had enough to finish this.

Cait lay like a dead thing. Christ. What had happened? Had one of the bastards bitten her? I booted the last of the dead abominations off her and stabbed skyward, intent on the one still flying above me. It remained just beyond the reach of my blade.

"So that's how you want to play it," I growled. Lethal magic flew from my ruined hands, and the thing exploded midair. The reeking shit that passed for blood rained down on me, but I didn't care.

I sheathed the blade and knelt next to Cait. Cradling her in my arms, I sent magic zinging through her trying to determine what was wrong. Relief seared me when I didn't detect poison. Wounds crisscrossed every centimeter of open flesh, but none of them were critical.

She writhed weakly in my arms. "I'm okay. Stupid. I was a dumbass. Ran my magic down to nothing."

"Ssht. It's all right. All of us have done that."

"Let go. I'm fine. We have to get out of here before Adva comes back. And we have to find Padhraic and Stacia." She made a gagging noise. I turned her head while she vomited into the dirt.

I tried to wipe her face but left bloody tracks from my ruined hands. "Can you stand?"

"Yes." The single word was laced with determination.

I helped her to her feet and held her until she stopped swaying. Her blade obeyed my command, albeit reluctantly, and I tucked it into her scabbard. Once I was sure she could stand on her own, I dredged up the beginnings of a teleport spell. Even if Paddy and Stacia were still prisoners, we weren't in any kind of shape to do anything but sacrifice ourselves.

Arawn punched through the wall that had thwarted my efforts to transit it. "I wondered what happened to the two of you—until I figured out this whole mess was a charade to trap you. Adva didn't give two fucks about the rest of us."

I stared at the wall. "How'd you go through it?"

"Adva's illusions are sloppy. If you'd taken a wee bit of time, you could have defeated it."

Hot words rushed to my lips about how quickly we'd been forced on the defensive, but I swallowed all of them. Warriors didn't offer excuses. I should have made a stronger effort no matter what foes materialized.

"Did you find Paddy and Stacia?" Cait asked.

The god of the dead nodded. "We did. They're back in Scourie Castle, which is where I'll be taking the two of you." He marched close, planting himself in front of Cait, and switched to Gaelic. "What ye did is forbidden."

"I had a feeling it was," she said and shook herself. Bird parts fell from her hair, splatting on the ground. "Death was clear we couldn't raise magic to force anyone to cross, but that rule went up in smoke with Vampires. Anything goes with them."

"And I'm ordering you never to do that again. 'Twasn't meant for those such as you, and 'tis why ye're weak as a newborn lamb." Arawn's dark eyes bored into Cait. The two of them had forgotten my presence.

I cleared my throat. "Which part, exactly, are you talking about."

"The song," Arawn and Cait said almost in unison.

"I didn't have access to it until Cathbad sang to me," Cait told Arawn. "And I wasn't certain it would work, but I was flat out of options."

Arawn placed a hand on Cait's shoulder. "Cathbad gifted the Sirens. It dinnae turn out well."

"Singing men to their doom and luring the dead to cross are different," Cait argued.

"Are they?" Arawn asked just before he wrapped us in magic and the blood-saturated, reeking cavern fell away. I had questions, but they could wait. Like had we made any progress at all today beyond effecting a rescue?

One thing was certain. If we'd harbored doubts about the dark mages still being attached to Vampires at the hip, we could jettison them. Vamps had rallied to Adva's call.

The liaison worried me. I'd thought once we corralled the Leanan, we could back off on the Vampire front. The only way we could do that was after all the dark mages were no more.

How in Danu's name could we capture the others and remand them to Hell along with Perrikus and D'Chel?

My mind traipsed in weary little circles, reminding me of a hamster running on a wheel. First, we'd clean up. Then we'd eat. If we got lucky, we might catch a couple hours sleep, but then we had to get back to it. Cait sagged against me. I'd see she got some rest, no matter what.

Maybe she could sit out the next battle...

In a pig's eye, she would.

She'd be by my side, kicking ass and breaking whenever rules needed breaking until we won. Love for her beat a path through me, hot and savage and protective.

We thumped down in the castle great room. It was empty, which meant everyone else was either cleaning up or eating.

"Do we understand one another?" Arawn was saying to Cait.

She nodded solemnly. "We do."

His somber expression lightened, and he actually winked at her. "Next time ye step outside the boundaries, doonae compound your sins with false promises—and to Vampires, no less."

Something like a snort burbled past her lips. "You got it."

The god of the dead shimmered to nothingness. "Feel like a bath?" I asked.

She plucked another bit of bloody bone out of her hair, grinned at me, and said, "Why on earth would you think I need one?"

CHAPTER NINE, CAIT

I leaned back against the wall of an old-fashioned clawfoot tub with water licking at my chin. This was the third change of water, and I was finally feeling halfway clean. I could still smell the burnt orange undernotes from the birds, but the sulfur and decayed meat stench were gone.

Liam had insisted I take the tub—by myself. Both of us remembered another tub in his flat in Malin where we'd first made love. Much as I hungered for him, sitting upright in the tub was about all I could manage. My energy was as depleted as my magic.

He'd crushed me against him before retreating to a shower on the other side of a small, neat bathroom. Perhaps half an hour had elapsed since he'd wrapped a towel around himself and told me he'd meet me in his chamber whenever I was ready. The shower was clearly an add-on since indoor plumbing hadn't even been a gleam in anyone's eye when

Scourie Castle was built. The bathroom wasn't luxurious, but then neither was anything else in the rambling old structure.

I remembered the days when I'd bathed in tubs like this one that had been filled laboriously, one bucket at a time, with water heated over a wood or coal-fired stove. But then I also remembered a whole lot of baths in icy creeks.

At least the water for this bath had been hot and plentiful. It didn't take much to imagine giant boilers somewhere in the castle's bowels. I lolled in the tub, hair floating around me, not in a hurry to get out. Arawn had been right to rebuke me. He must have felt an influx of souls into his realm—including the twenty-seven Vampires—and known I had to have done something.

My scythe and sword were propped against the far wall. The sickle seemed pleased with our work today. It hummed softly, a tune probably only I could hear. I didn't know quite what had possessed me to sing to the shades. At the front end, my plan had been to marshal the dead to my bidding, instructing them to form a shield between Liam and me and the Vampires bearing down on us.

Powerful magic has its own motives, though. Once I loosed even a few notes, I was lost. The song had dictated my next moves, but it was hard to argue with success. The power sheeting through me had impeccable instincts. I'd turned into a vehicle, rather than a master, though, which had broken every precept governing magic wielders.

The magic is never in control.

Death might have lied about a whole lot, but she hadn't lied about that, which meant the part about what happened to sorcerers whose magic led them around by the nose was also accurate.

Many more incidents like today, and I'd become too unpredictable to trust. I'd had the occasional tussle with magic that wanted its head. But rather like with recalcitrant horses, you had to step up to the plate and show them who was boss. If you didn't, next time you got on the horse, it would take off with you or throw you or bite whatever body part was handy.

Runaway magic was similar. Once it knew its mistress was weak, it would rampage through commands aimed at keeping it in line. I could conceivably find myself in a situation where my only choice was to give my power free rein or fight whatever enemy stood before me. The end result wouldn't be pretty. We'd lost a few Reapers over the years because their magic wrested the upper hand from them.

It had happened even without knowledge of the full spectrum of their skills, just the measly part Death let us mess with. Heh. Maybe that was another reason she'd been reluctant to teach us everything we could do. Bigger magic meant potentially bigger problems.

I shook my head to clear my thoughts. They were going nowhere, and I'd never ferret out Death's motivation. The odds of her ever having a reasonable conversation with me again were nil.

I got out of the cooling bath water, not liking the idea of magic besting me—not after all these years. There was only one answer. I had to practice. Had to get stronger in one hell of a hurry. Adding music to my repertoire would make my power more versatile—and far more robust—but only if I was at the helm.

Interesting. My interpretation of Arawn's warning wasn't to stand down, but to figure out how to make the music my ally.

Judging from his parting comment about "next time," he

knew I wouldn't be able to walk away. Telling boldfaced lies to the Vamps to manipulate them was off the table, though. Damn. Encouraging them to turn on D'Chel had been eminently satisfying, even if my power was in the driver's seat.

That part hadn't been a lie. Only what followed. That they'd be spared Hell's eternal torture if they helped me out.

Mmph. Maybe I wouldn't have to change too much. But would telling the Vampires I'd put in a good word for them have been enough? Probably not. They hadn't chosen Vampirism because they were trusting. Shrewd. Cunning. Eminently self-serving, maybe, but not gullible.

There had to be a line somewhere between outright lies and something that skirted reality closely enough to provide an inducement. Maybe I could brainstorm with the other Reapers —and Liam. That was it. Many minds were always better than one.

Together, we'd come up with a credible lure.

Liam had piled towels where I could get to them easily. I wrapped one around my hair before drying myself and letting water out of the bathtub. I'd just shrugged into a handy robe when the door opened and Liam slipped inside the bathroom. He'd changed into black woolen trousers, scuffed wingtips, and a pale-yellow cable-knit fisherman's sweater. He wrapped his arms around me, and I inhaled, soaking up the scents of Sidhe magic and clean garments.

They were a big improvement over Vampire-rot and feral-bird-monster stench.

"You're looking much better." He offered a warm smile.

"Thanks. I feel a thousand percent improved over when I climbed into the tub. My magic is even starting to recover."

He held me tighter. "Excellent news. I picked up your clothes. They're in the basement soaking in a laundry tub."

I chuckled. "What? No machines here?"

"No electricity."

I snuggled deeper into his arms. I hadn't thought much about it, but the fireplaces ran on magic, and the only lights I'd seen were mage lights. "Good thing I brought extra clothes with me."

"You can always borrow from my stocks too. And there's a wardrobe room with everything from ball gowns to hunting leathers. Ready?" He let go and offered me an arm; I latched a hand around it and grabbed my blade with the other, careful to touch its leather sheath rather than the hilt. The scythe would follow no matter what. Together, we traipsed up some corridors, down others, and finally down a staircase that came out close to Liam's chamber.

"How the hell do you keep track of this place?" I asked. "It's huge, and things seem to move around."

He chuckled. "They do move around a bit, but if the castle likes you, it makes certain you hit your destination." A small flare of magic pushed the door of his room open.

"Have you seen Padhraic and Stacia?" I walked into his chamber and set the blade in a corner. True to my prediction, my sickle bounced into the room and took up a position next to the Vampire-killing sword.

"I have. They're with the council answering questions."

I turned to face Liam. "Let's go. I want to hear what happened to them."

He cupped the side of my face in a hand. "Are you sure you wouldn't rather rest for an hour or two? They're safe, and their story will keep."

I wrestled with conflicting priorities. I was exhausted. My magic might be recovering, but it was a shadow of its usual strength. If anything attacked us in the next few hours, I'd be worse than useless. But supporting Stacia and Padhraic was important too. They'd gone out of their way for me on many occasions.

Tilting my chin up, I said, "I can sleep later. I want to lay eyes on them and hear what happened." I started for the door and then remembered I needed something other than the robe I'd found in the bathroom.

As I sorted through the clothing I'd brought with me, Liam said, "While I'd love to watch you change, it's not a good idea. I'll wait for you in the hall."

"What do you mean, not a good idea?" I called after his retreating back. It had been a rhetorical question, and he didn't answer me. I smiled. Restraining myself from making a grab for his naked body would be damn near impossible, so I understood precisely where he was coming from.

And why he'd left the bathroom when he was done showering. Tired as I was, I yearned for the touch of his hands on my body, for his lips pressed against mine, and for the thrust of his hot length inside me. Making love with Liam was such a joy, but we had other, far more critical tasks facing us.

Reluctantly, I dragged my attention away from the lust sluicing through me. Even a quickie would take time we didn't have.

A few minutes later, I'd donned a pair of khaki pants, a woolen top, and a violet sweater-jacket. I'd brought warm clothes, knowing how chilly the castle always was. Liam had cleaned bird gore and Vampire blood off my boots, and I slid my feet into them over a pair of socks I filched from one of his dressers.

I tossed my scythe over one shoulder and walked into the corridor. "Which way?" I asked.

"Everyone is in the dining room."

"Good. I'm hungry." Quite the understatement. I was famished. Ravenous. I'd expended magic until very little remained. The only remedies were food and rest. It was why Liam had pushed me to get some sleep.

"I hope you'll hang onto your appetite after you hear what happened. 'Tisn't a pretty tale."

Alarm ratcheted through me. "They're all right, aren't they?"

Liam nodded. "Mostly because Paddy's magic is...different. He retained elements of his Leanan nature, and it made his defensive strategy less predictable to Adva."

"Do we know why Stacia followed him?"

Liam stopped walking and threaded his fingers with mine. "What do you think?"

I shrugged. "Hard to say. It's why I asked you."

"She cares about him. What she did was pure emotion, nothing well thought out or considered."

Like I said, I'm exhausted and slow on the uptake. It took a while before I understood what he was trying to tell me. "Uh, does he return her affection?"

"I have no idea, but the two of them have just been through hell. Adva dragged Padhraic past maybe fifty portals. That amount of travel would cut most people to ribbons. Every gateway not of your choosing strips away a wee bit of who you are. It's particularly gruesome for magic wielders because we leave a little of our power on each portal as we're dragged through."

It was news to me. I used portals all the time. "Could you say more about that?"

"Certainly. The gateway wants us to bide a while. They all crave power. It adds to their visibility."

"They don't appear to have that effect on Adva," I mumbled.

"Of course not. They're his creations—most of them."

Which would explain why the portals I built didn't have that effect on me. Liam set a moderate pace to the dining room. Even though he wasn't walking quickly, I still had a hard time keeping up. He must have sensed my difficulties because he wove an arm around my waist and murmured, "Slow and steady. We'll get there."

The scythe hummed and funneled power into me. It seemed depleted too, but not as drained as I was. Voices rose in greeting as we walked beneath the arched entry into the main dining room. I nodded and waved. Considering what a lone wolf I'd always been, part of me was surprised how happy I was to see everyone.

My independent streak has always been one of my staunchest assets. It had seen me through hunger, homelessness, and Death's relentless pressure to perform. Although to be fair, Death hadn't been all that tough to deal with until the whole Vampire thing developed a life of its own.

Liam pointed to a bench near the front of the room. "Cait. You're shaking. Sit down before you fall down. I'll get you something to eat."

I hadn't realized I was trembling until he pointed it out, and

I made a grab for the coolheaded Reaper who flew airplanes. She had to be in there somewhere.

A month ago, no matter if I was ready to pitch facedown, I'd have told him I'd get my own food. But I recognized the wisdom in conserving what little strength I had. Pride was one thing, but sometimes it was misplaced. In this roomful of Sidhe, I still sat near the butt end of the magical totem pole.

I don't actually remember crossing the room, but somehow I ended up sitting more or less where Liam had pointed. Stacia and Padhraic were in the center of a horseshoe-shaped group of Sidhe and Reapers.

"We're nearly done," Krin was saying. "How are you holding up?"

"Fine." Padhraic nodded tersely.

"I've had better days, but I can get through relaying my part," Stacia said.

I felt guilty when I looked at them. Their garments bore long rips and were splattered with blood. Damn it. I should have done more, but the Vampire incursion had pinned Liam and me in place. And then, there'd been those infernal birds.

Padhraic wore a grim expression, his eyebrows drawn into a thick, dark line. Stacia's blue eyes held a haunted cast. The day she'd sought me out at *Carrick Sky Sports*, she'd still had a carefree air about her.

No more. She didn't appear old because Reapers don't age, but her slumped shoulders and the resolute set of her chin spoke to her having seen atrocities that would change her forever.

From the looks of things, neither Padhraic nor Stacia had had the benefit of time to clean up. Perhaps it had been offered

—the Sidhe weren't monsters—but both had wanted to get this over with.

Liam set a plate in front of me. Meat and cheese. Bread. Orange slices. I ate mindlessly and listened as Stacia began speaking. "You've heard this already from Padhraic, but at the beginning you"—she raised her gaze and looked right at Krin—"were clear about hearing from both of us."

"'Tis important," Krin said. "Mayhap your telling will yield clues his did not."

Stacia pushed to her feet and clasped her hands behind her as she faced the assemblage of Sidhe and Reapers. "Adva set a trap for us in an ancient abandoned shepherd's hut above Scourie Village. We assumed the Vampires who'd just fed selected it because it was out of the way and they could sleep off the worst of their blood-satedness."

She squeezed her eyes shut as if forcing unpleasant images away. "Even though there were more Vamps than we suspected, we had them on the run. They were just as sluggish as we'd anticipated. Between dead man's blood and silver stakes, we were down to only two when Adva burst out of nowhere. One side of the hut exploded. He swept through and grabbed Padhraic in a viselike hold."

"I couldn't escape," Padhraic concurred. "I tried. Sent enough magic into that bastard to stop a freight train, but it didn't have any impact at all."

"Which was why I knew I had to follow you," Stacia said. "I sensed the amount of power you raised against Adva. All he did was leer at us with that patronizing expression of his." She moved her arms until she'd wrapped them around herself as if she were chilled to her bones.

Damn. After what she'd lived through, she probably didn't believe she'd ever be warm again.

"I had to act fast. Something changed about Adva's magic. I'm not sure how I figured it out, but he was about to leave. My scythe was squealing at me too. I'm not all that adept at figuring out what it wants, but it seemed to be urging me to follow.

"So I did. I delayed until Adva executed a leap and bounded after him. If I'd jumped him too soon, he'd have flayed me alive. I had to wait until most of his magic was tied up in wherever he was intent on dragging Padhraic."

Paddy stumbled to his feet and stood next to Stacia, hooking a hand beneath her arm. "You were very brave, lass."

She shook her head. "Nah. I was terrified, but I couldn't let you face the darkness alone."

"What happened next?" Dena asked her.

"Adva yanked us through portal after portal. They flashed by so fast, they disoriented me until I couldn't tell up from down." She patted the scythe with its blade curved around her neck. "If it hadn't been for my sickle, I might not have made it. I never realized how much magic it holds. One more critical bit of knowledge Death hid from us."

A low rumble rippled through the room from disgruntled Reapers.

"Many of the gateways had sharp edges." She angled a shredded jacket sleeve for everyone to see. "Some were so tight, I didn't believe we'd make it through. Padhraic helped. He talked with me, told me Adva's magic wasn't endless and the rotating cavalcade of gateways had to stop somewhere."

"You could have let go of Adva anytime," Dena said. "Why didn't you?"

Stacia shrugged. "I have a stubborn streak, and I'd set a

course. Besides, I had no idea where I was or if I had enough magic left to try to teleport."

"Did he talk with either of you?" another Sidhe I didn't recognize asked.

"Mostly, he talked to himself," Stacia replied.

"Aye. And a stark, raving lunatic he is," Padhraic tossed out.

Stacia turned to him. "Well, he did make sense. He's infuriated some of his power was stripped away, willing to do anything to retaliate. You might have passed out for a short time because I think you missed this next part. After the fifty-first gateway—and yeah, I was counting—everything stopped. Adva dumped us in a stockade and vanished."

"'Twas the same spot I awoke," Padhraic said.

"By then, we'd been there maybe ten minutes," Stacia told him, "and I'd determined there weren't any easy ways out. Or any ways at all." She turned her somber gaze on the overflowing room. "Imagine a stockade with wooden walls that stretch hundreds of feet above your head. Impossible to climb—even with magic. Our enclosure was perhaps a meter-and-a-half around with a dirt floor."

She rocked from foot to foot. "Something blocked our magic. Telepathy didn't work, and Padhraic told me we couldn't teleport out of there. So we were stuck. At the mercy of Adva or one of the others.

"Arawn found us," she went on, "exactly like Padhraic described. And I've never been so happy to see that dour old soul. He barked a few power words that made my magical center feel like it was under attack, but the stockade-thing crumpled to nothing."

"Illusion?" Dena arched a black brow.

"Seemed to be," Stacia said, "but this is the second time I've been trapped by an illusion that fooled me."

"I feel like a rube," Padhraic growled. "I should have tested a few things, not assumed we were doomed to sit out Adva's pleasure."

"You did try a lot of things," Stacia told him.

"Pfft. Aye, but not the right ones. I admit our enforced flight through time and space was disorienting and demoralizing, but 'tisn't an excuse for not trying harder than I did."

"You can't blame yourself," Krin said.

"Och, and why not? Who else, exactly, bears the onus for my failure?"

Paddy's self-deprecating humor was one of his more endearing traits.

"Did you run into any shades?" I asked, curious if Vampire minions had been part of Adva's game plan.

"Glad you asked," she said. "I left that part out. Not intentionally, but I'm tired. There were shades who glommed onto me begging for passage, but I couldn't stop long enough to build a gateway of my own. Even if I'd tried, I'm unsure if my magic would have gained a toehold as we bounced through one portal after another."

"Were they true ghosts?" I persisted. "Or some of the ones who bode ill for us?"

She turned a hand palm upward. "In truth, I'm not sure. We didn't slow down until the stockade."

"We learned two key things," Krin said. "Adva may control portals, but passing through too many too quickly drains him."

"And the second?" Liam projected his voice.

"The dark gods favor illusion to trap us. Bear it in mind and assume if you're snared, it's illusion and amenable to destruction." He inclined his head. "Thank both of you so much for your cooperation. Rest. Bathe. Rejoin us when you're refreshed."

Leaning against one another, they shambled out of the room. I wanted to talk with Stacia, but it could wait.

Krin had begun talking again. I caught the tail end of a sentence. "Good opportunity. We leave tonight."

"For where?" I asked.

Liam leaned his head nearer mine. "A contingent will hit the seethe outside Dublin. The more of those fuckers we can immobilize, the fewer we'll have to deal with in places like the shepherd's hut near Scourie."

"I want to go."

His mouth curved into half a smile. "Get some sleep, Cait. If you're awake and up for it, I'd welcome your company. And your magic."

I started to argue that if he was going, so was I, but kept quiet. My best bet would be to sleep. I'd eaten. Between the two, my magic might, maybe, come back to half-mast in time for the raid.

Patting my plate with a hand, I discovered I'd eaten down to the crockery. Hedging my bets, I got up, wandered to trays spread along the back of the room, and selected a few more items.

Liam was waiting for me when I passed beneath the doorway. "I got enough to share," I told him.

"Thank you. Unless you'd rather we teleported to Malin, we'll hole up in my chamber here and sleep."

Malin sounded nicer, but wasting magic would be stupid. Plus, I hadn't forgotten my near miss with annihilation at

Death's hands. It hadn't been in Liam's flat, but it happened right across the street from there.

"Cait?"

"Here is fine," I said, certain I'd pass out the moment I was prone. Even if it ended up being in the middle of the drafty hallway.

True to my suspicions about elements in the castle swapping places, the door to Liam's chamber loomed in front of us. No way could we have arrived here this fast, but I wasn't about to complain. I don't remember laying the plate on a table, but it didn't clatter to the floor, so I must have.

The bed rose up to meet my body as blackness crashed around me.

CHAPTER TEN, LIAM

Cait must have been hanging on by her fingernails. She didn't stir when I pried her boots off and rolled her into a soft duvet with my arms around her. I dragged another blanket over myself, realized I hadn't bothered to remove my shoes, and sent a tiny thread of magic to undo the laces. That done, I toed them off, careful not to do anything that might disturb Cait.

She'd been through a lot. I wasn't satisfied she was all the way recovered from Death rampaging through her magical center. Having her crumple into a heap after she'd run her power down to bedrock wasn't reassuring in the least. Even more disturbing, Arawn had rebuked her for allowing her magic to get the upper hand.

I'd fully expected her to tell him he was full of shit. She hadn't. She'd meekly agreed with his assessment. Apparently, her transgression had been twofold. Power escaped her control, and she'd lured Vampires to her will under false pretenses.

I wanted to make excuses for her, but it would be a grave error on my part. Wielding power was a responsibility. Along with it came both rules and the duty to uphold them. Everyone had the occasional fall from grace, but it was brief. To hear Cait tell it, the music swept her into its maw, and everything else faded to black.

It was why she'd ended up comatose and on the floor.

There were good reasons for those like her—and me—to retain control of our power. The most basic was so we could titrate its flow. Once she'd ceded command, her magic turned into an independent element. It didn't give a goddamn if she fell on her face. Tossing magic about was intoxicating, exhilarating—another reason someone with a cool head needed to keep a firm hold on the tiller.

I pushed past the worrisome parts and focused on the miracle of the music that had gotten away from her. What a potent weapon it could be—if harnessed properly. Would Cathbad help train her? Probably not. Arawn mentioned he'd gifted the Sirens with their song. Given what a disaster that had turned out to be, the likelihood of Cathbad helping Cait was thin.

He probably wasn't even aware his music would have that effect on her, but I felt certain he'd sensed her making use of his brand of magic. I'd heard the same songs as Cait. While they'd soothed my soul, they hadn't augmented my magic. A blistering insight dragged my eyes open. Other Reapers had been in Scourie Castle when Cathbad had visited.

They'd heard him sing as well.

Did it mean they could incorporate music into their magic? It made a certain amount of sense. All the Reapers had been created from a single template. Cait stirred against me. I tucked the comforter more firmly around her and told the fire in the grate to burn brighter.

Despite my best efforts, my chamber wasn't as warm as I would have liked, although it was a good deal cozier than the rest of the castle. Except the kitchens. Cait turned in my arms again, and I touched her forehead gently, spelling her deeper asleep. Her breathing was gentle, regular, and the worry lines etched into her forehead and around her eyes had relaxed, leaving her looking young and vulnerable.

Her beauty had drawn me that first day when I'd strode into *Carrick Sky Sports*, unwitting ally to a nefarious plot hatched by Hollis Whitehall, my Sidhe warlord, to capture her. Something had happened to Hollis. I still wasn't certain how he'd been seduced by evil, but he was dead. An unpleasant end to an impossible situation.

Light filtered through my dirty window, highlighting the planes of Cait's striking face. Her beauty may have garnered my attention, but it wasn't why I'd fallen in love with her. I've known many stunning women. Cait has a warrior's spirit. It shines through everything she does. She might be terrified, but she doesn't let it stop her.

She'd get enough rest, goddammit. The same fierce protectiveness she always engendered swept through me, and I longed for a time we wouldn't have to be forever planning the next offensive.

I should rest too. I don't require much sleep, but my magic wasn't exactly in tiptop form, either. I'd expended huge amounts battling both birds and Vampires, and my right palm was in bad shape from the iron in the blade I'd used. I funneled healing energy into my hand. I'd need to swing that sword again, and it would be easier if the hilt wasn't hitting bone.

Both of us had a right to be exhausted. We'd been on the go ever since leaving Scourie Castle and stopping at the church where the dead were laid out. It seemed like weeks had passed, but it had only been a couple of days.

Kiko crossed my mind, and I winced. I hadn't thought about Cait's friend since we left Seattle. I hoped she was all right and that the amulet I'd made her was doing its work and keeping her safe from Vampires. In a perfect world, we'd check on her, but that wouldn't happen until we got a better handle on all the problems here.

Focusing the same relaxation charm I'd used on Cait inward, I drifted, floating in and out of consciousness as time ticked past. Guilt racked me. I had too much to do to sleep, but I needed my magic at full capacity. Every time I expended power, it levied a price.

I might not have fallen to my knees or sprawled onto dirt stained with ichor from birds and Vampires, but I'd had less and less power at my disposal. If I'd had to keep fighting, I'd have reached a point where I was using brawn and cunning instead of magic to hold everything together.

The realization had a sobering effect, and I pushed myself back into the fluffy oblivion that would allow my paranormal side to resurrect itself. We'd be on the move to obliterate the seethe as soon as everyone's magic was up to snuff.

I assumed Arawn and Hades would continue to extend aid, but we could use some of their fellow gods to make an end to this sooner rather than later. One of my last questions before I truly shut off my brain was whether Cathbad might join us. Surely, he'd sensed a disturbance when Cait added a musical component to her power.

It would either spur him to hasten to our side, or infuriate him no end. I didn't know him well enough to make a prediction in either direction.

I woke to the press of Cait's mouth against mine and the quicksilver feel of her arms around me, body pressed close as she teased my lips with her tongue. We must have shifted position while we slept because she was on top of me, legs straddling my hips. Opening my mouth to her kisses, I pushed everything else aside. We deserved a few moments to ourselves. Time we didn't have to share with Vampires or the dark gods or Humans Rule.

Or our respective councils.

As if she'd read my thoughts, she stopped kissing me long enough to say, "Five minutes. Surely, we've earned five minutes of us-time."

I smiled. "We merit a whole lot more than that, lass, but I believe we can justify enough 'us-time' to nurture our souls." I hadn't even quit talking before she crushed her lips over mine again, tongue pushing into my mouth. I sparred with it, loving her Reaper scent as it thickened around us.

Her hair was still damp, and I threaded my fingers into its curls as we traded deep kisses with little butterfly ones. Licking. Biting. Sucking. She had the most wonderful mouth with full, firm lips and an inventive, wicked tongue. Her nipples formed peaks against my chest, and her breath quickened. Mine did too.

Kisses were one thing. Did we have enough time for more? I reached between us and cupped her vulva. Heat from her raced up my fingertips to my hand and arm. My cock shot to attention, and I pressed my fingers deeper between her legs. She wriggled against me, hips moving as I touched her through her clothing.

She trailed a hand down my shoulders, across my chest and stomach until it stopped over my deliciously distended appendage. One finger at a time, she took hold of me, rubbing me. Something about touching each other through layers of fabric was unbelievably erotic. Almost more arousing than being naked.

I ran my other hand down her back until I cupped her ass and pushed her more firmly into my questing fingers. Images of the creamy globes of her behind filled my mind as I reconstructed when she'd faced away from me, inviting me to fuck her.

The memory snugged my balls against my body. I twirled my fingers in hard little circles over her clit, moving faster until she dissolved in a pool of heat around the hand trapped between her legs. I kept on rubbing her nub, riding her climax along with her.

Our mouths had been glued together; she broke the kiss. "Mmmm. That was yummy. And now for your two-and-a-half minutes."

I started to tell her it was all right. Sharing her orgasm had been a delight. Before I got any words out, she slithered down my body, tongue tracking along my neck, across my shirt, to trouser level. Muzzy with lust, I missed how she accomplished it, but my cock wasn't inside my slacks any longer.

She licked the head before plunging her mouth around me. Sensation roared through every cell in my body until I was drowning in pleasure, saturated in lust. Gripping my shaft, she worked me while licking and sucking. Every few strokes, she lifted her mouth from me and blew gently on the tip of my cock.

I'd let go of her head, but I wove my fingers into her hair again, holding her steady as I thrust into her mouth. Everything fell away. The only things in the world were Cait's mouth and her hands and the devilish things she was doing with them.

I gave up, ceded to the pleasure coursing through me. Semen spooled at the base of my cock, and then I was coming and coming and coming into Cait's hungry mouth. She kept on suckling me until the spasms played out, and then she laid her head on my belly.

I stroked her hair. "That was incredible. Thank you."

"I've wanted to do that for a while. We need more time."

"Aye, we need a lot of things."

She chuckled. "Guess our five minutes are up. Handy we didn't waste any of them getting undressed." Dipping from beneath my touch, she rolled to a sit and tucked me back together, buttoning my trousers.

I tossed my legs over the side of the bed and sat next to her. "Maybe the Sidhe and Reaper councils have come up with a strategy."

She angled a pointed look my way. "Wouldn't you have wanted to be part of it?"

"Aye. Of course." I shook my head.

"What?"

"We have so many irons in the fire, it's hard to know what to address first. Before I fell asleep, I thought about Kiko."

"Me too. But we're a long way from her." Cait tilted her chin up. "She's more resourceful than she looks. Because she's so tiny, people tend to discount her, but she has nerves of steel. Her parents spent time in a Japanese internment camp. They were in their fifties when she was born, and she was their only child. To hear her tell it, they ran their home like a camp. She didn't get anything she hadn't earned."

"We'll make a point of at least calling her as soon as we can."

"Next time we're in the village. Or if we go to Dublin to wipe out that seethe. They'll have good cell service."

I stood and drew Cait to her feet. "Let's find everyone, and we'll take it from there."

Her eyes widened. "Shit. They were leaving for Dublin tonight. Did we oversleep?"

"Nay. We're fine."

"How can you be certain?" She made a dive for her shoulder bag, dug her phone out, and made a face. "We're good on time. It's just four thirty, or sixteen thirty the way you guys do time. One of these days I have to remember to sign up for an international calling plan."

"Can you make calls without one?"

Cait grinned. "You really do need to join the modern world, Mr. Warwick. Yeah. I can make calls, but they're hella expensive."

"It's actually Lord Warwick, and I'll pay for it." I grinned back.

"My. A man of many secrets. You'll have to tell me how you became a lord."

"Bribery and extortion. Two useful skills that have faded into ignominy." I tugged the door open.

Cait snatched up her scythe and looped it over a shoulder.

I glanced at the longswords and opted to leave them in my chamber. We could collect them before we left. She turned her sparkling green eyes my way. "Thanks for the quickie."

"Anytime." I winked.

She batted her eyelashes, miming a coquette. Together, we walked into the hallway. I sent magic spinning outward to figure out where everyone was. Only two choices. The great room or the dining room.

Both appeared unoccupied, so I kept on looking. "That's odd," I muttered.

"What's odd?" she asked. Power flared around her, encouraging because it meant her magic had made at least a partial recovery.

"Everyone is outside in the courtyard," I told her.

Cait drew her dark brows together and ducked back into my chamber. When she emerged, the blade was tucked in its sheath and strapped around her hips. I flexed my sore hand. Flesh had knitted together over the worst gash. It was good enough. I retrieved my sword too, careful not to touch the metal part.

No point making things worse if I didn't have to.

"Do you think we should stop by the armory?" Cait asked quietly.

I thought about the silver stakes from our last go round. We'd used up all the dead man's blood. The stakes were in the coat I'd worn. Maybe Dena had more blood in her workshop.

"Let's do this," I suggested. "We'll stop by Dena's lab to see if there's more dead man's blood. Then we'll stop in the basement and collect the silver stakes from my coat.

"I have a few." Cait patted the leather satchel.

"How many?"

"Um. Three."

We'd begun walking. Cait's scythe glowed softly, lighting the way even absent a mage light from me. Dena's lab looked as if she'd left in a hurry. Papers lay scattered about. It wasn't like her. She liked everything neat and tidy. The spot where she'd stored the blood was empty.

"Oh-oh," Cait muttered. "None of this is looking good."

I quickened my pace as we left Dena's workshop and took the first set of stairs leading down. The laundry room sat next to huge boilers that provided hot water for the castle. Unlike the fireplaces, they ran on heating oil. My coat—and the stakes— were right where I'd left them. I counted ten and gave half to Cait.

"What I can't figure out," I said, as we retraced our steps, "is why no one summoned us if there was trouble."

"Did you ward your chamber?"

"Aye, but another Sidhe should have been able to cut through it." I ducked through a rounded doorway.

"Where are we going?" Cait asked.

"These old castles are famous for underground passages. We're taking one that will spit us out in the carriage house."

"Why not teleport? Never mind. Sorry I asked. We don't want magic to give us away."

"Exactly."

We entered a dank-smelling corridor hogged out of dirt and rock. I couldn't quite stand up inside it. The walls ran with water and were slick with moss and lichens. We emerged through a trap door set in a corner of the carriage house. Light had leached from the day, and it was raining.

What a surprise.

Along with rain pelting the roof, the unmistakable din of angry voices reached me. We'd been wise not to sashay through the castle's front doors.

"But they're mortals," Cait protested. "What the hell are

they doing here?"

I had a feeling it had something to do with the trio murdered by Vampires. For all I knew, they were only the leading edge of a bloody massacre.

The Humans Rule chant started up with its drivel about mortal superiority. What hogwash. I'd never listened to it before, and I wasn't about to start now. I grasped Cait's hand, and we walked out of the building.

Reapers stood grouped on one side, Sidhe on the other. A small mob faced them. Perhaps thirty humans, some decked out in Humans Rule regalia. Christ. Had the entire village turned out?

"We demand you leave," a burly Scott thundered. Black hair spilled down his shoulders and mingled with a black beard. He was garbed in an old-fashioned tartan in a red-and-black pattern that was no doubt clan-related.

The English only thought they'd chased the clans out of the Highlands. All they'd done was drive them underground.

"Aye, we had no troubles till you came," another man shouted. His tartan was blue, green, and black.

Krin spread his hands before him. "We own this piece of land, have for centuries."

Yet a third man came forward waving a sheaf of papers. "No more. We filed with the magistrate to relieve you of your tenure." He hesitated before reciting in a singsong voice. "Whenever a property sits vacant for a period in excess of one hundred years, it shall be deemed abandoned—"

"But Scourie Castle is far from vacant," Krin cut him off. "As you can see, we are living here. In truth, one of us has lived here all along. Just because you didn't know we were here didn't mean we weren't. The castle has always had a caretaker."

I smothered a snort. I'd never realized Krin could be such a smooth liar.

Angry shouts met his words, punctuated with, "What did this caretaker live on? Air?"

"We don't require sustenance in the same way mortals do," Krin replied, weaving credibility into his words.

I scanned the crowd, searching for Deidre, and found her toward the back. Anger fanned from her in waves. I recognized other men and women I'd seen during my few excursions to the village.

None of the men wearing Humans Rule paraphernalia looked familiar. They must have come from outside the region. No doubt sent by some central office to stir up shit in the wake of the Vampire killings.

But it was conjecture on my part. To set things straight—at least for me—I walked to Krin's side with Cait next to me. "Have there been more deaths?" I asked.

Relief surged when I met a sea of head shakes. Not that three wasn't bad enough, but thank all the gods the carnage hadn't spread.

"I provided passage for your loved ones." Cait spoke in a clear, ringing voice. "They are safe on the other side."

A low hissing ran through the crowd. "Abomination!" one of the Humans Rule men shouted. The same cry was taken up by others.

"Quiet!" Cait shouted over the din. "Would you rather your dead wandered aimlessly on this side of the veil, forever refused the gates of the afterlife? I've known ghosts like that. Many of them. Each has reasons not to cross, but things don't go well for them. They grow more sad and confused with each passing year until they lose all sense of who they were."

"Abomination," the HR fellow shouted again, but this time fewer throats took up his cry.

"Where are you from?" I pointed at him.

"What's it to you?" he growled.

"My guess is you're not from here. Someone sent you to whip up trouble."

"Why, you bastard." He lunged toward me, but I sent a wave of magic his way. It lifted him a few meters in the air and plopped him onto his arse in the mud.

"I didn't hurt him," I told the crowd. "I don't want to hurt any of you. None of us do."

"We take the loss of your kinsmen very seriously," Dena said. "Many of us are recently returned from dealing with Vampires, and we have another sortie planned. We can kill them. You cannot. Go home. Let us do our jobs."

Compulsion ran thick beneath her words.

It's a rare mortal who's immune to our power. This batch was no exception. Slowly, they turned for the group of cars sitting near the gates. All except for the Humans Rule contingent.

"You haven't seen the last of us." A short, beefy brown-haired man dressed in jeans and a woolen shirt shook a fist our way.

"We'll get our solicitors working on evicting you," another yelled.

"We own Scourie Castle," Krin repeated. "No one gets evicted from a place they own."

Padhraic walked toward the half dozen men sporting logos identifying them as HR associates. "I haven't had a very good few weeks here, mates. I used to be a Vampire myself, but my kin cured me. One of your bosses kidnapped me. I'm not kindly disposed toward anything either Vampire- or dark-mage-related right now. You can leave the easy way." He pointed at the cars pulling through the castle gates. "Or we can send you packing. Your choice."

"You threatened us," one shouted.

"Nay. Merely stated facts." Paddy walked closer to the men, standing his ground. "Let's get a few things clear. Nothing, and I mean nothing, you can do to me will be one millionth as horrible as what I've lived through."

I sensed weak magic emanating from the men and cursed myself for having missed it before. Double damn it to fuck. Was the cancer of humans dabbling with power spreading?

"Mortals have no right to magic. None," I told them. "It upsets the psychic balance of Earth."

I'd dealt with this before. Running to Padhraic's side, I murmured, "Remember what we did in Seattle?"

"You bet."

Alarm bounced from man to man. "Magic is an outrage," one sputtered.

"How dare you accuse us of—?"

"I accused you of nothing." I spat the words. "But you rose to the bait handily."

"Now?" Paddy asked.

"No better time," I agreed.

The men turned as a group and ran, but no one can outrun a Sidhe spell. Shrieks and squeals rose from them as we yanked magic out of their twisted souls.

"If you return to the well and attempt to resurrect your ability to cast magic, 'twill mean your deaths." I projected my voice so there would be no doubt.

No one so much as turned around. They dove into two

black sedans and sped away from the castle.

"Good call." Krin clapped me across the back. "I was so intent on finding a peaceful solution, I totally missed their misshapen magic."

"Are we still going after the seethe?" Cait asked.

"Aye, that we are, lass," Krin told her, "but we have yet to select who will tackle the problem."

Stacia hurried to Cait and threw her arms around her. "Good to see you."

"Make that a double from me," Cait replied as she hugged her back. "You gave me quite a fright."

"We do what we have to," Stacia said and made a fist. "I'm in this to my eyeballs, and I won't rest until those dark fuckers are dead."

Music heralded Cathbad's entrance. I wasn't as surprised to see him as I'd been the first time he dropped by Scourie Castle.

"Aw crap," Cait muttered. "Time to face the music or pay the piper or do whatever I have to to convince him I'm sorry."

"Shouldn't be hard if it's true," I said softly. "You are sorry, aren't you?"

She screwed her face into a grim expression. "That the magic got the upper hand, yes. That I used it in the first place, no. It felt like it belonged to me. Just like all that unused Reaper power."

"Tell the truth," I murmured. "Everything else will work out."

I hoped.

Cathbad wasn't exactly a god, but he was ancient, and he'd kept company with the Celts for long enough to become as arbitrary and temperamental as the rest of them.

CHAPTER ELEVEN, CAIT

I'd be damned if I'd cower behind Liam. If Cathbad had made a special trip to censure me, I'd take it like a woman. I'd been a reluctant recruit in Death's army for too long to hide behind anyone's skirts. Or in Liam's case, trousers. Detaching myself from his side, I walked toward the silver-edged portal that had disgorged the Druidic bard, stopping a few feet from him.

He nailed me with his keen dark-eyed gaze. Dressed the same way he'd been the last two times I'd seen him, he wore leather garments embellished with red-and-blue dye that accentuated his tall, broad frame. A war axe swung from a sheath by his side, and a broadsword was attached to his back by a scabbard with thongs that wrapped around his body. Boots laced to just below knee level. Dark hair hung loose to the middle of his back. Unlike before, it wasn't braided.

He raised an arm, index finger pointed at the center of my chest. I steeled myself for the blast of magic I was certain would follow. It scoured me from head to foot and back again, leaving a trail of raw energy in its wake. Swinging a few degrees to the left, he targeted Stacia with the same volley.

Other than a muted gasp, she remained stoic. After Adva's not-so-tender ministrations, Cathbad's power probably felt downright agreeable.

He narrowed his eyes my way. "You used music to coerce Vampires to your will."

No point in denying it, so I nodded.

"Why?"

It was an excellent question, one I'd asked myself after the fact. I took my time answering, testing my words to make certain I wasn't sugarcoating anything. "As you know, Death concealed a great deal of our magic. This isn't an excuse, but I'm still figuring out how to manage everything beyond my original ability to construct gateways with Reaper power."

"Go on." Cathbad never took his gaze from my face. It was unsettling and encouraging by turns.

"I didn't mean to do more than hum a couple of notes, but once they were out, the song took over. I admit I didn't try hard enough to stop it at the very front end. If I had, maybe I'd have managed to establish the upper hand. By the time I recognized I'd lost the battle, the music was everywhere. It felt right. Natural. Like it belonged to me."

I stopped long enough to lick my dry lips. My heart was beating faster than it should have been, which told me how nervous I was. This next part was the crux of my faux pas. "So long as the music was loose, and clearly in control, I had two choices. I could have panicked. Instead, I listened to the song's suggestion and used its power to, erm, manage the Vampires."

"Define manage," Cathbad ordered.

There was no way not to answer him. Holding silence was impossible. "I encouraged them to turn on Adva, and they did. He wanted them to go through a mirror, but I lured them to choose my gateway, instead. He might have been somewhat depleted magically, but when it became clear his minions were no longer under his control, he loosed a flock of monster birds on us and left. Then we only had the birds to deal with."

After another shaky breath, I plowed on. "I lied to the Vampires to get them to cross the veil. Suggested I'd put in a good word for them and they might escape Hellfire when I had no intention of doing any such thing. Arawn has already rebuked me and made it clear what I did was both wrong and forbidden.

"But I already knew as much. Death wasn't truthful about many things, but she made it abundantly clear cajoling shades through a gateway with lies was prohibited."

"How did you get any Vampires to cross if not by chicanery?" Cathbad furled his dark brows.

"I tricked them in other ways that didn't involve overt lies."

I'd run out of words. I've found it's best not to use too many when confessing sins. It avoids the temptation to try to make myself look better than I am.

Cathbad turned until he faced the group of Reapers and repeated his magical scan. Was he done with me? I had a feeling the answer was no. He hadn't dismissed me, so I shifted my weight from foot to foot, waiting for him to pronounce my fate.

There'd be a price for my actions, but I had no idea what it might entail.

He crossed his arms over his leather-clad chest. "I hadn't anticipated some of you would have an affinity for music.

Perhaps two-thirds who heard my song have some talent for incorporating music into your castings."

Shaking a finger our way, he said, "You must not give in to the temptation to let the music out. None of you have been trained, and if even a few notes escape, you'll find yourself in the same position as Cait, where the music took over.

"That's the most dangerous part," he went on. "Allowing magic to gain the upper hand. 'Tisn't that you'll never be able to incorporate it, but like any new skill it requires instruction."

I gathered the shards of my courage and asked, "Do you suppose Death knew we had an affinity for musical enchantment?"

"Nay. I'm certain she didn't."

I wanted to urge him to say more, but receiving any reply at all was more than I deserved.

"I will be forthright with you," the bard continued. "My single instance of entraining musical magic was with the Sirens. It could have gone better. I had no idea they'd latch onto wickedness along with the music and use it to murder mortals."

"Did it happen right away?" Liam asked from somewhere behind me, his rich baritone ragged.

"Aye. From nearly their very first time. They stuck with me long enough to learn how to summon the power, but then they disappeared. I chased them down time and time again, but they used my songs against me." Cathbad unfolded his arms, made a fist, and punched the air.

Liam strode to my side, facing the bard. "Then I believe the Reapers will be safe enough. I was there when Cait raised her voice and sang the Vampires across her portal. She didn't turn into a modern day Medusa. She was just Cait, with an added magical dimension. The biggest problem with the magic operating as its own mistress was it drained her to nothing, and she collapsed unconscious."

"You didn't tell me that part." Cathbad's attention was back on me.

"With everything else, it didn't seem important," I murmured.

The bard nodded, perhaps lost in thought. His next words were a question directed at all of us. "What do you have planned next?"

"We have chosen a seethe on the outskirts of Dublin," Liam told him. "Seems simpler to eradicate Vampires in their nests than to deal with them when they're in thrall to the dark gods."

"You'll be waiting until daylight, aye?"

Liam shook his head. "Enough of them have learned the art of daywalking—courtesy of the Leanan and the dark gods— we're not sure it would make much difference."

"I see. Will it require all of you?"

"Nay. The seethe is large," Krin replied, "but we'd planned on selecting a contingent. Too many of us will confound things."

"I will work with the Reapers who have musical skills while you're gone. Provide basic instruction aimed at knowing the point at which they must cut the flow of magic to the music."

"But I want to help take the seethe down," I blurted, and quickly clapped a hand over my mouth. Cathbad's offer of instruction was probably a rare concession, one I'd do well to take advantage of.

"I'll pass his lessons on when you return," Stacia told me.

"Good enough," Cathbad rumbled in his deep voice and stabbed his index finger at the group of Reapers. "You and you and you and you..." He continued until a subset of Reapers had stepped toward him.

"Come on. Sooner we're gone, the sooner we'll be done with this," Liam said to me.

I nodded and walked closer to Cathbad, bowing my head. When I straightened, I said, "Thank you for not being angry."

Something close to a smile played about his generous mouth. "Music is a great deal of what I am, child. How could I be angry with another who felt its call?" He dropped a heavy hand onto my shoulder. "You've felt its pull. You must be vigilant, or it will slip its noose again. Once freed, it will want the same again. Absolute control. The more times it happens, the lower the odds you will ever be able to successfully wield it."

"I understand. I'll keep my guard up. Now that I have access to the full spectrum of my Reaper power, I have other ways to force Vampires across the veil, methods that involve beheading or staking them first. Once that's done, the rest is simple."

Cathbad nodded curtly to me. I recognized it as a dismissal —for now.

He sang a few notes. The group of Reapers flowed nearer to him, mesmerized. I felt the same pull but fought it as I hurried to join Liam, Krin, Dena, and Padhraic. They were tapping other Sidhe and some of the remaining Reapers until we had a group of twenty-five.

The plan was to weapon-up and meet in the courtyard in a quarter hour.

"I'll have more dead man's blood," Dena told everyone.

"And a cache of silver stakes," Krin said.

"We have stakes." Liam nodded tersely.

"And swords." I patted mine.

"Fine. Wait here, then," Dena said before she loped toward the dark bulk of the castle.

"How about if we wait in the carriage house?" I suggested.

Liam swiped rain off his face. "Better to wait at the top of the castle stairs beneath the overhang."

I followed him to a relatively sheltered spot. "Sheesh. I thought it rained a lot in Seattle. Does it ever do anything else here?"

"Rarely." He smiled at me and drew me close, arms wrapped around me. "I was proud of you."

"For what?" My voice was muffled against his shoulder.

"You didn't whitewash anything."

"He would have known." I hesitated, not sure whether to give voice to the next part, but Liam was intuitive as hell.

"What makes you so certain?" he asked.

"From the moment he scoured me with magic, something inside me kindled. It's as if the musical part of my magic recognizes him as its maker. I wanted to sing my answers to him, but if I had, the magic would have broken free again."

"Interesting." Liam's expression grew wistful. "I'm almost jealous."

"Of wild magic that's just waiting to get away from you? Nah. You only think you want that."

"Nay, of the untapped power in that 'wild' magic. I've always liked a challenge."

I tried to muffle the snort that wanted out and only partially succeeded. "I liked it better when my main challenges were airplanes with engine problems."

He pulled my head against him until I heard the reassuring beat of his heart beneath my ear. "We'll get back to *Carrick Sky*

Sports, someday. Even if you've lost every customer, we'll rebuild it from the ground up."

"It's a kind offer, but I can't let you—"

"We're a team," he spoke over me, and then changed the subject. "Have you ever visited a seethe before?"

I reared back to look at him. "Of course not. Why would I have?"

"I thought not. They're unusual places. Some of the very old Vampires never leave."

"But how do they feed?"

"Vampire society is arranged in hierarchies. The old ones have minions who hunt for them. They bring mortals to the seethe and hold them there for months or years while they slowly drain them of everything that made them human."

I rolled the idea around in my head, thoroughly disgusted by the concept of human slaves. "Why not keep them alive for longer? Seems like it would simplify their blood problem. All they'd have to do would be to keep feeding the humans so they don't die."

Liam shook his head. "It's more complicated than that. If they drain them to the point of death, they can make new Vampires, but then they can't feed from them nearly as efficiently. Vamps resist providing sustenance for anyone but the one who made them, and even then they're reluctant. If they keep their victims human, eventually their humanity withers until they no longer care about anything. It's why they die. Not from starvation but from hopelessness."

"Can they still turn them into new Vampires at that point?" What I didn't know about Vampirism could have filled volumes.

"I suppose they could." Liam frowned. "But they don't

want to. More Vampires means more mouths to feed. They've always paid close attention to keeping their raw numbers in line. And new Vampires require a great deal of oversight."

"The ones I sang through my portal were newly made," I muttered. "I figured it was why it was so easy to convince them."

"Not necessarily. It might have made it harder. New Vampires feel the pull of evil more strongly than older ones. It should have made Adva's gambit irresistible. Instead, they chose your option."

From the far side of the courtyard, Cathbad's song ebbed and flowed, punctuated at intervals by notes from Reaper throats.

The castle doors slammed open; Sidhe and Reapers clattered down the stairs to where we stood. "Ready?" Dena asked and pressed a few vials of blood into Liam's and my hands.

"Aye. Never readier," Liam replied.

"We plan to emerge half a kilometer from the graveyard with the crypts," Krin said.

I worried it might not be far enough, that the fallout from our combined power would alert the Vampires a magical army was bearing down on them, but no one else voiced a concern.

"The plan is simple," Krin went on. "Kill on sight. No conversation necessary. In fact, don't let them engage you in conversation. They can snare your mind, trip you up. Once we have a mass of bones, Reapers will see the spirits cross to the far side."

"Not all of them will be in the seethe. Some are probably out hunting," I cautioned.

"We'll deal with them if they return," Dena said. "The

point isn't necessarily to kill every one of them, but to levy enough damage they shutter the seethe."

We split into four groups of six to teleport. Scourie Castle's gray stones frittered to darkness, and then the bustle of Dublin formed around us. Liam had taken care to ward our small contingent, so no one ran screaming for a pub—or a constable—when we emerged. Dublin had to have a sizable Humans Rule contingent, and I'd had enough of them for one day.

No one saw us, and we slipped into a sheltered alleyway before Liam dismantled the ward keeping us hidden from view.

My magic was maybe 75 percent recovered, and I felt the musical part champing at the bit for freedom. It was reassuring and unnerving at the same time. As soon as we got back, I'd huddle with Stacia and let her teach me what she'd gleaned from Cathbad.

Half a moon provided soft illumination, and a few stars shone overhead. Unlike the Highlands, it wasn't raining here, and the pavement was dry. Liam knew where we were headed, so we hurried after him. Our group was made up of him, me, Padhraic, Abby, Pavel, and Griselda, a rather bloodthirsty Sidhe with steel-gray hair and dark eyes.

We passed from the town center to an older section of the city. From there, we skirted vestiges of what had once been the town wall. Outside its boundaries sat a protestant church. It had seen better days. Paint was peeling off its boards, and it appeared abandoned. No wonder the Vamps had set up shop in crypts peppering its graveyard.

The other three groups of Reapers and Sidhe slithered from shadows, and we held a quiet conversation where Krin pointed out which crypt held the seethe. It didn't look like much from my vantage point, but according to him a substantial dwelling had been hollowed out underground.

I wondered how he knew, but it wasn't important. We needed to get moving. Any Vamp worth his salt would know we were close. Those bastards had noses like bloodhounds. Rather than storming the main door, we teleported. Probably a smart move. If the entrance was anything like normal doorways, we couldn't pass through more than perhaps two abreast. It would give the Vampires an opportunity to try to pick us off—or blockade themselves inside.

The church disappeared, replaced by something that looked like I've always envisioned an opium den. Dark. Lush. Muted jewel-toned lighting. Rather than the sweetish reek of opium, though, the place stank of rot and putrid open sores. The room was large. Maybe fifty feet long and thirty wide. Vampires had formed rows at one end, facing off against us.

I couldn't see how many, but a lot of them. More than I'd faced in Adva's cavern.

A tall, beautiful man strode toward us. Red hair spilled down his shoulders, and he had violet-gold eyes. An old-fashioned dark-blue frock coat covered a white shirt and black velveteen pants. He looked much like a nineteenth-century gentleman of leisure might have.

"We do not wish to battle with you," he said in a mellifluous voice. "We might win today's skirmish, but in the end, you will overpower us. Vampires have survived because we've had the good sense to remain mostly out of sight."

I remembered Krin's warning about not talking with them. What the fuck were we doing?

"If you're so invisible," Krin said, "why have you aligned

with the dark gods and taught humans what is forbidden to them?"

The Vampire nodded. "Both were mistakes, but we are only one seethe. There are many, and we so rarely agree on anything."

"What does that mean, exactly?" Liam asked. "That this seethe isn't part of the problem?"

"Aye. 'Tis precisely what it means." The Vampire beamed, displaying what looked like rows of teeth.

"We can keep the others in line," another Vampire, this one female, spoke up.

While we'd been talking, more Vampires had joined the ones lined against us. God knew where they were coming from, but the number arrayed across the chamber from us had doubled. I gripped the hilt of my sword; a shudder of pain shot up my arm. If I led out, Liam would follow me. But I wasn't the commander here.

"Liam?" I resorted to mind speech.

He caught my eye and nodded very slightly. Too bad I had no idea what he meant. I hadn't fought with Sidhe enough to be attuned to their favored strategies.

"So nice of you to stop in," the red-haired Vampire continued. "But unless you prefer to feast on blood, you're wasting precious time. Ours and yours."

"Now." Krin's voice rang in my mind. The swish of blades being drawn filled the air, and we charged the Vampire horde. They weren't expecting it. Perhaps that had been Krin's tactic all along, to put them at their ease. Make them believe we were two steps from being gone.

Lamps crashed to the earthen floor, shattering and adding the cloying scent of oil to everything else in the large chamber.

Small fires burned smokily in pools of lamp oil. My hands still ached from our last go round, but I swung my blade, cleaving through sinew, muscle, and bone. Eerie music filled the room, one of the ways Vamps lured their victims.

My own music battered against the wall I'd barricaded it behind. If notes were part of this fight, they wanted a piece of it. "No." I shrieked. Didn't matter who heard me with all the noise in the Vamps' erstwhile living room.

Squeals, howls, yipes, cries, screams. With it all, surprisingly little blood. These Vamps had been around long enough, all they left were piles of moldering bones.

The next time I drew my blade back, something grabbed it. I pivoted, twisted, and finally got turned around enough to see the Vampire who'd tried to convince us he was one of the good guys hanging onto the end of my blade.

He was about my height, but Vamps are ridiculously strong. I yanked and jerked and pulled. He lost one finger, and then another, but it didn't seem to faze him. He'd moved from the tip of my sword about a third of the way up. Clearly, I wasn't going to get it back by brute force, and if I let go, the first thing he'd do would be to use it against me.

I only had one option. It wasn't great and would require split-second timing, but no one was about to ride to my rescue. Not that I expected them to. All around me, Sidhe and Reapers were engaged with an endless stream of Vampires. Someone had said this seethe was big, but from the looks of things, it must house hundreds.

They could engage in telepathy, so they'd probably called everyone home.

I shifted the hilt to my left hand to let it take some of the pain. My right one was on fire from the proximity to metal. In one fluid motion, I reached into my pocket, grabbed a vial of dead man's blood and pulled the stopper out with my teeth.

"Darling," the Vamp purred. "I can make your death far more pleasant than drinking poison."

His words put one of my fears to rest: that he'd smell the contents of the vial and wrest it from me. Or run like hell.

I spat the cork onto the ground. "Thanks for the offer," I growled and waited. The Vampire was convinced I was about to off myself. He edged closer, ignoring the bite of my blade. When he hit the halfway mark, I raised the flask and tossed its contents right into his face.

Good stuff, dead man's blood. After a garbled cry, he released my blade and I finished him, severing his head from his body. Breathing as if I'd just run a marathon, I kicked the head out of the way for good measure.

I was so tired, I was staggering, but I couldn't quit now. At least the music had stopped raising hell with me. Maybe somewhere along the line it realized I'd drawn a line and wasn't about to cross it.

Cathbad's prediction about each loss of control being cumulative had sunk in. I wanted to work with the music someday, and if I gave in to it, that day would never come.

Abby and Pavel called for me. Apparently, we'd moved from the part where we joined the killing to shepherding shades across the veil. We tag-teamed with other Reapers, building three portals and booting Vampire ghosts on to what would come next.

I was proud of myself. I cursed them. No promises of a cushy afterlife from me. I've always been efficient that way, good at learning from my mistakes.

A harsh cry brought my head spinning around. One of the

Vampires had Griselda in a headlock and was about to sink his fangs into her neck. Power flashed and flared around her, but it didn't dissuade the Vampire. No one else was close enough to intervene.

I didn't have a good angle on his neck, so I dragged a silver stake from the bag still wound around my body and charged him, sinking it between his ribs. Had I been quick enough? Had he bitten Griselda before withering to a pile of bones.

As his flesh fell away, I saw his jaws, fangs piercing the Sidhe's neck. "Noooo," I screeched.

Padhraic leapt into view. Grabbing the Vampire's skull, he twisted it until I heard vertebrae snapping. His jaws relaxed their hold on Griselda, and she moaned softly.

"Hold up," Padhraic said and slapped a hand over her neck. It glowed blue white as magic flowed from him.

"Will she be all right?" I shouted over the din around us.

"Maybe. Depends if I neutralize all the venom. It works fast in combination with Sidhe power."

I did my best to stand, but my legs were wobbly. I refused to engage in a repeat of my ignominious collapse in Adva's cave and sucked in a steadying breath. It reminded me how raw my throat and lungs were.

"Can I help?" I asked Paddy.

He removed his hand, inspecting his work. "Nay. I'm done."

"You bet you are, Sidhe," Griselda snarled and threw herself at Padhraic. They ended up on the floor, each working hard to wrest control from the other.

Fangs gleamed in the muted light of the wrecked chamber as she tried to bite him, jaws snapping, spittle flying.

I yanked out my last vial of dead man's blood and doused

her with it. At least it would give us time to come up with a solution.

"Good woman." Padhraic sprang upright.

"You weren't kidding about a quick transformation." I gawked at the tip of a fang extruding from her mouth and added, "It won't hold her forever."

"Aye, but it gives us an opportunity to save her."

The question about what if we failed danced at the back of my throat, but I didn't let it out. I knew the answer. She'd join all the other dead Vampires littering the floor of the seethe.

CHAPTER TWELVE, LIAM

I'd never viewed Vampires as much in the way of adversaries, not the Earth-bound variety, anyway. The Leanan had posed a different problem since they'd begun their lives as Sidhe, and many of us are warriors at heart.

Vamps are territorial as hell, which meant their seethes were widely spaced. No new ones had formed in a very long time. Until the dark gods had lured the Leanan to their purposes, Earth-bound Vampires had been fading. The twentieth century version was far less noticeable than their eighteenth century counterparts had been.

With good reason. A proliferation of television shows and movies had popularized all the ways to kill them. Groups of real-life Vampire hunters had driven them even farther into the shadows...

All those thoughts and more circled through my brain while Krin made small talk with the master Vampire. He had to be centuries old but appeared around forty. I understood Krin's tactics, and felt the sly unraveling suggestions of a subtle spell riding beneath his words.

He was doing his best to cut the heart out of the Vampires, so they'd back away, much as the Master Vamp was urging us to do.

Nice try. Too bad it hadn't worked very well.

Despite all my research into Vampires and their nefarious ways, I hadn't run across anything to prepare me for their viciousness. Because they were already dead, a total disregard for their own safety made them tricky opponents. It wasn't all that different from battling immortals, something I hadn't taken into consideration.

Or maybe it was a matter of critical mass. The other Vamps I'd taken on had come in much smaller numbers—and hadn't been protecting their home base. Seethes were created by master Vampires as they engaged in empire-building. I had no idea how many minions they needed—and sub-minions of the minions—before they figured they had enough to start their own seethe.

My hands weren't nearly as recovered as I'd hoped, but I couldn't think about them. I added magic to my blade until its swings and thrusts and parries turned into a blur as I beheaded one Vamp after another. I still had stakes—and dead man's blood—but they wouldn't be as efficient.

I stopped counting after separating twenty heads from their respective shoulders. What difference did numbers make? We'd fight until we were done. Breath came hard, and my heart rose to the occasion, pumping fast enough to keep me upright and fighting.

I'd imagined the Vamps would teleport out of here in one hell of a hurry once it became obvious we didn't plan to leave any of them alive. Instead, they jumped Sidhe and Reapers from every angle, sinking fangs into any body part that was handy. They weren't in this for feeding.

Nay, they wanted to exact maximum damage.

If they turned too many Sidhe, we'd have a resurgence of the Leanan all over again. I'd once told Cait even a scratch could transmit the building blocks of Vampirism. We were nothing like mortals, who had to be drained to the point of death and then drink willingly from their brand new master.

Dena had switched from killing to treating the fallen. I caught the occasional brief glance of her drawn face and intuited the news wasn't good. She'd do what she had to, even if it meant severing souls from bodies, the same way we'd ended Hollis's life.

A Vampire jumped me from behind. He no doubt expected me to fall on my face, collapsing beneath his weight. It was iffy for a moment, but I recovered. Switching up my grip on my blade, I angled it behind me and drove it through something.

An infuriated howl followed, but the weight clinging to me fell away. I twirled and brought the blade down, cleaving a shoulder and cutting off one of the Vampire's arms before I beheaded him.

Black blood sheeted from my blade. It was having a good old time, glowing with the magic that had gone into its forging. Despite all the carnage, the blade made me smile. It was a simple implement, created for a single purpose.

If it could speak, it would have told me the best days were massacres, exactly like today.

My shoulders and arms ached from the constant output of effort. I wasn't in bad shape, but neither was I battle-hardened. Hundreds of years had passed since the Sidhe had to fight our way out of skirmishes on a daily basis. A glance around the room told me we'd finally made a difference.

Fewer Vampires were on their feet, and the floor was littered with so many stacks of bones, tripping over them had become a hazard. I'd forgotten how good killing felt. The clean joy of vanquishing an enemy partially offset my physical discomfort.

Between Sidhe and Reapers, we seemed to have demoralized the remaining Vampires because they were finally, finally teleporting the fuck out of their ruined home.

I scanned the chamber hunting for Cait, and found her near Padhraic. He was on his knees next to Griselda. I threaded through skulls, spines, and assorted long bones. When I got close, I understood he was engaged in more than aiding a fallen Sidhe.

"Dena has a field hospital set up," I told Padhraic.

"She probably has her hands full, and I've almost got this. You understand how these things go, mate. If I quit now, we'll have to start over. Link to me, and add water to my healing." Paddy didn't even look up. His entire focus was on Griselda. She was crusty and outspoken, but I'd always appreciated her no-nonsense approach.

I opened a channel for Padhraic. He sorted through my magic and drew water into his casting. "What happened?" I asked.

"Shit. What didn't? She turned into a Vampire as soon as one dug his fangs into her." Cait sounded rattled. "I had no idea the transition would be so...immediate."

A whitish glow around Padhraic's hands changed to blue. Griselda's neck quivered beneath his touch. Stinking, black ichor oozed from open wounds the fangs had made.

I pushed more water into the spell. We were winning. I felt certain not all the Sidhe had been as fortunate. And I had no idea how Reapers succumbed to Vampire poisoning, other than it was certain to turn them unless someone intervened.

Breath rattled from between Paddy's clenched teeth. He finally looked up at me. "She'll be fine. She should shake off the enchantment from dead man's blood now we've removed the rest of the Vampire taint."

True to his prediction, Griselda groaned and shook herself weakly before struggling to sit. Her dark eyes flickered open and landed on Padhraic. "I take back every bad thing I ever said about you," she rasped. "Thank you."

He made a grunting noise. "For a while there, I wasn't certain I could fix you."

She made a sour face. "Living it from the inside was no picnic, either. Goddess's tits. How do Vampires do it? Even a few minutes biding as they do was hideous. 'Twill take liters of mead to wipe it from my mind."

"Mead, eh? You'll be fine." I bent to clap her across the shoulders.

"Thanks to him." She jerked a thumb Paddy's way.

"I'm going to see if Dena needs help," he said and rolled to his feet.

"Can you stand?" Cait asked Griselda, offering a hand. The Sidhe grasped it and let Cait haul her upright.

"What's left to do?" Griselda asked me.

"Not much," I told her.

"I have to help the Reapers," Cait said. "You probably can't sense them, but the chamber is thick with shades. Pissed off shades who weren't ready to turn loose of their bodies. Sheesh.

They're pounding fists into each other. And us. Good thing they're not corporeal."

"How are you holding up?" I kept my question neutral, open-ended. She looked tired, but we all were.

Cait cracked a weary smile through a face streaked with gore and Vampire remains. "What you're really asking is if the music got the best of me. It didn't, but not without quite a struggle before it retreated."

"Excellent news. See you in a bit." I gave her a quick hug.

Griselda and I walked through the room making certain no Vampires were hiding in corners or behind anything. She moved with more alacrity as she shook off the aftereffects of her near brush with disaster. Side tunnels led off the main room, so we checked those too.

"I can't believe how big this place is," she muttered after the tenth channel yielded rooms with mortal prisoners. Obviously a convenient food source, most jumped at a chance for freedom, bolting into the corridor as soon as we freed them. Others merely stared at us with rheumy eyes, clearly no longer understanding much of anything.

"What should we do with them?" Griselda asked.

I had no idea if they could recover, but we had to give them a chance. "Let's finish searching," I said. "Once we figure out how many are like them"—I jerked my chin at a room packed with drooling, vacant-eyed husks who'd once been human beings—"we'll come up with a plan."

"Good enough." She shuddered. "Not much bothers me, but this turns my stomach. How could Vampires be such heartless fuckers?"

"They were human once too," I reminded her. "The transformation turns them into beasts. They still look like people, but that's where the similarity begins and ends. Nothing about them is human any longer."

"I still can't believe how fast my magic glommed onto Vampirism," Griselda muttered. "Gives me a whole new view of the Leanan."

Two more empty tunnels, and we returned to the cave with its glut of living food sources. We'd opened the gate our first time through. A few more people might have left, but at least thirty remained.

Scraps of clothing clung to their emaciated forms. Fury and disgust filled me, along with a need to somehow make things right. If it was possible. "Let's try a bit of magic," I said to Griselda.

"I was thinking the same," she replied in a soft voice. "Perhaps a wee bit of fire and air to energize them, so they can walk out of here."

"We'll anchor the spell with earth," I said, "and feed in fire and air in very small amounts."

"Got it." She scrunched her eyes in a distasteful expression.

"If you're not up to it—" I kept my voice gentle, devoid of judgment.

"Nay. I'm girding myself to touch my magic. Last time I did, it was tainted."

"Your choice."

"I'm good. Let's do this," she gritted.

I had to hand it to Griselda. She had balls of steel. We'd butted heads more than once over the years, but I've always respected her strength and determination.

I tapped into her magical center and controlled the casting, adding power a tiny bit at a time. The mortals were so weakened, I didn't want to make a mistake and kill them inadvertently. Griselda helped, funneling our power in dribs and drabs to each person in turn.

One by one, they rose to their feet and shambled from their prison. A few thanked us, but most plodded, one foot ahead of the other, gaze downcast. I assumed they knew the way out and wouldn't wander aimlessly.

"We did a good turn here today," Griselda said after the last of the mortals had cleared the low doorway.

"Aye, that we did. This is worse than a prisoner of war compound."

Our magic had gone a small way toward cleansing the stench of long-unwashed bodies, but the holding cell was dank and grim. No wonder the mortals had checked out mentally.

She fixed her unremitting gaze on me. "Appreciate the boot in the arse to trust my magic."

I smiled. "I didn't do anything."

"Aye, but you did. You trusted my power enough to tap into it without so much as a preliminary assessment."

"Wasn't much of a risk. Your fangs were gone, and, from what I saw with the Leanan, Vampirism is kind of either all on or all off for our kind."

She looked away. "I feel ashamed for doubting Padhraic. I was one of the most vocal advocates for dumping him into the pit with the others."

"It's all right." I squeezed her shoulder lightly. "'Tisn't often we get a chance to redeem ourselves. You'll have plenty of opportunities to be less...biased in the future."

"You always were his friend. Do you suppose he'll forgive me?"

"He already has. He knows he did wrong, and he wasn't

expecting any of us to forget about his transgressions. Come on. Let's see if we can help with the cleanup."

We walked back to the main room. The Reapers were dismantling their gateways. I glanced at all the bones and decided to leave them where they lay. In a different situation, I'd have made piles and burned them, but no reason to tidy up a domicile I hoped was never occupied again.

Krin strode to us. "Glad you're all right," he told Griselda.

"Makes two of us," she said crisply.

"Did a bunch of humans walk through?" I asked him.

He nodded. "Once we understood you'd found the Vampires' food supply, we escorted them out of the crypt. I alerted the authorities, so someone will provide at least temporary shelter and sustenance for them. Poor sods. Some of them were in terrible shape."

"Aye. They were," Griselda said. "So much so, we had to rouse them with magic, or they'd still be back yonder."

I rolled my tired shoulders straighter. Somewhere along the line, I'd sheathed my blade, but I'd be damned if I could remember doing it. "Losses?"

"A Sidhe and two Reapers," Krin said. "We've already moved the bodies outside so we can transport them back to Scourie."

I bowed my head, grateful we hadn't lost more but sad and angry any of us had died.

"Dena did an amazing job," Krin went on. "Our casualty list would have been far longer were it not for her skills and refusal to give up."

"We learned something," Griselda said. "Or at least I did, but it has universal applicability. We must ward ourselves. It will hamper our fighting to some extent, but I never want to be hanging in limbo again, where I feel Vampire taint creeping through my body and am helpless to stop it. I fed magic into the equation, but all it did was make the poison spread faster."

"Good to know," Krin said, tightlipped.

"Is the master Vampire dead?" Griselda skinned her lips back from her teeth.

"Very," Krin told her. "He'll never form another seethe."

Cait materialized by my side. Black smudges caked both cheeks, and the cut places in her hands had reopened. "If we're done here, I'm going outside and try to call Kiko."

"We're done," Krin said.

I looped an arm around Cait's shoulders and said, "I'll go with you."

We climbed a long set of rickety wooden stairs that led to the graveyard. I was certain the original crypt hadn't been this deeply excavated. Dawn was breaking, adding a pale edge to the night sky. This late in the year, my bet was it might be nine in the morning. The British Isles were far enough north that winter daylight began midmorning and ended between fifteen and sixteen hundred.

Cait plopped down on a headstone and dug her cellphone out of her bag. After a bit of fiddling, she tapped the display until a likeness of Kiko flared across the screen.

Perching on the tombstone's edge, I watched the tiny display and willed Kiko to pick up.

Six rings later, a tinny voice said Kiko Tanaka wasn't available. Cait left a message. All she said was hello and she hoped Kiko was doing well. After that, she switched to the message screen and sent a text.

We waited, but Kiko didn't reply.

"Damn it." Cait balanced the phone on her knee. "Usually,

Kiko is surgically attached to her cell. Maybe I should call the pharmacy."

"It's a good idea," I said. "They can at least tell you if she's been there."

Cait shook her head. "Nah. They're not supposed to disclose anything about their employees. It's one of a bunch of new privacy rules. I could pretend to be a relative, except she doesn't have any. Her parents are dead, and she had no brothers or sisters."

"Aunts? Uncles?" I prodded. "Maybe she has family in Japan."

"Eh. Like I can do a credible Japanese accent."

"Magic could help with that. So can I."

"Maybe so. Just a moment. I need to block my number from showing up at the pharmacy end." She tapped the display, cycling through screens before handing the cellphone to me. I waited until the pharmacy's recording came on. None of the options fit, so I selected the one to patch me through to a pharmacist.

"Twenty-four hour pharmacy," a crisp male voice said.

"I am looking for Kiko Tanaka." I adopted what I hoped was a credible Japanese twist. If it came down to it, I spoke Japanese. Not well, but enough to get by.

"Who is this?" The voice didn't sound as friendly as before.

"Her uncle, Daiki Tanaka, calling from Sakura. Many apologies for bothering her place of employment, but she is not answering her telephone or her messages."

A long pause followed. Good. The fellow on the other end didn't have clue one about whether Kiko had blood kin in Japan.

"Is there some problem?" he asked at length.

"So kind of you to ask. Yes. My wife is quite ill. She was fond of Kiko, and I fear…" I let my words trail off. Sometimes too little information was better than too much.

"Ms. Tanaka isn't here at the moment," the man said a bit stiffly, "but I'll pass on your message."

"Are you expecting her?" I pressed.

"Uh, she's on vacation."

"Oh. When will she return?"

"I don't have that information." The line developed a hollow sound, and I knew he'd disconnected.

Cait took the phone back. "Damn it. She's in trouble. Pretty much has to be."

"Or she's gone to ground and left all her electronics elsewhere. I'm not totally up to snuff on these things, but aren't cellphones a primary way to trace someone?"

"They are, but it doesn't make me feel any better."

I placed a hand on her thigh. "What do you want to do?"

She leaned into me. "I don't know. It's hard to pick one thing out of a sea of critical stuff. Everything is important, but I can't be two places at once. Or three or four."

"We could teleport to Seattle."

"I know we could," she said, "but both of us are dead on our feet. We need rest and food; the Sidhe and Reapers need us here. Besides, even if we went to Seattle, I wouldn't have the first idea where to look for Kiko. She could be anywhere."

"I can find her. So long as she still has my crystal."

Cait twisted until she faced me. "Man of many surprises. Did you know when you fashioned it, we might need to use it that way?"

I nodded. "Let's return to Scourie. We can pay our respects to the fallen, and then we'll make a quick side trip to Seattle."

Her eyes sheened with sudden tears, and she threw her arms around me. "Thank you."

I scooped her against me and stood as I summoned a teleport spell. "We may not like what we find," I warned.

Cait nodded. I felt the motion against my chest. "Yeah. I get that part, but knowing is better than not. And maybe if she's in trouble, we'll get there in time to intervene."

I let the spell take us. I hoped Cait's optimism was justified. She felt guilty for Kiko's plight, and tonight's slaughter could amplify her problems. Word of what we'd done to the Dublin seethe would spread. Vampires around the world would be outraged, running scared, a dangerous and volatile combination.

They'd already set their sights on Kiko because of her connection to Cait. I said a quick prayer she'd be the only element of collateral damage in the war rapidly rising around us. Except I didn't believe it.

We could only tackle one problem at a time. We'd see the fallen to their rest, but we'd go after Kiko immediately afterward. Cait said she was resourceful. Hopefully, she'd found a safe spot to hide, one where the Vampires couldn't kill her or turn her into one of them.

But I didn't believe that, either.

CHAPTER THIRTEEN, CAIT

The funeral for the dead Sidhe and two Reapers made my heart hurt. One look at Dena's face, all planes and angles and pain, told me without words how much she'd suffered. The Vampires had turned all their targets. It was their only option since Sidhe are immortal. Perhaps the Vamps hadn't been certain about Reaper status in that regard.

And they weren't taking any chances.

I stood over the biers, saying goodbye and doing my best not to lose it. Dena hadn't gotten to these three in time to reverse the blood-borne curse. They'd died by her hand because she had no choice.

The Sidhe's name was Jonathan. The Reapers were Merry and Christine. They'd been assigned to a big chunk of South America. I hadn't known them well, but any loss was unacceptable. The bodies on their raised biers were committed to magefire after everyone told tales of their bravery and wished them the pagan equivalent of Godspeed.

Stacia and I formed a gateway and welcomed their spirits to the afterlife. I'd managed not to cry before the shades latched onto my magic, but by the time they were done, my cheeks were damp with tears.

Such a shame.

Such a waste.

Anger rushed through me in a scorching tide that dried my tears and left me feeling like an empty husk. Worse, I kept looking over one shoulder or the other for Death. Surely, she'd felt her Reapers die. Eh, maybe not hers any longer. We'd severed the connection, so it was possible she had no idea. Regardless, I was grateful she didn't splat through a portal to chide us for how badly we'd failed.

I had enough on my plate, so much my perennial concerns about *Carrick Sky Sports* had vanished from center stage.

Once the gateway was down, Stacia gripped my upper arm. "I promised Cathbad I'd tutor you."

I shut my eyes for a moment. They felt hot and gritty. I hadn't forgotten, not exactly, but it meant I couldn't go after Kiko quite yet. "How long will it take?"

"Hard to say. I figured you'd need to get some rest first, and then—"

"No." The word came out harsher than I'd meant, and I winced. "Sorry. A friend of mine is in trouble because of me. Liam and I were headed for Seattle to see if we can't find her."

Stacia nodded, her eyes pinched at their corners. "You can't go anywhere else until I impart Cathbad's instruction."

I drew back, nonplussed. "What do you mean, can't go anywhere?"

Stacia rolled her sleeve back, revealing a short gash on the inside of her wrist. "He made me swear a blood oath. He probably knew better than any of us how quickly things would heat up. He only left a couple of hours ago. The rest of us were growing concerned about you. No one expected you'd be gone all night dealing with the seethe."

"We didn't exactly anticipate it, either," I muttered.

Liam walked to my side. "Ready to leave?"

"I will be, but first Stacia has to teach me a little bit about the musical magic."

"Won't it keep?" Liam's hazel gaze slid from her to me.

Stacia shook her head. "Nay. Cathbad bound me with my blood. He wasn't taking any chances."

"How'd it go keeping that part of things under wraps at the seethe? You didn't say much when I asked before." Liam furled a blond brow.

"It was really difficult at first, but then things were happening so fast my attention was elsewhere." I swallowed hard, trying for bedrock honesty. "Apparently, Vampires use a variant of musical magic to lure their victims. When they started up humming and crooning, my song wanted out in the worst way, but I quashed it."

A corner of Liam's mouth turned downward. "I believe I just put two and two together. Vampires must use music as one of their control mechanisms for the newly turned too."

It took a moment for me to make the connection, but then I muttered, "Which was why they responded to my song in Adva's cave."

"Exactly. Mind if I sit in on the lesson?" Liam asked Stacia.

She crinkled her forehead in thought. "I don't see why not. Cathbad didn't add secrecy as a condition. He'll know what I do through the blood link. If he doesn't approve, he'll have ways to let me know quick enough."

I didn't doubt it for a moment.

Smoke from the funeral pyres was still puffing into the night sky when Liam herded us to a workspace in Scourie Castle's lower level. It wasn't any warmer inside than it had been in the courtyard, but at least it was dry.

"Go ahead and start without me," Liam told Stacia. "I'll run upstairs and brew us hot tea and see what I can find for finger food."

"I'm so lucky he likes to cook," I murmured to Stacia after Liam had left. "I've lived on TV dinners and takeout forever."

She smirked. "Only the past few years, sweetie. Before that, if you didn't cook, you didn't eat."

"True enough, but I was never much more than a toss-grains-in-boiling-water-and-wait type." I shrugged. "Some talents never take. Speaking of which, I was grateful Death didn't make a cameo appearance today."

"Aye. Me too. I kept reminding myself she couldn't spy on us any longer, but I didn't truly believe it. Kept expecting her to bounce through a portal, shake her finger at us, and scold us for walking away."

I dragged a chair out of a corner and fell into it. "Ready when you are."

"Close your eyes," she instructed, "and reach for your magic. Make certain you have a good handle on the earth element and sort out at least half a dozen strands. Keep them separate from one another. Let me know when you're ready for the next step."

It took me several tries. Sitting wasn't working. Not with my eyes closed. I was so wiped out, my attention wandered in unexpected directions, mostly toward fragmented visions of the seethe and Vampires with glittering eyes and shining fangs dripping blood.

Somewhere along the line, Liam pressed a mug of steaming tea into my hands. I was standing by then, and I took a sip of the hot liquid. It cleared my head almost immediately. Had he spelled it, or was it a combination of carefully selected tea leaves?

Didn't matter. I was finally able to sort out six strands of earth-imbued magic. "Got it," I told Stacia, grateful she hadn't prodded me or asked why it was taking me so long to accomplish a simple task.

"Good. This next part is the crux, and it's not easy. While holding onto the filaments, let a few notes escape. As each group of notes is free, wrap it with a strand and move to the next."

Sounded simple enough not to merit her warning. Once I was certain I had a handle on the filaments, I redirected my attention to the music I'd buried deep. Its response nearly flattened me.

Rather than a short riff, an entire song burst from me, the notes evocative, haunting as the music mourned last night's losses. Before the song caught me up entirely, I forced it aside and punted it back under wraps, panting with effort.

Stacia wrapped a steadying arm around my shoulders. "Aye. See? It wants to be free. Once you figure out how to only let a tiny bit escape at a time, you'll have most of the battle won. You wrap the sections in earth to make them amenable to your command. That way, they don't get away from you."

I was still trying to catch my breath. I hadn't expected the music's strength, but then I'd freed it once when I didn't know any better. Even that single misstep was costing me now.

"Did all the Reapers manage to establish control?" I asked.

Stacia shook her head. "Cathbad did something to five of us. He couldn't remove the musical part, but he clipped its wings or something. Reassured us his intervention had solved the problem."

"Were the Reapers disappointed?"

"Oh hell no." Stacia rolled her blue eyes. "By then, they'd decided they housed the Devil himself and were delighted to be relieved of the burden."

Good to know there was an option—if I failed.

The specter of washing out didn't sit well. I'd made it through tougher things than this. "Going to try again," I told them. Bending, I placed the cup on the floor and focused on my magical center.

If you want to be part of my magic, I told the music sternly, *you cannot be in charge.*

When I reached for the music this time, I lightened my touch to a mere feather brush. I imagined a trap door and slid it up, but only an inch or two, slamming it fast. Three notes emerged from my throat, and I wrapped them in one of the filaments that still stood ready.

"Do it again," Stacia instructed. "And again. Until this part can happen without thought."

Time passed. I had no idea how much. My sides were heaving and slick with sweat despite the castle's damp chill. I'd built six more filaments. An even dozen clumps of notes floated around me muffled by earth magic.

"What's next?" I asked Stacia.

"Allow two of the groups to join. You'll have to alter the earthen wrap to accommodate it. Once you've got it, add another and then one more, until you have an entire song wrapped in earth."

I'd moved beyond tired long since, so much so my brain had developed an eerie observer aspect where I was both here and watching myself at the same time. The joining part was far simpler than the original assignment had been. Part of a song emerged from me while I was working, but I maintained the upper hand. And with far less effort than I'd imagined it would take.

"Now let go," Stacia said.

"Let go, as in?" I was still concerned the music would take off at a gallop once I released my iron grip on it.

"The same way you'd dissipate any spell. Simply release it."

I did. Surprise rolled through me when the music behaved itself, slinking quietly away once I withdrew the power keeping it alive. I stood blinking stupidly at Stacia.

"You've got the basics," she told me and smiled broadly. "I'd wait on practicing until you're more on top of your game."

"No shit," I muttered. "Thank you. You're a good teacher."

"Because you're an easy student. You follow directions and you've got determination. There was one point when I was afraid you'd throw in the towel, but you didn't."

"I'm still jealous." Liam moved toward us from the wall he'd been leaning against. "I poked and prodded and tested various combinations of my power while you two worked and convinced myself music was nowhere in my repertoire."

He pointed at a tray. "Finish your tea and have something to eat. Both of you."

My eyes widened. I hadn't even noticed the mug clasped between Stacia's hands. Bending, I selected a croissant that looked as if it had been baked with cheese and maybe ham. The first bite brought saliva rushing into my mouth as I realized I was half-starved.

Footsteps clattering down stairs spun my head around. Padhraic strode into the room and straight to Stacia's side. "How'd it go?"

"Ask her?" Stacia tilted her chin my way.

"Fine," I said around a mouthful of food. Once I'd swallowed, I added, "It went fine. I know what I need to do. Now what I require is practice. Until then, the music remains buried."

Paddy snatched a sandwich off the tray, took a bite, and nudged Liam. "I'd recognize your work anywhere."

Liam shrugged. "I like to cook. So shoot me."

For a while, we ate and sipped tea in relative silence. "Ready to go?" Paddy asked Stacia.

She offered him a warm smile and hooked a hand beneath his arm. "I am. See you soon," she told me. "Good luck in Seattle."

Padhraic stopped dead. "What's in Seattle this time?" He aimed his words at Liam.

"A friend of Cait's might be in trouble. She's dropped off the radar."

"Vampires targeted her. Because of me," I blurted. "We rescued her once, but now she's not answering her phone or text messages. Her work doesn't even know where she is."

"Did it occur to you to take reinforcements with you?" Paddy's dark eyes radiated concern.

"Nay. We planned a quick trip. In and out," Liam replied. "I didn't wish to deflect any resources from our problems here."

"Does Krin know you're leaving?" Padhraic persisted

"Nay, and I suppose I should tell him." Liam drained his mug and set it down. "I assumed we'd leave right after the funerals, but then Stacia had other priorities. Cathbad must have had his reasons for not wanting Cait to go too far without instruction—"

"Doesn't matter how we got here," I cut in. "We should leave. It's been hours since I tried to raise Kiko and got nowhere."

"I'm going with you," Padhraic said.

"Well then, I'm coming too," Stacia announced.

A long, burbling sigh rose from Liam. "Fine. I'll tell Krin or Dena, whoever I locate first. Stacia will need a sword, and we could use more dead man's blood. Just in case."

"I'll take care of the sword and dead man's blood," Padhraic said.

"Back soon, one way or the other," Liam told us.

I understood what he meant. We were going to Seattle no matter who lodged a protest or told us we had to remain at the ready in Scotland.

"We'll stay here." Stacia turned to me, guiding me to the chair I'd once occupied. "Sit. Shut your eyes while you can."

My legs were shaky, and I didn't require a second invitation. I'd have laid on the floor if it weren't so cold. All the sweating I'd done while working magic had left my clothing damp, and I shivered from time to time. Using magic to warm myself was kind of a crapshoot. When I drifted off, the magic became less effective. Shivering woke me up, and the whole process started anew.

The buzz of voices alerted me others were in the basement. More than just Liam and Paddy. I opened my bleary eyes, blinking a few times to focus them. I'd been right about there being lots of folk milling about. Stacia lifted the arm she'd folded around my shoulders. I'd been leaning on her, and she'd supported my weight so I didn't tip the chair over.

"Thanks," I said, swaying a little as I planted my feet and got my bearings, promising myself I'd stand up soon.

"No worries, sweetie. Liam's here, and Paddy's back too," she told me. "Paddy brought me a blade, but it's pretty big. I'm going to make a trip to the armory and see if I can't find something I'd rather fight with."

Liam knelt in front of me. "Did you get some sleep?"

I nodded. "What's all this about?" My words were slurred. Damn. I had to pull myself together, so I didn't sound like I was coming off a two-week bender.

"I ran Krin down and filled him in. He was of Paddy's opinion."

"What? That we shouldn't go alone?"

"Aye," Liam concurred before continuing. "The more Vampires we can stamp out, the easier our job with the dark mages will be. Once Krin rustled up more Sidhe, we did a little research. Dena is certain a seethe is located north of Seattle. So long as we'll be in the area anyway, and have a system halfway developed, we'll take it out."

Something didn't quite add up. I struggled to get my brain to kick in. "Uh, but what about Vampires all talking to each other. Won't all the seethes be on high alert?"

Liam's solicitous expression shifted to one with vicious edges as he morphed into warrior mode. "We don't have much in the way of options. It's coming down to either us or them, and I vote for us. If we crush enough seethes, the others will do what good little Vampires learned long ago. They'll retreat deeper into the shadows and stay there."

I thought about it. Vampires have been around for a very long time. They always were abominations, but they'd never created havoc before. They'd gone on the occasional rampage, but nothing like this. The dark mages were egging them on, painting pictures of a rosy future full of all the blood they could drink. Our job was to pound home the point that continuing to follow their lead wouldn't end well.

"Too bad we can't get hold of a list of all the seethes," I mumbled.

"I'm certain such a thing exists," Liam said.

"It's a stretch, but maybe it's all written down somewhere in an electronic file. Something we could hack into. If we had any idea where to begin."

Liam patted my knee. "Cait. These are Vampires. What makes you think they've made the leap to the digital age?"

I shrugged. "We did."

He made a snorting sound. "Nay, lass. You did. I've come along kicking and screaming, but much of it seems like an arcane set of runes. In truth, I'd have far better luck with them than chasing down information on the Internet."

"It's worth a shot," I argued. "I can see where the dark mages wouldn't have bothered with computers, but Vampires spend a lot of time with humans. There are legions of dating sites and other meet-up opportunities where they could lure prey."

"Too rich a resource to ignore?" Liam eyed me.

"Something like that."

Sidhe and Reaper power flashed and flickered around us as teleport spells kindled. I got to my feet about the time Stacia and Padhraic joined us. "Ready to leave?" Paddy asked.

Liam stood too. "Aye. I'll manage the spell."

Good thing he offered. I was still depleted. Hell, I hadn't ever fully recovered from my last run-in with Adva. In the background, the musical part of my magic seemed to be the only portion relatively unaffected. It took scads of magic to manage, though.

Might be true today, I reminded myself. If I put in the time, it wouldn't always be like that.

Scourie Castle's basement took on an insubstantial aspect, and I felt the distinct bite of Sidhe power as Liam's journey spell ignited. "What's our destination?" I asked.

"One of the small, uninhabited islands in Puget Sound. We all mind-linked the coordinates."

"How many of us, and why there?"

"A few more than in Dublin," Liam explained. "Ten groups of six signed on, and we needed a spot we wouldn't generate undue attention. Once we're within striking distance, you and I will hunt for Kiko—"

"With us," Padhraic tossed out.

"No point telling you otherwise, I don't suppose," Liam muttered.

"None at all," Paddy agreed. "You saved my life, mate, vouched for me. I owe you, and I take my debts seriously."

"I've told you"—Liam's voice held a bristly edge—"any debt has been discharged. You owe me naught."

"We can agree to disagree on that point. Anyway, the four of us will attempt to locate Kiko, and—?"

"The others will track down the seethe." Liam stopped there, but I'd come to know him quite well.

"What aren't you saying?"

"'Tis possible Kiko's been turned. If we locate the seethe, we'll find her too."

An outraged scream formed in my throat. I contained it, barely. I could rail against fortune all I wanted, protest Kiko was too canny to be taken, but Vampires had entered her house and marked her. It didn't bode well—even with Liam's protective amulet.

"If she's been..." I stumbled over the word turned, unable to choke it out. "Is there anything we can do to fix it?"

Stacia gripped one of my hands. "You know the answer. If she's turned, it means she's dead."

I nodded once, short and terse. I did, indeed, know that answer, and all too well. Dead was dead. We couldn't resurrect her. The only kindness we could offer was passage across the veil. If it came to that, I'd rustle up Arawn or Hades and beg them not to consign her to Hell.

I cut my thoughts off at the source. I was way ahead of the curve. First we had to find her. Maybe it wasn't that bad. Perhaps they were just feeding from her. Or maybe she wasn't their prisoner at all.

Urging myself toward positive thoughts, I rode out the remainder of the journey spell. I'd find out soon enough. Until then, I'd be damned if I'd go into mourning, or mark Kiko down for the count.

If there was a good end to be had, I'd find it. And I wouldn't give up until I'd exhausted every avenue. Finally. I felt more like the old me. The one with grit and spunk and determination.

Deep in my mind, a melodic riff purred encouragingly, almost as if the music could read my thoughts and approved.

CHAPTER FOURTEEN, LIAM

I'd hesitated before voicing my fears about Kiko's fate. Cait had flinched, but she'd held her emotions in check. I kept returning to her suggestion about a master list of seethes being available somewhere. Personally, I thought it more likely to be etched in blood on parchment and secreted in a tomb than digitized. Except, there had to be more than one list. Back in the days before Xerox machines, scribes had copied important documents.

If any magical group had been laggardly joining the electronic age, it had to be Vampires, although Cait had raised a good point about them perhaps using online "get to know you" sites to scare up victims. I'd always looked at the myriad news articles about missing persons and wondered where they truly were. If law enforcement couldn't come up with a corpse, my money was on Vampiric possession.

We came out on a small islet between Blakeley and Cypress Islands in the eastern portion of the San Juan Island chain. Most everyone else had already arrived. This had been Griselda's suggestion. She remembered a string of deserted summer beach homes but had warned us they might not still be standing.

None of us thought we'd need a place to hole up, but we had required a location one of us knew about. Once we'd agreed, Griselda shared a mental image with coordinates.

We'd lost about eight hours, perhaps nine, and it was the middle of the previous night. This area was somewhat warmer than Scotland, but no drier. A fine drizzly mist spit from the cloud-shrouded sky, and I turned up the collar of my jacket. It didn't help much, but I've never favored hoods. They restrict my field of vision.

As soon as the magic from my teleport spell cleared, I changed things up and set a seeking vector in place, hoping against hope it would yield Kiko's location. I was certain I'd find the amulet, but it didn't necessarily mean Kiko would be with it. The magic I'd utilized to craft it was anathema to Vampires. If they'd taken her, they'd have jettisoned the stone.

"Well?" Cait stood next to me, teeth closed over her lower lip hard enough to leave small indentations.

The ping I was waiting for plucked the threads of my spell. "Found it," I said.

"Where?" Krin and Dena hovered near.

I did some quick mental calculations and then doublechecked them for accuracy. Grabbing a handy stick of driftwood, I kindled my mage light and drew a rough map in the wet sand. "Near as I can tell, the amulet is here." I jabbed the point of the stick into the map.

Cait crouched, examining what I'd drawn. "Looks suspiciously close to the airstrip."

"My guess would be one of the buildings that line up along both sides of it," I told her.

"Means she's not at the seethe," Krin said.

I shook my head. "Nay, doesn't mean that at all. They could have separated her from the amulet and left it."

"No reason why there couldn't be a critical mass of Vamps near my office," Cait said slowly. "I always wondered why the bastards showed up so fast. Could be because they didn't have to travel very far."

I gazed around the assemblage. "Do any of you recall something like a list with all the seethes? Have you ever heard of such a thing, or come across it?"

"Why would they do that?" Dena asked. "They hate each other. A list would make it easier for them to engage in tribal warfare."

"I don't know. To keep track?" I resisted rolling my eyes. My innate need for order was tripping me up. Same way it had when I'd been on the hunt for a single spell that would wipe out every Vampire on Earth.

That effort had run aground too.

"We have to go right now," Cait urged. "If we find the amulet, maybe there will be enough of Kiko's energy left on it to track her."

"Perhaps." I kept my tone noncommittal since it seemed unlikely.

"If we don't find her," Stacia said to Cait, "we can visit the realm of the dead. At least it would rule out one possibility."

Cait set her lips in a thin line. "If she's not there, and not with the amulet, it does narrow the field. Means she's either been turned or conscripted for food."

Pavel and Abby trotted close. "We had an idea," Abby said.

"Aye," Pavel chimed in. "We'll take a few Reapers and drop in on Arawn and Hades. If there's a Vampire seethe anywhere near here, they'll know its location."

"Excellent idea," Krin sounded almost jubilant. "They might even want in on the action. They seemed to enjoy the battles we've shared."

"We'll be in touch," I told him, anxious to get moving now that I had a direction mapped out.

"Cuts both ways," Krin said. "I'll transmit what we find too."

"Goes without saying," I replied.

"I'll manage the spell," Padhraic said as his Sidhe power swept us into its net. The island dropped away replaced by the rounded walls of Cait's Quonset hut office. "Figured we'd begin here," Paddy murmured. "Plus, it offered a protected spot where I didn't need to ward our presence."

Vestiges of Vampire energy floated in the room, but they'd spent enough time here, it didn't surprise me. The vector I'd engaged burned brighter, and I started for the door.

"She's close, isn't she?" Cait asked.

"The amulet is close," I corrected her, not wanting to raise false hope.

"Vampires have been here," Stacia said.

A disgusted grunt emerged from Cait. "You might say that. For a while, they may as well have taken up residence." Her scythe had begun to glow, but it didn't feel like a warning.

Intent on tracking the amulet, I tugged the door open and strode through it. My magic ebbed and flowed as I wove my way around buildings peppering this side of the airstrip.

Stacia's sickle glimmered too. She shook her head and

batted the air with a hand, muttering, "Go away. I'm not as stupid as you think I am."

"Yeah. We've gotten better figuring out which shades want passage and which ones are Vampire spawn," Cait said.

It explained why their scythes were activated. Ghosts must be jockeying for a gateway. Most of my focus was on my tracking spell, but even if it hadn't been, my ability to sense spirits was weak compared with Reapers.

"In here." I stopped next to a darkened hangar with blinds over the windows.

Cait frowned. "This is—or was—Doug's place."

"The one who loaned you the defective plane?" I asked.

"Yeah. And who used it to commit suicide. He's still here, by the way. He's one of the shades giving me grief. At least, according to my mechanic, he was highly placed in Humans Rule."

"Serves him right to be stuck in limbo." I narrowed my eyes. "Vamps wouldn't want him once he was already dead. Even if he'd fiddled with magic, it wouldn't work anymore. Wonder what the fuck he was thinking when he took that plane up?"

"Maybe that I'd exaggerated how damaged it was?" Cait shrugged. "We'll never know, and I don't care."

Padhraic stood in front of the hangar door; small jots of magic puffed from his outstretched hands. "I don't sense anything living inside." he said. "Can't sort out Vampires, either, but there's a residual taint just like at Cait's place."

I started to tell Cait to stay back, but she wouldn't have listened. Kiko was her friend. Done hesitating, I twisted the door latch expecting to find it locked. It wasn't. The barnlike door swung sideways on well-oiled tracks. Airplane smells—

leather, plastic, gas, oil, and metal—leached through the open door.

I searched for the slightly sweet rotten smell of decay, but didn't find it.

Cait rushed past me. Her scythe was glowing brighter, illuminating the cavernous interior. Three planes sat, wings overlapping with one another. Stacia hastened after Cait. The two of them started at opposite ends, searching the hangar floor.

Meanwhile, I followed what had turned into a lighted trajectory, courtesy of the pull of the amulet. It led me to the largest of the three planes, a two-engine job that looked a lot like the one in Cait's hangar. The amulet wasn't on the ground, so it had to be inside the plane. I walked around it, looking for a way inside.

Cait and Stacia caught me up. "If she's here, it's nowhere obvious." Cait's voice was thin, strained. "Did you find the amulet."

"It's in there." I pointed at the plane.

The words were no sooner out of my mouth than Cait sprinted up a couple of metal rungs to the wing on the passenger side and tugged on the door. "Fuck," she shouted. "It's locked, and my magic won't budge the tumbler. Look on the corkboard for something that says Piper Chieftain keys or just Chieftain keys."

"Got 'em," Paddy shouted and came on a run. He tossed the keys to Cait, and she opened the plane, stepping inside. A harsh cry carried my worst fears to full bloom.

Kiko must be inside—with the talisman. Cait wouldn't have sounded so frantic over a piece of quartz. I followed the same path she'd taken and wove past rows of seats to an empty spot in the tail of the aircraft.

Cait knelt on aluminum struts next to Kiko's comatose form. "She's not dead," Cait said in a tense voice. "Almost, but not quite."

Padhraic joined us, falling to his knees on Kiko's other side. Blue-white power flared from his hands as he ran them the length of her slight form. Dark hair fanned around her, and fang marks stood out on her neck. Lots of them. Damn it to hell. Vamps had feasted on her, and then left her for dead.

But why would they have locked her inside an airplane?

The only explanation that made sense was she'd managed to drag herself this far before losing consciousness. Sure enough, a key was clutched in one hand.

"Kiko loved this plane." Cait's words were garbled; tears had to be close to the surface. "Flew it whenever she could." Her anxious gaze followed Paddy's every move, but then mine did too.

Stacia worked her way around the seats but stopped there. Four of us was tight in this confined space. Her scythe had taken on a silvery edge; Cait's too. Perhaps they recognized the proximity of a soul on the verge of seeking passage.

Padhraic looked at me. "We need Dena, but if we try to transport Kiko, she'll die. That she's still alive is a miracle."

"Can we take her to a hospital?" Cait pleaded. "They'll have blood. They can transfuse her."

"Blood is only part of the problem," Padhraic said. "Vamps drained her and tried to force her to drink from them. She refused, but some of their blood dribbled into her mouth. Not enough to turn her, but it's the only thing keeping her breathing."

"She got here under her own steam," Cait said. "She must have. Vampires would never have known to put her into an airplane, and particularly not this one. My guess is she knew she was dying, and wanted to die in a place that was special to her."

A strangled sob followed, followed by another, followed by, "Say something, Padhraic. There has to be something we can do."

"I might be able to funnel magic into her via the amulet," I said.

"How did you craft it?" Padhraic asked in as sharp a tone as I'd ever heard from him.

"With fire and water, heavy on the water. She'd been marked, and I shaped power to eradicate the Vampires' ability to locate her again."

Breath whistled from between Paddy's teeth. "Might work, but we need the talisman." He ran his hands over her lightly, locating the stone in an inner pocket. She lay so still, she looked like a broken doll. Her slender chest barely rose and fell. When Padhraic moved the amulet, she made a gasping sound as if she were drowning.

He tucked it back into the pocket. "I was mistaken. 'Tis your magic holding her on this side of the veil."

"Healing isn't my strong suit," I told him, "but you already knew that. Tell me what you need from me."

"Establish a connection with the amulet and strengthen the magic you used to create it. Go very slowly. Any changes at this point could backfire on us."

Cait moved to a cross-legged sit and gently maneuvered Kiko's head into her lap, crooning softly.

Padhraic constructed a canopy over Kiko's inert form. I recognized the intervention; healers only used it as a last-ditch effort. "While Liam is making her stronger, I will attempt to leverage his magic to remove the tiny bits of Vampire toxin in her body."

"Will it hurt her?" Cait raised her green-eyed gaze to Padhraic's somber face.

"It shouldn't, but the most I'm hoping for is allowing her to slip peacefully away. So long as she plays host to Vampire poison, she'll hover betwixt this world and the next. Not dead, but not alive, either."

"I see," Cait said woodenly and smoothed hair from Kiko's face. The woman's high cheekbones stood out beneath skin that had developed a translucent aspect.

"Ready when you are," I told Paddy.

"Begin," he said.

I was already joined with the amulet, so feeding magic into it was simple enough. I shut my eyes, feeling my way. The closer I got to Kiko, the more aware I was of the frayed threads of willpower keeping her alive. That she'd managed to walk to this hangar, let along crawl into the plane, was miraculous.

Paddy's magic braided with mine. I followed his seek-and-destroy mission. Once I identified the parts that didn't belong—the Vampire contamination—I obliterated them too. Meant we could work more quickly.

Cait's voice rose and fell. Sometimes I caught a few words and heard her exhorting Kiko to hang on, to be strong. That we would save her if we could. Stacia hummed a few notes, and then a few more, and the distinctive feel of Cathbad's song wrapped Kiko in its weave.

I'd almost forgotten the music. It was an unknown entity. As such, it could cut either way. I strengthened my connection to Kiko and asked Danu for divine intervention. We could use a break, and Cait would always blame herself if Kiko died.

Observing the tenderness in her touch almost broke me. If I could have shielded her from pain, I would have, but I couldn't protect her from this any better than I'd sheltered her from Death's onslaught.

"Almost there," Paddy said.

"Are you sure?" I eliminated two more spots.

"Quite. The question is what will happen afterward."

Cait didn't react. Maybe she hadn't heard. Her head was bent over Kiko's, and a soft tide of violet magic sheeted from her, warm and soothing. "I know, darling friend," she said, "but you can't leave. Not yet. We're fixing this. Be strong for just a little longer."

Kiko straddled two words. Cait's words clinched it. She was requesting passage, and Cait had refused.

"Yes, dear. I promise," Cait murmured.

"Our task is complete." Padhraic's words were gentle. "Time to withdraw and see if she can stand on her own."

Stacia had moved until she knelt next to Padhraic. Music still flowed from her. Would it be enough to keep Kiko alive? Paddy was reeling in the power that kept his canopy in place. One change at a time would be plenty. I waited until the canopy had turned to streamers of light before I began withdrawing my magic. I took my time extracting my presence.

Usually, I have complete confidence in my magic, but I was in over my head. We all have talents, and this has never been one of mine. Cathbad's music had been one of the elements that kept Cait alive after Death tried to kill her. Perhaps it would have the same effect for Kiko.

Maybe. Kiko wasn't magical.

I was down to a single filament, and I let it dissolve.

For long moments, nothing changed, but then Kiko made a

gagging sound, struggling to breathe. Cait propped her up and rubbed her back and shoulders, turning her head to the side in case she vomited.

I leaned forward, feeling helpless. We'd done all we could.

The same tortured sounds of Kiko fighting to breathe went on so long, I kept expecting a sudden silence. Surely, there'd come a time when her depleted resources wouldn't be up to the task of dragging air into her lungs.

The cadence of Stacia's song changed, and then changed again.

Cait never stopped touching Kiko, talking to her, stroking her hair. "I'll be here for you," she said, "but this isn't your time."

Maybe the resolve in Cait's words turned the tide, or maybe it was Stacia's music, but Kiko's breathing grew less labored. When it shaded to normal, Stacia's song ceased.

"We need to get her to a hospital," Cait said.

Kiko's dark eyes fluttered open. "It's really you," she rasped. "Thought I dreamed you. Thirsty."

"There should be a refrigerator somewhere in the hangar," Cait told me.

"I'll bring water. Tea if I can find it," I said.

By the time I got back, Kiko had moved to one of the passenger seats. Cait sat on one side, Stacia on the other. Paddy stood over them, keeping a watchful eye. He'd always had an understated aspect, but I knew he was pleased. He'd expected her to die. That she hadn't was an unexpected gift.

I handed a mug with tea and sugar to Kiko. She drank greedily and asked, "Is there more?"

I'd anticipated her and refilled the mug with more tea from

a flask. I'd used magic to heat the water, not wanting to wait for the hotplate I'd found in a corner.

"You need to be in a hospital," Cait told her friend. "You lost a lot of blood. They can transfuse you."

Kiko shook her head and shivered. "Not safe. Nowhere is safe."

"Do we know what happened?" I asked Cait, not wanting Kiko to have to recount the tale a second time.

Cait shook her head and pointed to a cabinet. "There should be blankets in there."

I grabbed a couple and wrapped them around Kiko, who'd begun shivering in earnest. It would take more than hot tea and blankets to restore her.

"They were sure I was as good as dead," Kiko said. "And I refused to drink from them. It's why they left."

"How'd you get here?" Cait asked.

"Not sure. Can't remember, but it wasn't far. I was sleeping in your hangar. Maybe not the best choice." Kiko shrugged her thin shoulders. "I ate some of your food."

"Don't worry about it. They found you in my hangar?" When Kiko nodded, Cait went on, "What happened then?"

"I tried to run, but they caught me. Shit. They're fast. They did horrible things before they sank their fangs into me." She shut her eyes for a long moment. When she opened them, she said, "Not drinking from them was one of the hardest things I've ever done. I kept telling myself I didn't want to become like them, but there was this drive, this insidious push from within telling me all the pain would go away, and I'd turn into this wondrous being."

Padhraic knelt in front of her and took one of her hands. "I know all too well. I spent many years as a Vampire. You were stronger than me, and I applaud your courage."

Spots of rose formed on Kiko's cheeks. She drank more tea and murmured, "Thank you."

"My car is over by my hangar," Cait said. "I'm going to take you to one of those walk-in clinics. I'll stay with you until you've gotten blood and maybe some lactose."

"And then what?" Kiko looked from one to the other of us. "I can't go home. If they could track me here, even with the talisman thingy protecting me, it means they could find me anywhere."

"They won't be looking for you," I said. "Not since you refused them. They believe you're dead."

"*We located the seethe.*" Krin's voice blasted into my mind. The others must have heard too—except for Kiko, of course—because their heads snapped up. An image and coordinates followed the words.

"I'll join you as soon as Kiko is squared away," Cait said.

"What's going on?" Kiko asked.

"We have work to do," Cait told her. "If we're successful, Vampires in this region won't be a problem any longer."

"Can I come with you?"

Cait shook her head. "For magic-wielders only."

Kiko smiled softly. "In my dream, you told me you'd be there for me when I die."

"I will be." Cait patted her hand. "And I build the best gateways, ever."

Stacia chuckled softly. "Mine are pretty awesome too."

"You're like her?" Kiko furled her brows.

Stacia nodded.

"You sang to me."

Stacia nodded again. "It was a gamble, but one that worked. Welcome back, dear."

"I'll go and collect my car," Cait said.

"We'll have her outside," I replied.

It took Paddy and me, one on each side, to support Kiko and get her out of the plane and the hangar. "Do you want your amulet back?" she asked.

"Nay. Keep it. If nothing else, I'll be able to locate you again if need be."

"I would have died, otherwise. Thank you." She extended a hand, and I shook it. This wasn't the time to mention she wouldn't exactly have been dead.

Cait's battered SUV rolled up in front of the hangar. I opened the passenger door and helped Kiko inside before going around to Cait's open window. "I'll let you know how things are going."

"Save a few Vamps for me," she joked and gestured at her sickle and blade, both in the back seat along with her shoulder bag.

"Be careful," I told her.

"Always. If I can't come up with any good alternatives here, are you okay with me leaving Kiko in Malin?"

Her question caught me off-guard. Normally, mortals had no place in Sidhe strongholds, but this situation was scarcely normal. "Sure, Cait. Whatever you come up with that keeps her protected so she can recover."

I waited until they drove off the field. Paddy tugged the hangar door shut, sealing it with magic. In case I was wrong, and the Vamps came looking for Kiko, we didn't want to make things easy for them.

"I do believe your music turned the tide in our favor," I told Stacia.

She smiled. "I had no idea what it would do, but desperate times require desperate solutions."

"As in we had naught to lose." Padhraic threaded an arm around Stacia's shoulders.

"Nothing," she agreed. "Kiko's spirit was loose. I had one foot in the realm of the dead, and I saw her arguing with Cait, begging for passage. Cait was amazing and strong. Her Reaper magic was activated, but she didn't built a gateway, even though it went against every magical bone in her body."

"I bet she was waging war on two fronts," I murmured.

Stacia nodded. "You know her well. Her music wanted out in the worst way, particularly once she understood mine was working to salvage her friend."

"Enough of this." I rolled my shoulders straighter. "Every Vampire I slay will help even the score for what they did to Kiko."

"I missed the last Vamp battle," Stacia said. "It should make me eager for this one, but those bastards make my skin crawl."

I resurrected the image Krin had sent. "Did any of you recognize where we're going?"

"No, but dawn is breaking. At least some of them should be simpler to dispatch," Padhraic said.

"I'll manage our journey spell," Stacia said. "I need the practice."

The hangar melted away, replaced almost instantly by the dark maw of a long-abandoned mine, outraged howls, and the unfettered rotten-egg stench of Vampires.

CHAPTER FIFTEEN, CAIT

Kiko and I spent quite a while in one of those doc-in-a-box clinics. They were pushy, insistent she needed a hospital, but she refused and signed herself out against medical advice.

She was looking a thousand percent improved to me after a couple of bags of blood and one of saline, but what do I know? I'm just a dumb Reaper, not an MD. Once we were back in the car, I turned to her. "What do you want to do?"

She rolled her eyes. "Go home. Shower. Burn my clothes. Sleep for a week."

"I could teleport you to Ireland. Or Scotland. To one of the Sidhe strongholds."

Kiko shook her head. "Nope. I thought about it after I overheard you asking permission from that hunky dude of yours. I wouldn't feel right. It's kind of you to offer, but I'm human, and my place is here."

I'd had a feeling she'd take that tack, so I had a fallback

position. "All right. We're going to the market. We'll stock up on food and salt. Then we'll stop at a church, and I'll filch some holy water."

"Did I drop into a bad *Supernatural* episode?"

"More or less. All those programs have some basis in fact."

AN HOUR AND A HALF LATER, I pulled away from Kiko's condo. I'd seen her inside with enough groceries to feed an army and left her instructions about placing a salt trail in front of every window and her door. She had syringes from a flu clinic she'd run for the pharmacy, so I offloaded some dead man's blood. She'd asked if it mattered where she injected it and had seemed relieved when the answer was no.

The vial of holy water was a last resort. If Vampires broke in despite everything—and she ran out of dead man's blood— she was to toss it into their faces and make a run for it.

I grabbed my cell phone out of my bag and plugged it into the charger. I'd told her I'd be close for at least the next day or two if she needed me.

Satisfied I'd done all I could, I nosed the SUV back toward *Carrick Sky Sports*. May as well teleport from there. I hadn't heard from Liam, but then I hadn't expected I would. He had to be knee-deep in Vampire ass by now.

My phone trilled. A glance showed me Kiko's likeness and her number. As soon as I picked up, she said, "I'm so sorry to be a pain in the ass from hell, but is there any way you could come back?"

My throat tightened. Kiko had a tendency to downplay everything. I choked out, "Are they outside?" If Vamps had found her already, we had to go to plan B. I'd teleport to her and move her to Malin.

"Oh my, no. Sorry. Of course, it would be the first place you'd go. My car is still at the airfield. In case things go south, and I have to leave here fast, calling a cab—and then waiting for it—will be awkward."

Relief pounded a path through me. "Pfft. Worse than awkward. It wouldn't work at all. I'll drive your car back to where you are. Do you have a hide-a-key somewhere?"

She told me where to find it, and I altered my plans. In truth, it wouldn't add more than perhaps an hour to my timetable, so long as traffic didn't trip me up. After trading cars and driving back to Kiko's, I teleported to my office. My estimate had been woefully optimistic, and it was getting dark by the time the Quonset hut took shape around me.

I still hadn't heard from the Sidhe/Reaper contingent, and it was beginning to worry me. A lot. I didn't bother with lights or looking around. I'd checked for Vampires, and their reek wasn't any worse than it had been earlier. My plan was to retrieve my blade—my sickle had followed along everyplace I'd gone—and beat a track to the coordinates Krin had sent hours ago.

I filched a couple of energy bars from my bottom drawer and was on my way out the door when familiar magic pummeled me. The scythe jumped from where it had been balanced across my shoulder blades to my free hand.

Oh-oh. Not good.

The magical Reaper tool believed I'd have to fight my way out of something. I contemplated a quick teleport spell, but Death was faster than I'd ever dreamed of being. She blasted through a gash in the ether and stood regarding me, an unreadable expression on her ageless face.

Somehow, I'd never viewed her as having much of a wardrobe, but she was garbed in a flowing emerald-green gown with long sleeves and a high neckline. Modest, yet revealing, the silken fabric clung to her. The same necklace with a large red stone hung from her neck. Her favorite high-heeled boots peeked from beneath the hem of her dress.

Her silver hair had been braided out of the way and streamed down her back in several plaits.

My chest and throat felt tight, and an iron bar of tension sat between my shoulder blades. She'd nearly killed me. Was she back for another go?

Cathbad's music battered the cage I'd locked it within.

Death furled her gray brows. Before she could say something bitter and scathing, I straightened my tired back and said, "Why are you here?"

"Child." The word held hurt with a side helping of rebuke.

I ignored the label, which had always irritated me, and repeated my question. "Why are you here? I'm kind of short on time."

She spread her arms, and her scythe shimmered out of nowhere, blade hooked around her neck. Today it was gray, and I wondered if its color had anything to do with her mood.

"No one is holding you," she observed. "I'd hoped for thanks, but perhaps I overestimated you."

I unclenched my jaw. I'd played this game with her before. I should leave before she sucked me in too deep. Unfortunately, "should" has never bought me much.

Instead, I snatched the bait. "Thanks for what?"

"How do you imagine Ms. Tanaka made it from the parking lot to the place you found her?"

I shut my eyes, hoping I was so trashed I'd hallucinated the whole thing. No such luck. Death still leered at me, decked out as if she had a ball to attend. "If you helped Kiko, thank you. Don't you have better things to do than spy on me?" I growled.

"Now that you mention it, no. Once upon a time, I had a cadre of Reapers to watch over, care for. Thanks to you—"

I sliced the energy bar hand downward. "Stop right there. You dug your own grave. If you don't like the consequences of your actions, so be it, but I'll be damned if I'll stand by while you pin them on me." I was on a roll, and I kept on talking. "Apparently, you didn't learn a thing. Have you given even a single thought to why over a hundred of us ran for the gates the moment we had an opportunity?

"I believed I was the only one you mistreated, but—"

"How can you say that?" She sounded genuinely aggrieved. "I watched over you, showed up whenever you needed help with Vampires."

"You fed and housed all the other Reapers. Why'd you single me out to stand on my own?" I waved a hand in front of me. "Never mind. You're sidetracking me. You're good at that. There's a battle, and I'm not there. I need to leave."

"I was grooming you, ensuring you were resilient enough for the next steps."

Part of me wanted to shout, "What next steps?" but she was baiting me, banking on curiosity overpowering my judgement. No more.

"I'm leaving," I went on. "If you want to continue this conversation, find me in Scotland in a few days."

She closed the distance between us, and I felt the bite of

her magic. Music surged; I swallowed the notes back. Death was one problem. Last thing I needed was for the music to subsume me, bury me in a spot where I'd never be able to command its power.

"We are leaving," she corrected me just before the jaws of her teleport spell snatched me, and the Quonset hut vanished in a swirl of Reaper enchantment.

I fought against it, but she's always been stronger than me. Even using the full force of my Reaper magic didn't buy me much. Where were we going? Had she kidnapped me to finish the job she'd begin in Malin? This time, she'd take far better care and wouldn't stop until I was well and truly dead.

I raised my mind voice, intent on calling Liam, but it bounced back at me. Figured my magic wouldn't work within the net of Death's superior power. We floated in blackness long enough I lost track of time. My scythe clung to my side, still warm, but even its magic was muted.

Death's energy cut like a two-edged blade. Familiar and deadly, it enticed me and iced my bones with fear. I knew the feel of her power nearly as well as I knew my own. I'd depended on it. Many a time, I'd been relieved when I knew she was close.

Not this time. My inner voice was stern.

All the while, Cathbad's music poked, prodded, and hammered against my resolve. It could free me, it insisted, if I but believed in it. At least it provided the illusion of an ace in the hole.

The compound in the Arctic shimmered around me, taking shape in stages. Of course. Where else would she bring me? This was the only spot that was truly hers. It pulsed around us, empty of life. I hadn't been here since

Reaper school. Then, the place had bustled with Reaper energy, Reaper voices, Reaper enthusiasm for learning our trade.

I hated to give up even a smidgeon of ground, but I understood why Death was bereft. Her entire *raison d'être* had been snatched away. She'd done it to herself, but it was beyond the point. She'd never see it that way.

We stood in the practice arena, a spot I'd honed my skills building gateways and learned the underpinnings of my craft.

Death dropped her scythe on the wooden floor and crossed her arms beneath her breasts. "You, child, are my heir. I wasn't planning to leave quite so soon, but as you can see, there's little reason for me to remain."

Rolling my eyes, I relegated the whole heir thing to just one more lie. "Bullshit! You did your damnedest to kill me," I sputtered. "What would you have done for an heir then?"

"Eh. I was angry. I knew the Sidhe could patch you back up." She dusted her long-fingered hands together. "They did, and here we are, having a conversation I hadn't planned on for a few hundred years."

"What if I'm not interested?"

"What if you have no choice?" she shot back.

I stuffed the energy bars into a pocket and shifted my scythe to my other hand. "That's silly. Of course I have a choice. Reapers have a council now." I quit before saying something along the lines of no longer requiring a despot to run the show.

"These things go in cycles, child." For once, her tone was neither patronizing nor angry. "No one gave me a choice when assignments were being parceled out."

I didn't understand enough about her origins to say much

beyond, "The world has changed since those days. A lot. The Sidhe don't have warlords anymore. Maybe—"

She cut me off. "Three constants in the realm of the dead have been Hades, Arawn, and me. We did not design the system, but it is in balance with them below and me above." She hesitated for a moment before going on. "We are in agreement, my time has come to an end, but there must be another in my stead."

"Pick someone else." I gathered my magic, intent on leaving if I could, but it was sluggish. I'd never amass sufficient to kindle a teleport spell.

"Let. Me. Go." I inserted space between each word.

"In your dreams, child." She picked up her scythe. "Fight me. If I prevail, I shall continue, although I do not wish to. If you win, you will take my place." A harsh laugh burst from her. "I cannot imagine two more reluctant combatants. Neither of us desires the fruits of victory."

I stood staring at her, not certain I'd heard her right. "But I don't want to fight you. I concede. You can remain the goddess of Death forever."

"Not how it works," she informed me and lunged my way, blade swinging.

I jumped out of her path, heart thudding in my chest. Out of all the things that had flitted through my head once Death made off with me, this scenario hadn't been so much as a glimmer. I couldn't believe Arawn or Hades would have agreed to such a plan.

Nope. This had Death's slimy fingerprints all over it. Maybe they'd ordered her to cede her position—since she'd abused it—and this was her way of trotting back to them and reporting I'd insisted on a fight to the death.

What a fucking joke since she was immortal.

What would have happened if I'd acceded to her offer? It was a non-question. She knew me well enough to understand I'd never have smiled and jumped on her proposal.

Which meant everything had been choreographed, and I was in my usual one-down position as her pawn.

She swung her scythe again. I ducked beneath it and got my own weapon in a two handed grip. My bag was tangled around my body, but I couldn't do shit about that. I'd fought with it before.

I'd stated what I wanted. It got me nowhere. Anger pushed through me in a steaming tide of resentment. It centered me, and I started thinking like a warrior rather than a victim. I was ready for her next attack. I'd fought with her enough to anticipate her moves.

So far, all I'd been doing was staying out of her way, but that was about to change.

The next time I leapt, I added a spin to it and sliced my blade down. It caught the edge of her shoulder, leaving a bloody track and a flap of skin. She didn't even flinch, just swung, bringing the tip of her scythe down hard. It caught in my upper arm, but I twisted away.

I had layers of clothing on, and she hadn't done more than rip my jacket. It occurred to me she'd scarcely dressed for a fight, yet she'd anticipated there would be one.

"Where's your armor?" I called.

She didn't answer, just came at me from the other side like a whirling dervish, dipping and swaying. No wonder she'd chosen the arena. No furniture to place between us like there would have been in the study or the living room or the library.

Her expression hardened into an unreadable mask, and

something akin to a shining black cage dropped around me, its weave impenetrable as it pushed closer. "Thought you said you didn't want to win," I taunted.

"I changed my mind."

The glowing links circling me touched my back. Soon, they'd crush the breath from me. My scythe buzzed angrily, resenting the hell out of being trapped. One look at Death reminded me she'd gone over the edge, lost her grip on reality long ago. If her plan was for me to die here, and in a desperately unfair contest, I should use every avenue open to me. The music clamored for ascendancy. I loosed it, letting notes flow from my mouth in a rush. The cage shattered, and I lunged forward, blade swinging as I sang of death and destruction and victory.

The music was in control, but I didn't care. I'd deal with it later. Its magic married with my own, feeling like it belonged there. Fury fueled my song. Anger from every time Death had yelled at me, belittled me, smirked at me—or the time she'd tried to kill me.

I sliced with my blade, hacking at her until blood ran hot and free, staining the green silk of her gown in a grisly parody of Christmas colors. She sliced and parried and thrust. The backs of my hands were crisscrossed with cuts all the way down to bone. Blood ran down my ribs from places she'd stabbed me with the pick end of her scythe.

It took time before I understood my music outshone Death's magic. Lunge. Thrust. Parry. Do it again. And again. I backed her into a corner, forcing her to her knees with a string of forceful notes. My blade sat dead center in her throat, ready to cleave head from body when something odd happened.

The music retreated. My head cleared. Along with it came

the realization I didn't want to kill her. I needed her to go away, but I didn't want her to be dead—assuming the music could accomplish such a thing.

Nor did I intend to be the instrument of her unmaking. Such a deed would haunt me even worse than she had.

"We are done." My voice was harsh, so bleak it didn't sound anything like me. "I am done. Tell Arawn and Hades whatever you wish. Or tell them nothing. It's the same to me."

She bowed her head, for once out of words.

I walked across the room, putting space between us. Hooking my bloody blade across my shoulders, I set a teleport spell in motion with the dregs of my magic. The music had retreated to a soothing hum. It was in high spirits. I'd trusted it, and it had won the day for us, somehow knowing when to stop.

My blade glowed silver, pulsing in time with the music's hum. Had the two become linked through my magic? I'd sort it out later.

"You won the contest," Death called across the expanse of floor between us.

I wasn't about to let her off the hook that easily. If part of some psychic balance required her front and center, so be it. "Neither of us won," I corrected her. "I refuse to accept your mantle. Go where you will, and I shall do the same."

I let my spell take me. I didn't want to talk with Death ever again, but I didn't imagine I'd be that fortunate. I'd have to ask Arawn or Hades about the balance thing. Fingers crossed, Death had made it up to force me to agree to take her place.

As I floated between locations, I wondered where she'd planned to go once she draped the unwanted mantle of Reaper leadership over my shoulders. Or had the whole thing been a ruse? Maybe she'd planned to kill me all along, not counting on Cathbad's musical gift to trip her up.

I splatted down on the floor of my office, too trashed to cushion my fall. Hell, as drained as I was, I was shocked I'd hit my destination spot on and not ended up outside on the asphalt.

My hands ached. My ribs burned. I wanted to drag a sleeping bag out of the cabinet, curl up in it, and not think about anything for a while. The stink of blood drove me to my feet and to the small bathroom where I rinsed the worst of it off my hands.

The scythe cleaned itself, one of its more endearing traits.

I removed my jacket and shredded shirt to tend the wounds along my ribs. I couldn't reach one of them midway up my back, so I sent a tiny bit of magic to encourage it to close. That done, I filched a clean sweatshirt from the closet and shrugged it over my head. My hair had blood in it, but I wasn't about to wash it over the sink.

Where was Liam? Why hadn't I heard from him or anyone else?

I tried for a teleport spell, but my effort was laughable. I was running on fumes.

Food and sleep, I reminded myself.

Sleep would be an indulgence, but I retrieved the uneaten energy bars from my jacket pocket. One package had a slice through it from Death's many sword thrusts. I ate it first, washing it down with water from the sink.

My legs were wobbly, but I forced myself to remain upright afraid if I folded to the floor I'd never get up. I ate the second energy bar and walked to the desk for a third. Somewhere along the line, I made a pot of coffee. I was partway through my second cup when I tested my magic to see if I had enough to leave via teleporting.

My fallback position was driving closer to where everyone was, and then walking if I ran out of roads. Surely, the battle had to be over.

But if it was, where was everyone?

Worry outshone my injuries until the Reapers and Sidhe were all I could think about. I didn't want to burn through what little magic I'd resurrected, so I decided to drive. I sorted through my bag to make sure I had what I'd need. Blood flaked off it in the process.

A quick check of my phone told me Kiko hadn't called. At least it was one piece of good news. I hoped she was sound asleep as her body recovered.

The bite of Liam's magic flickered and withdrew. He was trying to get to me, but something wasn't working. I raised my mind voice, but he didn't answer. The scythe bounced across the floor to me, glowing like it did when I entered the realm of the dead.

Was it trying to tell me something?

I cracked my Reaper magic, and my office ceded to a familiar muted gray half-light. For once, no shades accosted me. I scanned the barren landscape. Damn it. I'd been hopeful my scythe knew something. I was about to close off my Reaper power when light pulsed to one side, growing brighter.

It might have been anything, but I took a chance and walked toward it, feeding small bits of power into the light and urging it to take shape. I might be very sorry. It could be anything from a Vampire minion to Death—if she hadn't given up following me.

But I'd set a course, and I'd stick it out until it blew up in my face or turned out to be a dead end.

Liam's bright hair shone through. Heart in my throat, my worries from earlier ratcheted up several notches. I waded past layers of obfuscation until I got my arms around him. He hugged me back, and I released the magic holding us in the realm of the dead.

The curved walls of my office were welcome as they took shape around us.

"What happened?" I asked.

"We walked into a trap." His words were terse; bloody streaks marked his face and clothing. "Had to get out of there to find help. Adva ran me a merry chase with his infernal, fucking mirrors. I'm deucedly grateful you never showed up at the seethe, but why didn't you?"

"Long story. It'll keep."

His hazel gaze bored into me as if he was reassuring himself I wasn't an illusion. Grabbing my half-empty coffee cup, he chugged it and made a face, probably because it was so strong and bitter.

"We can trade war stories later," he agreed. "Next stop, the *Dreaming*."

I looked away. I'd known I'd have to face Cathbad one day but hoped it wouldn't be quite so soon.

"What? Come on, Cait. We have to go now. It's the nearest place to secure help."

Cathbad would be furious with me for letting the music loose—again—but I didn't want to add to Liam's worries. "Nothing. I'm ready. My magic is pretty low, but maybe it will perk up joined to yours."

"We don't need much to enter the *Dreaming*," he said.

"Good thing because you saw how hard it was for me to break away from Adva's spell."

I had a pile of questions. But they'd keep just like my go round with Death would. "Is everyone snared in the seethe?" I asked.

"I hope a few broke loose. They'd all have gone after reinforcements like I'm doing."

"Losses?"

He shook his head. "I don't know."

It would have to be good enough for now. I felt him reach for my magic and opened myself to him. Energy bars and coffee wouldn't go far, but I'd share everything I had.

CHAPTER SIXTEEN, LIAM

The welcoming golden glow I associated with Reapers in the realm of the dead punched through. I'd caught a sense of Cait before that, but at first I didn't trust it was her. I'd been snatched up by Adva's insidious portal system, running through one mirror after the next until I'd lost all sense which way was up. He'd tricked me good this time, setting a mirror as bait. I'd tested it, but the moment I tumbled through, I understood I'd been duped.

I'm getting ahead of myself, though.

The seethe was right where Krin thought it should be. I never did ask him how he figured it out, and I should have. Somehow, the dark gods had intercepted his search, and they'd been ready for us.

Since we'd found the lair so easily, the rest should have been a slam-dunk. Hell, I figured I'd join Cait before she and Kiko were even finished with the clinic. Coming fresh off our victory in Dublin, I'd made a bunch of assumptions. All of us did.

We were fools.

It's what comes of being out of practice. The few skirmishes we'd been drawn into lately weren't enough to get our "battle legs" back under us.

The Reapers who'd gone in search of Arawn and Hades had yet to return, but we weren't concerned about them. Turned out, they were the lucky ones since they missed the worst of our sheep-to-slaughter dance.

Located in a series of caves that had once housed a copper mine, the Vampire den sat many miles off a main east-west highway. We'd split into the same groups we'd used before, adding more contingents to accommodate our additional numbers.

We'd stuck together as we entered the cave. So far, we hadn't seen a single Vampire, but the place stank of them, and it was daytime, when they reverted to playing at being truly dead. As we went farther into the caverns, my elation slipped a few notches and then a few more.

"Has all the makings of a trap," Paddy had whispered.

Maybe someone heard him because the corridor—reinforced with rebar and wood—collapsed at one end. Two of our groups were on the far side of the cave-in, but they could teleport out of here.

I was beginning to believe it was the wisest course for all of us, but I hated to retreat. Nothing untoward had happened. Not yet. Old mines were notorious for cave-ins. No reason to believe the one filling the corridor with dust and grit had been anything other than a natural occurrence.

"Where are the Vampires?" Stacia whispered.

"Sleeping in several side caves we have yet to locate," I whispered back, "but they should have posted sentries."

Padhraic set his jaw in a tight line. Apparently, my comment resonated with his suspicions about a trap. When he shouted, *"Retreat!"* his telepathy was so loud it made my brain hurt.

Adva chose that moment to leap from the top of the rubble heap, power jetting from his hands.

"Dark gods. Escape if you can. Return with help," Krin ordered on the heels of Paddy's command to retreat.

I looked around for the remainder of my regiment, but I was alone with Adva. How the fuck had he finessed it? I hit him with lethal magic dialed as high as I could make it. He laughed in my face.

"That's the thing about paybacks," he hissed. "Sweet for me, and a bitch for you."

I pulled power like a madman, intent on teleporting the fuck out of there, but my power boomeranged back and slapped me hard enough to drive me to my knees. How had Adva managed it? My magic should be more than a match for his, but somehow, it wasn't.

The Vampire cave had vanished, replaced by a vast chamber lined with mirrors. Dragging air deep into my lungs, I surged to my feet and began a painstaking process of examining the mirrors. I tried testing them with magic, but they all felt the same even after I drilled down seeking subtle differences.

I'm not sure how much time I wasted going from mirror to mirror. In betwixt and between, I tested my teleport magic, but it was just as ineffective as it had been during my last attempt.

I've never been one to shy away from hard truths. The one staring me in the face was I had to do something, and it meant picking a mirror. Maybe all of them were boobytrapped. I wouldn't have put it past Adva. He was furious with me for losing face in front of his Vampire minions when they'd chosen Cait's inducements over his.

If I didn't jump through a mirror, I'd be stuck here forever. It didn't matter which one, so I feinted sideways and hit one with my shoulder, feeling it give way to the accompaniment of Adva's maniacal laughter.

Our esoteric game of cat-and-mouse via mirror had begun. Some of them had sharp edges that tore at my skin and clothing as I passed through. Others held threatening beasts that I caught glimpses of. I'm certain Adva figured I'd exhaust myself and get stuck in one of the worlds in his macabre version of a funhouse. I still wasn't quite sure how I'd escaped. When I saw a shimmery figure that looked like Cait, I'd been sure she was one more hallucination courtesy of Adva's endless collection of mirrors.

But she'd been real, goddammit. And she'd been hunting for me.

I'm convinced it was her magic added to mine that pulled me away from the god of portals' alternate universe since I'd been unable to break free on my own.

Who knew how long I'd been passing through mirrors? Judging from the sorry state of my magic, hours had slipped by. From the frantic look in Cait's eyes, she'd been as worried about me as I was about her. We held one another close. I still didn't quite believe she was real. She looked like she'd lived through as rough a time as me with new lines etched into her forehead and around her eyes.

No time to talk about any of it. We had to head for the *Dreaming*. It was the closest spot we might find help.

Krin had asked for aid a long while ago. Who knew if anyone had returned with anything viable. Or if any Sidhe or Reapers were still salvageable? I didn't believe for a moment Adva was working by himself. Tokkhots' bite was poison. Majestron Zelia was ruthless, and Slototh drowned you in filth.

The Leanan were proof Sidhe could be turned to Vampirism. Reapers were vulnerable as well, but the dark mages might simply kill them to get them out of the way. Too many brand new Vamps would require a big infusion of magic to control them.

The *Dreaming* formed around us. For once, I welcomed its touch, hoping it would replenish my magic. It sensed my unease, and surrounded me with images of Sidhe victories.

"Never thought I'd be glad to see this place," Cait murmured, "but I could use a break."

"Is Kiko all right?"

"Yeah. Seems to be. No crisis messages from her, so I'm going to assume the best."

We came to an open area, the *Dreaming's* signal for us to stop. Cait seemed uneasy.

"What's wrong?"

She made a face. "The condensed version is Death kidnapped me. I had to fight my way out of her compound in the Arctic, and I used the music. Not the way Stacia taught me, either."

"You left out a few things," I observed.

Cait nodded. "A whole lot. But the music was stronger than Death's power. I won and then walked away."

I frowned, doing my best to understand. "Did you injure her?"

"Maybe her pride." Cait swallowed hard. "Somehow, the

music knew I didn't want to end her. I had her cornered, on her knees, and then the music just stopped. My will was my own again, and that was when I left."

I understood why she'd hesitated when I said we were coming here. She'd been afraid Cathbad would rebuke her for violating his instructions.

"I didn't have any choice," Cait was saying. "First Death told me she didn't want to win. Then she dropped a black mesh cage around me and said she'd changed her mind. The links would have crushed me, so I freed the music. It took off full tilt, shattered the cage, and fashioned my offense until I'd won."

"Did she say why she kidnapped you?"

Cait nodded. "Apparently, I'm her heir, and—"

"What a steaming pile of horseshit. She almost killed you," I cut in, battling incredulity.

"She said her temper got away from her. It's actually believable. Anyway, I don't think she'll bother me again."

"Why?"

"Just a feeling. Once she made a commitment to fighting, she didn't believe she'd lose."

A figure strode toward us from the far end of the clearing. My initial take was it wasn't Cathbad. Not broad enough, and not dripping with weapons. Mists swirled around the figure, so thick I wasn't certain if it was male or female.

"Who's that?" Cait adopted a battle stance, scythe in one hand, knees slightly bent, and feet shoulder-width apart.

I didn't blame her for her lack of trust. But this was the *Dreaming.*

"It's all right," I reassured her. "Naught here will harm you."

She cast a quick glance my way and then went back to

staring at whomever approached us. "Might be true for Sidhe," she muttered, "but I'm an outsider."

"Oh come, Liam. It hasn't been so long as all that," a familiar voice issued from the mist.

My head snapped back. Heedless of my perilously low magical reservoir, I sent a volley to split the illusion. Sure enough, Hollis emerged. His black hair hung loose to shoulder level. On the tall side, but slender, he wore traditional Sidhe battle leathers in buff tones. Deerskin boots laced to just below his knees.

So long as my power was deployed, I poked and prodded. "You're just as dead as you were in Malin. What are you doing here?"

"A stint in the *Dreaming* resurrected my spirit." He tossed his head back and regarded me with the same dark-blue eyes I remembered all too well. He'd been my Sidhe battle lord for millennia.

A low hiss issued from Cait. She hadn't let loose of her scythe. "You," she growled. "You sent him"—she jerked her chin at me—"to capture me and feed me to the Vampires. Go away. We have enough problems."

Hollis bowed low and switched to Gaelic. "I doonae expect ye'll forgive me. Were our situations reversed, I would hold a grudge until my verra last breath. My loyalty to the Sidhe was never in question, merely my assessment we'd be better off leaving Earth and allowing its inhabitants to self-destruct—"

Hollis always had a tendency to pontificate. We didn't have time for a long, convoluted "I told you so" moment, so I cut him off. "Save the 'Aude Lang Syne' commentary for later. We're in the *Dreaming* to rustle up aid. Haste is of the essence."

"Why do you think I'm here?" Hollis shifted back to

English, and adopted an aggrieved tone. "Even sequestered in our ancestral retreat, I've felt shockwaves from both times my kinsmen battled Vampires. This latest episode isn't working out especially well."

I rocked back on my heels, fighting frustration. "I'm well aware how badly it's going, but I fail to see how you can do aught beyond harboring guilt for anything you did to assist those Undead fuckers."

"We have to get moving," Cait said. "If there's no help here, let's try the realm of the dead."

Hollis was sputtering. Death hadn't improved his temper, or his need to have the last word. "But you must hear me out," he insisted.

"Two minutes," I told him. "They begin now."

The old Hollis—the live one—would have stalked off in a huff. Perhaps dying had knocked a hole in his arrogance because he nodded tersely and began talking.

"The only way you'll rid yourselves of Vampires is by thinking bigger. Beheading them one at a time is ridiculous. They can make new ones faster than you can rob them of their Undead lives."

I folded my arms across my chest. "I spent nearly a month trolling through the Sidhe library. Never found even a whisper of a spell that might work."

"Because you were looking for something to destroy them. It's a waste of magic."

Hollis had my attention, and he knew it, the bastard. He took full advantage of my one-down position to draw things out. I wanted to grab his shoulders and shake him, but my hands would pass right through what only looked like a body.

Now that I'd spent more time with him, the outlines of his illusion had become clearer.

"Only the dead are a match for other dead," Hollis said at last.

"Won't work. I've tried it," Cait said. "Shades hate Vampires. They see their evil in ways even we don't, and give them a wide berth. Except for Vampire minions, and they have a pathetic feel to me."

"Exactly." Hollis clasped his hands together, fingers moving through one another in an eerie ballet.

I stared at him. "Look, mate, your two minutes have been up for a while, and I'm not any closer to understanding what you have in mind than I was before."

"Those who are dead at Vampire hands, but not turned, were the strong ones. The ones who resisted the call to drink. Because Vampires drained them, it's given the Undead a residual hold on their souls. They obey because they have no choice, but they wish to cross to the other side."

"And you're proposing to use them how?" Cait sounded suspicious. "They've nearly been the end of me more than once. They hate Reapers."

"Only because their masters have promised if they only do this, that, or the other thing, they'll free them. But wait, the rest of my plan is brilliant. I always was quite the tactician, and—"

"Stuff it, Hollis. What is the rest of this brilliant plan?" I cut in.

"I rustled up other Sidhe spirits—from the Leanans' pit. They've seen the error of their ways, and—"

"Nay!" I thundered. "Tell me you haven't freed them."

"Now how could I have done that?" He shook his head. "Your problem was always a lack of imagination. No spirit of adventure. No willingness to tread the ragged edges of the possible."

Anger twisted my stomach into a knot. Before I could banish his illusion with magic, Cait spoke up. "How do you envision using the Leanan and the Vamp minions to deal with Earth-bound Vamps."

"At least one of you hasn't quit thinking." Hollis set his mouth in a simpering line that made me want to punch him. "There are a lot of seethes, and a lot of Vampires. The Leanan know the location of all the seethes. They would send an emissary to each with a simple message.

"It's past time for all Vampires to join forces—and knowledge. The very first ever all Vampire gathering will be held at our old enclave in Canada. The same spot the Leanan were lured into the pit. The message will be that the Leanan escaped. All of them will be there, and they stand ready to share every secret that's made them able to do things Earth-bound Vamps can't."

"It won't work," Cait said flatly. "Master Vamps have never worked together. On anything."

"We'll never get all of them," I protested. "Some won't trust it. Others will be sleeping off a blood glut and won't get the memo."

"I'm not concerned if we miss a few," Hollis said. "Don't you see the beauty of this? We can lure them back to the same pit where we buried the Leanan. It's how I convinced them to cooperate. They hate that pit, and they're delighted to do whatever it takes to trade spots."

"But then they'd be free." I spun one hand in a circle, waiting for Hollis to make the obvious connection.

"Padhraic appears to have transitioned back into the fold," Hollis commented.

"Not without a huge amount of work on the part of a group of us who labored over him reshaping his magical center to remove the Leanan taint," I clarified.

"Mmph. Didn't know that part." Hollis dusted his hands together. "Still seems like a winning strategy. You'd have all the Vamps, Leanan and otherwise, in the same spot. All you'd have to do would be to pile the lot of them back into the pit."

"It's a pretty tall order," Cait said.

"Aye, we barely managed it last time, and we'd have hundreds more Vampires to cope with." I drew my brows together running magical equations through my head and not liking what I came up with.

"Even if the dark mages don't show up to rescue their pets," I said, "we wouldn't have enough magic to manage the Vampires and the liminal space. It holds unimaginable energy, and it lives for opportunities like this, times when it can get up and romp."

Hollis shrugged. "I did my part. I've planted seeds with the Leanan."

I narrowed my eyes. "They'll want an update. What will you tell them?"

"That you're considering their offer."

"And you'll stop there." I put steel in my words. They weren't a suggestion.

"Of course. I may be dead, but I haven't lost my wits. I understand full well the gravity of this, and the complexity. I'll enjoy watching it unfold from the sidelines."

The mist rose once again, swallowing him with much less

fanfare than his arrival. He'd probably run out of the magic powering his illusion.

Cait planted the scythe handle in the dirt. "I don't like any of it. Can we trust him?"

"Probably. He was quick to suggest chucking the Leanan into the pit along with the others. If he was on their side, he wouldn't have been so hasty. Hollis is a lot of things, but he'd chose his kin over the Leanan any day."

We had to get moving, but we weren't any closer to coming up with aid for whoever was still trapped by the dark gods and Vampires in the seethe northeast of Seattle. Maybe we should return to Scourie Castle and collect the rest of the Sidhe and Reapers who hadn't come with us.

"Oh-oh," Cait muttered.

I turned in time to see Cathbad hustling toward us, flanked by Arawn and Hades. Cerebrus bounded ahead and threw himself into Cait's arms. She crouched and scratched all three sets of ears.

"Yes. Yes," she crooned. "At least you still appreciate me."

CHAPTER SEVENTEEN, CAIT

I thought I'd gotten a reprieve from dealing with Cathbad, but such was not to be. I gathered Cerebrus close, enjoying his warm, doggie breath as he licked me enthusiastically. It was a nice diversion, but I wanted to get this next part over with.

I pushed to my full height and walked to Cathbad, chin up. I'd be damned if I'd be too apologetic for using his gift to save myself from annihilation. "Stacia did her part." I made certain to lead off with that, so his ire wouldn't be directed at her. "Problem was what she taught me will take practice—lots of it. And time. I used the music, or let it use me more accurately, because I was flat out of choices."

A corner of his mouth twitched downward. "And you believe I doonae already know everything that transpired with my music?"

Heat rushed from my chest up my neck, suffusing my face. "Um, I'm not assuming anything. Just explaining."

"Justifying why you disobeyed?"

"Something like that. Look. I'm sorry, but I can't guarantee I wouldn't make the same choice again. If you're going to punish me, could you either get on with it? Or save it for later because Liam and I have our hands full."

His heavy, ham-sized hand plopped on my shoulder. "I like you, Reaper. You have spirit. I doonae fully understand how the magic works within you. The topic is not closed, but 'tis tabled for now."

Cerebrus leaned one of his heads against my ribcage, almost as if he sensed my relief. I was stretched so thin as it was, I couldn't bear the specter of more animosity. Cathbad was an ally. He'd gifted me with something amazing—never mind he hadn't planned to do so—and I'd be forever grateful to him.

"We must leave," Arawn said.

"Aye. If we hurry, we should be able to add a couple more of those dark bastards to the two we've already detained," Hades added.

I patted my pockets. They were empty, so I dug through my shoulder bag and found a crushed and battered energy bar in its depths. God only knew how old it was, but I ate it anyway. Those things had so many preservatives, it could have been buried in a tomb and not rotted.

"I have no idea what we'll find at the seethe," Liam cautioned.

"We'll figure it out once we get there," Arawn growled. "I'd hoped when they lost the Celtic portion of their magic—and two of their cohort—the dark mages would back off. Instead, they've grown bolder."

"Anger does that," I muttered. Grateful to let someone else

deal with the teleport spell, I conserved my magic and waited until we plopped out in the midst of a thick, evergreen forest.

Liam and I followed Cathbad, Cerebrus, and the gods of the dead until we stood at the edge of a clearing. The maw of an old mine marred an enormous cliff. It was midafternoon, and for once it wasn't raining. I wanted to ask if we had a plan —so I could do my part.

I sensed power flow from Arawn. Thick and relentless, it made the air crackle with untapped possibilities. He turned to Hades. "Should work. Shall we try this?"

"Try what?" Liam asked.

"A drawing spell with Vampire written all over it. Once we've cleared them from their lair, it will be simple enough for you to retrieve whoever is left within," Arawn said. "Or for them to find their own way out. I suspect Tokkhots crafted a labyrinth. It would be very like him. He and the Minotaur were close back in the day."

A tiny flicker of hope took hold. Maybe my friends were neither dead nor turned. Perhaps they were just lost in a maze. I liked that explanation far better than the other possibilities.

Arawn and Hades wove magic into something beautiful and terrible, careful with their working until they were certain it would do what they wished. It glowed in tones of black and gold, edged with hellfire. A cyclone force gale blew up out of nowhere and chased their spell into the cave. I'd known the two gods controlled the dead, but even Death had problems binding Vampires into herds and coercing them to her bidding. I was expecting something like her intervention, kind of a one-Vamp-at-a-time endeavor.

I couldn't have been more wrong.

Waves of power—mostly water married to earth—sheeted

from Hades and Arawn, chasing after their initial spell. Within moments, Vampires stumbled from the cave mouth, looking dazed. Some got their bearings and bared their fangs as they hunted for someone to blame for being disturbed.

Perhaps sixty or seventy Vampires were milling about when a woman sashayed forth. Black hair tumbled to ground level, and she wore a sky-blue gown reminiscent of the eighteenth-century Italian Court. Low cut with full sleeves and many layers, it swirled as she moved. Dark eyes glared at us from beneath winged brows that cut across her alabaster skin.

The woman, no doubt the seethe's mistress, stalked to Arawn and Hades. "I have not broken my vows. Why do you disturb our rest."

Cerebrus growled. In a very un-Vampire-like reaction, the woman cringed away from his snapping jaws.

"You have allowed dark mages into your seethe," Hades intoned. "Such cannot be overlooked."

"Or go unpunished," Arawn said.

The woman nodded once. "I understand. Take my minions. I can begin anew."

My eyes might have widened. Damn. No loyalty among Vampires. She'd just sold out her entire seethe. It wasn't lost on them. They turned as a unit and converged on her, hissing and spitting like a pack of feral cats.

I had no idea how power passed from Vamp to Vamp in a seethe. But judging from the scene about to play out, Ms. Mistress-of-the-Seethe had no chance in hell of escaping her minions. Hades and Arawn exchanged a pointed glance and fell back a few feet. I felt certain they'd had plans, but perhaps a horde of angry Vamps would do their work for them.

Liam grabbed my hand, and we headed for the cave

entrance. No reason for us to hang around and observe the carnage. No one called after us, but Cerebrus bounded to my side.

"Good boy," I told him. "You can help us hunt for our friends."

He woofed as if he understood, which I'm certain he did.

Liam stopped a few feet inside the cave. I felt him deploy seeking magic, so I opened myself to it. Between the nasty reek of Vampires and layers of dark-tinged magic, the air was unpleasantly thick.

A mage light bloomed next to Liam's shoulder. My scythe took on its soft glow. Between the two, we had adequate illumination as we began covering corridors and side corridors.

Cerebrus ran ahead, woofing from time to time. When his barks turned strident, I said, "He found something."

"Aye, and far quicker than us."

I shrugged. "He has a better nose. And magic."

It took us a while and many wrong turns that led to dead ends. Several places in the sprawling warren of tunnels had recently collapsed. Dust clung to everything and made me cough. I had a bead on Cerebrus, but following him often meant backtracking and trying again.

"Why can't we teleport?" I asked Liam.

"Too many competing magics in here. They'd divert whatever spell we set in motion. Come on. It's not much farther."

I zipped my tattered jacket, hoping to stem the tide of shivering that had begun a few moments before. The cave was cold. As if to verify my observation, we passed a bevy of icicles hanging off rock outcroppings.

Two more twists and turns and we entered a downward

sloping walkway. The stench of human waste and unwashed bodies hit me like a wall.

"I wondered where they kept their food supply," Liam muttered.

Ice crunched under our boots as we dropped lower in the cave system. Cerebrus bounded toward us, woofed a few times, and turned back the way he'd come. I took a chance and called our friends. "Stacia! Dena! Padhraic! Krin!"

No one responded. Of course, those four might have escaped, but someone would have answered—if they could have.

"Maybe you should stay back." Liam angled a worried look my way.

"Maybe you should," I countered and shook my head. "Sorry. I'm edgy."

I sensed the spell before I saw its edges vibrating hypnotically. The casting was exotic, beautiful. It sang to me, intimating my life would change if only I entered its territory. Liam grabbed my arm before I walked right into its force field.

I shook myself hard, fighting its thrall. "Do you recognize it?" I asked.

"Aye. 'Tis a casting to induce stasis in multiple victims. I understand why the Vampires would employ such a tool to keep their dinner in line. What I can't determine is how it snared Sidhe and Reapers."

"We don't know how many are here," I reminded him. "A bunch might have escaped—like you did."

He snorted. "I didn't exactly escape. You found me and pulled me away from Adva's clutches."

If the god of portals had been angry before, I'd just given him one more reason to want to gouge my eyes out.

Cerebrus came into view, dragging someone. He'd latched onto the person with two of his mouths in an efficient maneuver that kept most of the man's body off the ground.

"Krin!" Liam dove next to him, hands extended as power probed and prodded, assessing damage.

Cerebrus let go, barked, and vanished back within the knockout spell. Apparently, it didn't impact the dog.

I knelt on Krin's other side, checking for fang marks in his neck and relieved when I didn't find any. The Sidhe groaned; his dark eyes shot open, and he struggled to sit. "The others. Where are they?"

"Slow down, mate," Liam gripped his shoulder. "How many were with you?"

"Ten. No nine. The ten included me. Shit. I'm not thinking. We were running around in bloody circles, chasing our tails. Dena found a cache of humans, most of them barely alive. Seemed like the last place Tokkhots would look for us, so we barricaded ourselves in."

"This is your spell?" I asked about the time Cerebrus reappeared with Dena balanced between his three mouths. He laid her next to Krin and turned back to retrieve someone else.

"That was stupid of me," Liam muttered. "I recognized the spell, but assumed it came from other magic. Call the dog back, and I'll take the whole thing down."

I had no idea if he'd come, but I whistled and followed it with his name. The big dog padded back to me, and I wrapped my arms around two of his necks while Liam and Krin withdrew the magic powering the spell. The dog's warmth was welcome. I couldn't wait to get out of this icebox deathtrap. I've never minded caves, but this one had a huge creep-factor.

Dena's eyes were open, and she was shivering. "Told you it would work," she rasped.

"You might have frozen," I chided her.

"Nah. Immortal. Remember?" She pushed to a sit.

"Can we save the humans?" I asked.

"Aye," she replied. "Most of them. A few were already dead. Vampires are a bunch of bastards. They shanghai humans, starve them, and chuck them after they're not useful any longer."

The spell collapsed, changing to red-and-blue streamers as it settled to the rock-strewn dirt floor. Cerebrus's tail slapped my side. "Come on, boy," I urged. "Show me where everyone is."

A few steps brought me to a barred doorway. I started to direct magic to defeat the lock, but the dog bumped me and headed off to the right. Figured he'd found a path since he'd not only come and gone, he'd carried the fallen with him. An indentation in the earthen walls proved to be illusion; I followed Cerebrus through.

My scythe took on a healthy glow, illuminating a large, open room littered with bodies. Humans lay in their own filth, moaning and miserable. Some had torn out huge hanks of their hair. Sidhe and Reapers were lurching to their feet, shaking themselves to clear the muzzy aftermath of Dena's spell.

Stacia pelted toward me and threw her arms around me. I hugged her back. Padhraic joined us along with the other Sidhe and Reapers who'd chosen this cavern to hide out from Tokkhots.

"We need to move the mortals out of here," I said.

"We'll manage that part." Padhraic motioned to three other Sidhe, who nodded agreement.

Shades battered against me, more than I could count. So many humans had died in this dank, miserable place, it made me sad. And furious. Maybe Hollis's suggestion about tricking the Vamps to their doom was worth a shot.

Stacia and Abby gripped my hands. "We have to help them," Abby said, her eyes damp with tears.

I understood what she meant and closed my jaws so hard my teeth ached. The shades had been trapped here far too long. Not that shades are ever stuck in one spot, but perhaps these had given up on any semblance of free will long before their deaths. So much so, leaving to locate a Reaper had never occurred to them.

I focused Reaper magic until the half-light of the realm of the dead formed around us. Stacia and Abby built a gateway. I built another. One by one, the dead passed through me and the other Reapers. By the time they were done, all of us were crying. The shades' misery and despair clung to me after I'd shut the portal and reeled in my Reaper power.

Cerebrus hadn't left my side, but he was no stranger to the realm of the dead. It was his home. All of us made our way back through the main door. Someone had broken the lock with magic, and it stood open. The humans—the living ones—were gone, presumably transported to the surface via magic.

The only people left in front of the Vampires' holding cell were Liam, Padhraic, Abby, Stacia, me—and the dog.

"Are you done tending the dead?" Liam wrapped an arm around me.

"Yeah. Let's get out of here."

A rush of prickly magic smelling of sulfur buffeted me. Fuck! I knew that magic. "Look sharp," I yelled. "We're about to have company."

A low snarl from Cerebrus was followed by a menacing woof. The short hair on his three necks stood up, and all three mouths displayed long, sharp teeth.

"Well, well, well. There you are." A man wearing black trousers, a white shirt, and a tweed jacket bounded out of nowhere. Hair so black it appeared blue was trimmed to shoulder level. Dark eyes regarded us intently. I had the uncomfortable sensation of being relegated to a mouse facing a cagey cat. Medium height and slightly built, the man didn't look all that threatening, until I focused on his eyes.

"Tokkhots." Liam made the name sound like a curse.

The man parodied a sweeping bow. "At your service. No. Wait. You're actually at mine."

The air around us took on a glistening aspect as he tossed magic about. Before it could coalesce into something that would sweep us into a labyrinth, Liam dragged his blade from its sheath in a single, fluid motion. Padhraic did the same. So did I.

Abby raised her scythe to a fighting stance. Stacia notched an arrow from a quiver strapped across her back. First I'd noticed either bow or arrows. Perhaps she'd shrouded them with magic. Nor had I known she was an archer.

Tokkhots rolled back onto the balls of his feet, regarding us. "Five against one? Where's your sense of sportsmanship?"

"Where's yours?" Padhraic countered. "Losing our way in your labyrinth was poor man's sport."

"Worked, didn't it?" Tokkhots leered at him.

Padhraic shrugged. "Worked is a relative term, mate. We hid ourselves from you. And we escaped."

Laughter blatted from Tokkhots. He borrowed Paddy's phrase. "Escape appears to be relative as well...mate."

Liam danced forward, light on his feet as he swung his blade. Tokkhots leapt out of the way, spinning midair. Stacia let an arrow fly. The dark god caught it before it could burrow into his body. Padhraic attacked from one side, Liam from the other. Between them, the god twirled and jumped and somersaulted, laughing all the while. He did his damnedest to bite them but couldn't get close enough.

I got in a few thrusts, but the field was crowded, and I worried about becoming an inadvertent target. Stacia kept arrows flowing. One lodged in Tokkhots' shoulder, another in his leg.

When he twisted away, intent on dragging them out, Cerebrus jumped on his back, all three sets of jaws snapping. His bites were deep, vicious, and drew blood. Best of all, they finally got the dark mage's attention. He wrapped his fingers around one of Cerebrus's necks, but the dog just bit harder with another head.

Not that Cerebrus required a cheering squad, but I danced closer yelling, "Good boy. Get him."

A swoosh of familiar power swept over me just before Hades shimmered into being. "Strong work, now come," he told the dog, who obediently jumped off Tokkhots and ran to his master, blood dripping from every mouth.

All of us cleared a path between Hades and Tokkhots. The dark mage seemed sluggish as he stumbled to his feet. I felt him try to draw power to leave, but it stopped shy of his outstretched hand.

"What did you do to me?" he whined, sounding dazed, confused.

"You're not the only one whose bite can immobilize." Hades buried a hand in Cerebrus's neck.

I filed that little bit of data away.

"Do you require us?" Liam asked in an oddly formal tone.

"Nay. Leave. I shall be along presently."

We hurried back the way we'd come, avoiding all the dead ends that had tripped us up the first time. After a while, Tokkhots' shrieks and howls faded, absorbed by the cavern's thick walls.

"Nice trick with the arrows," I told Stacia.

"Thanks. I found the bow when I went to the armory after your nap. It was a good fit for me, and I'd rather use it than a blade any day. Easier on my hands."

"Why couldn't I see the bow or quiver before you used them?"

She shrugged. "I suppose it's wrapped up in how they were made. Good to know they can be invisible, though, just like our sickles."

A small square of fading light told me the entrance wasn't far, but it took longer to reach it than I anticipated. I'd passed beyond weary hours ago. So much had happened since we went after Kiko, just thinking about it all was a daunting prospect.

Shades batted against me from all sides.

"No rest for the wicked," Abby muttered.

"It's all those Vamps," I said. "They're finally truly dead."

"We have to send them packing." Stacia blew out a tired-sounding breath.

I agreed. If we left them, they might turn into Vampire fodder, something that could be used against us. "Let's get outside, first," I suggested. "The energy of this mine sucks the life out of me."

"Yeah, me too. They'll follow us," Abby agreed.

Stacia made a snorting sound. "Not because they want passage. They're furious and still trying to glom onto my neck. Good thing their fangs don't work anymore."

Dusk had fallen by the time we staggered outside. The other Reapers had a gateway going and were tossing Vampire shades through it with help from the Sidhe. It would go faster with one more portal, so I cracked my Reaper power. At least the process was smooth given how resistant the Vampire shades were. Liam and Padhraic tag-teamed scooping up groups and booting them through the gateways.

One detached herself from the mass of ghosts and headed right for me. The erstwhile mistress of the seethe. "I hope you're happy with the ruin you caused, Reaper."

"You should talk," I retorted. "We found your food supply. I wouldn't force a mouse to remain in such horrific conditions."

"But they were happy," she protested.

"Yeah, right," I mocked.

"You don't understand our ways." Her somber tone got the point across loud and clear. Damn if she didn't believe her own propaganda.

Liam and Padhraic moved behind her and gave her a shove. She didn't move. Hands still glued to her hips, she glared at me. My scythe vibrated, reminding me I had its power at my disposal. Grabbing it, I swung hard, lopping off dead body parts. As soon as the head rolled free, Liam kicked it through a gateway. Once an arm followed, so did the rest of her.

"I can't believe how strong they are, even after they've been beheaded," Liam growled.

The field cleared, and I let go of my gateway, leaving the realm of the dead. Standing was suddenly too much, and my knees buckled, depositing me on the ground.

Liam hauled me to my feet and hung onto me. "We're leaving."

"But Hades isn't back yet," I protested, wanting to see things through to the end.

"He doesn't need us, and you ran the well dry. Again."

I winced. It was getting to be a bad habit. The last gateway had drained the dregs of my magic. It wasn't coming back around until I fell on my face for a while.

Arawn strode from shadows. "I have shades to attend to. Hades and I will meet you at Scourie Castle at this time tomorrow."

"Is Tokkhots out of the way?" Padhraic asked.

Arawn nodded. "He has joined the other two. Three down. Three to go. The odds are improving."

I wanted to nuzzle Cerebrus, tell him he'd been amazing, and I'd see him soon, but Hades and his dog were nowhere in sight.

"Come close." Liam projected his voice to get the attention of the few Sidhe and Reapers who hadn't yet left. Once everyone was gathered, he wrapped us with magic and set a journey spell in motion. "Once we're underway, I need to tell you about my run-in with Hollis in the *Dreaming*."

"Surprised the *Dreaming* accepted him," Padhraic muttered.

"Aye, well, that will be the least of your surprises. He's been in touch with the Leanan..."

I must have fallen asleep as Liam recounted our exchange with Hollis. The next thing I remembered was his chamber in Scourie Castle, and even that faded fast as blackness rose up and claimed me.

CHAPTER EIGHTEEN, LIAM

I held Cait close, willing her to sleep deep and well. She'd developed a pinched look around her eyes, and her skin had taken on a translucence I didn't care much for. She needed to eat, and something more nutritionally robust than those premade bar things she crunched down as if they were actually food. I'd feed her once she awakened.

My own magic wasn't in that great a shape, but I wasn't the one holding gateways. Hundreds of shades had passed through Cait, probably far more than her power had been designed to accommodate.

I've mentioned I don't require much sleep, so I took advantage of the spot of downtime to take stock. Three dark mages remained. Out of Majestron Zelia, Slototh, and Adva, the latter was the most dangerous. His power didn't outstrip Majestron Zelia's, but his resentment probably did.

Maybe.

We'd captured her son, Perrikus. It might make her angry enough to be plotting retribution. According to Nemed, leader of the third race of men and a shade Cait had sheltered across the veil, Majestron would spare no quarter where Perrikus was concerned.

Except it had been a while since we captured him, and she hadn't made an appearance.

I reminded myself not to misjudge Slototh. Because of his love affair with filth, I'd always viewed him as inconsequential, and it was probably a mistake. We had yet to lay eyes on him or Majestron Zelia. Did it mean anything? As in they weren't involved in this?

Aye, wishful thinking on my part. Even if Majestron Zelia had decided to sit this one out, the loss of her son would have changed her mind. Not much we could do but wait and see if she showed up. I was certain Adva would. He was egotistical enough to want the last word. Slototh remained an unknown quantity.

My thoughts tumbled onward. I'd been surprised to see Hollis in the *Dreaming*.

More than surprised. He must have said a whole bunch of Hail Marys to someone to be forgiven sufficiently to be allowed into the *Dreaming*. Since Sidhe are immortal, he was probably the only one there who'd actually died. A minor moon goddess, Selene, had ripped his soul asunder from his body. She'd been in league with the Vamps and dark gods, and her action had ensured his silence.

At least until he'd resurrected the spirit part of himself.

His alliance with Vampires was disturbing. He'd been eager to share his master plan to rid the world of them. Even more troubling, he'd been in communication with the Leanan Sidhe in their pit of doom. The question was why? Had he switched sides—again? Or was he working as a double agent, tossing out a juicy tidbit and hoping the Sidhe would jump on it?

To our undying distress we'd been so stupid.

Except that part would come later. After a full understanding of how we'd been duped sank in.

I closed my eyes and rubbed grit out of the corners. We had to hold a conversation with Hollis, drag him out of the *Dreaming* if need be, and layer him in truth spells. We'd drill down to his motivations quick enough that way. Until then, I was spinning my wheels.

Cait drowsed with her head on my chest and her legs and arms sprawled at odd angles. I'd drawn the comforter over both of us. A bath would have been lovely, but her most pressing need was sleep. I wanted to know more about Death dragging Cait to her compound. The tale about her being Death's heir was preposterous.

As I understood things, Death was part of the beginnings of the world. Even older than Hades and Arawn—though not nearly as powerful—she and a few others were the mainstays of Earth's foundations. She might nurture delusions of passing her mantle to another, but it would never happen.

Cait had seemed certain Death was out of the picture for now. I hoped she was right. Death's earlier appearances had been helpful, but her more recent ones had only added to our troubles.

I spelled Cait deeper asleep and slid from beneath her, tucking the duvet close. While I was about things, I unlaced her boots and slipped them off before leaving the room. My first stop was the kitchen. I piled an assortment of biscuits, cheese, leafy greens, and butter on a generously sized plate and returned to my chamber with it. A mug of strong, black tea laced with honey was clutched in my other hand.

If Cait woke, she'd see them right away, and hopefully tuck in.

I returned to the kitchen and made something similar for myself before trotting to the basement room I'd designated as a study. For some reason, Scourie Castle didn't feel as unpleasant as it had. I muffled a snort. Easy to see why. In comparison to the two Vampire dens we'd frequented of late, it was downright homey.

Padhraic looked up from where he sat at my worktable. "Hello. Hope you don't mind me helping myself to your lore books." His dark hair was still wet from a recent shower, and he'd looped it behind his ears.

I set the plate and mug down. "Not at all. Did you find anything helpful?"

"Maybe." He tilted a flagon of something that smelled like mead and drank from it.

"Skipped the tea, eh?"

He smiled. "Nope. Started there, and this is actually a mixture. The reason I'm here is because of what Hollis suggested."

I pulled up a stool and perched next to him. "Aye. It bothered me too."

Padhraic focused worried dark eyes on me. "Bother is a wee understatement. He's spoken with the Leanan. How is that even possible? We—er, you—buried them with the help of liminal magic. They should be beyond reach. Of everyone. If Hollis can communicate with them, who else can?"

"Mmph. Hadn't considered that part."

"Which part did you consider?" Paddy asked.

"He's who sent me to kidnap Cait, although at the time, it wasn't how he described it. He knew better. He fluffed it up in 'bring us the special Vampire Reaper to help with our Vampire problem' wrappings. I didn't find out until I returned without her that I'd have been delivering her right into the center of a pack of Vamps."

Padhraic brought a fist down on the desk. It was so solid, it didn't even creak. "That does it. We can't trust him."

"Same conclusion I'd come around to. What the hell is in it for him?"

"Revenge for him being dead? Who cares." Paddy shrugged. "Nothing says we can't come up with our own Vampire solution, but 'tis a mistake to put any credence in his. First off, we do not want to disturb the Leanan. Unlike Earth-bound Vamps, we were never dead."

I'd known that part but never focused on its implications.

I frowned. "Not dead means no shades."

"Means they can resume being Leanan Sidhe as soon as they escape from the pit."

I crooked two fingers into the universal sign against evil. "Earth helped us. Their prison is secure. For now."

"Unless we open it, like Hollis suggested."

"Do you think there's any truth in his assertion the Leanan offered to help trap the Earth-bound Vamps?" I asked.

"Probably a whole lot of truth, particularly if their reward was freedom. Hollis was quick enough to say we could toss them back into the pit, but I'm not so certain of that. The only reason you won that day was because we"—he cleared his throat and looked embarrassed—"weren't expecting you."

"Aye. I suspected it wouldn't be so easy a second time," I muttered and stuffed a few bites into my mouth, washing the food down with tea strong enough to stand a spoon.

"Do you want to hear what I may have unearthed?" Paddy asked. At my nod, he went on, "The part about the all-Vampire meeting might work. We've taken down two seethes. Two master Vampires no longer walk the Earth. Out of the remaining seethes—"

"Any idea how many we're talking about?" I broke in.

"Not more than twenty."

I furled my brows. It was a more manageable number than I'd guessed. "Continue," I urged. "Out of the remaining seethes, what?"

"They'll be in an uproar, wondering which one will be the next target. Vamps have never banded together outside their respective seethes. They don't know the meaning of joining forces. Each master Vamp jealously guards his—or her —own."

"So how does an all-Vampire meeting even happen?"

"Someone they trust would have to suggest it." Padhraic offered me a mouthful of teeth. "I was thinking about Selene."

My mouth gaped open. I shut it fast. "Where would you even find her?"

"The gods will know where she is."

"All right," I spoke slowly. "What's in it for her?"

"That's quite the stumbling block," Padhraic agreed, "but worth bringing up when Arawn and Hades show up in a few hours."

I clapped him across the shoulders. "Selene would be

perfect. She was obviously in league with the Vampires before, and she can be quite...persuasive."

"Speaking from experience, mate?"

I laughed. "Nay. She missed me."

"It would make you one of the only ones. Moving forward, if we could come up with a way to get the Vampires to agree to a meeting in a central location, then we could beg aid from Earth and craft a second pit. We might miss a few Vamps, but if we immobilized the bulk of them..."

I nodded, liking the idea. "Absent Vampires to order about, whoever is left of the dark mages will like as not lose interest."

"Leaves the Humans Rule contingent, but mortals have never posed huge problems. If no one is feeding them magic, the little they have will die, and then they'll just be one more bunch of bigots without much force behind their rhetoric."

I mowed through the rest of the food on my plate and finished my tea. Paddy drank from his flagon and offered it to me. The mead was sweet and spicy, warming my mouth and throat. If it was mixed with tea, the tea part wasn't noticeable.

"Absent Selene's cooperation, do you have a backup plan?" I asked Padhraic.

He nodded slowly and held up a hand. "You're not going to like it, so let me get through talking before you yell, 'Nay,' in my face."

"Fair enough." I waited, intrigued by what he had in mind.

He squared his shoulders and sat back from the desk. "The Sidhe removed my Leanan essence. If you put it back—"

"Not just no, but hell no," I thundered, completely forgetting my promise to hear him out.

He eyed me. "Leanan are useful with the Earth-bound Vamps. They looked up to us, and rightfully so. We had real magic that ran beyond making new Vampires and superhuman speed and strength."

I shook my head. "You nearly died. If it weren't for Dena's skill, you would have. It hasn't been all that long since we reshaped your magical center, and—" I narrowed my eyes as an idea took shape.

It was Paddy's turn to say, "Don't even consider it, Liam. I know that look. You'd never pass. You've never been a Vampire. Besides, they'll remember me."

"Fine. I could employ a glamour."

Padhraic stood and twisted my stool until he faced me, then he dropped his hands onto my shoulders. "Nay. We will find some other method that doesn't include you turning into a sacrificial sheep."

"How is me adopting the Leanan mantle any different than you doing it?"

"I've been there. I spent hundreds of years as a Leanan. I can pull it off. You might view Vamps as a bunch of dumb fucks, and I agree they're far from mental giants, but they have a strong intuitive side. It's what keeps them fed and out of the line of fire from mortals."

"So far, you haven't launched any argument that's insurmountable," I said.

He squeezed my shoulders. "How about Cait?"

"What about her?"

"Do you think she's going to stand still and watch your kin chop up your magical center and turn you into a Leanan?"

Almost as if she'd sensed we were talking about her, the door to my study swooshed open, and she strode inside. "Thanks for the food," she told me and looked from Padhraic to me and back. "Why the grim faces?"

"Liam thinks he can go undercover as a Leanan and fool the Earth-bound Vampires," Padhraic said in a level voice. At least he unhanded my shoulders. Cait slid between us and wrapped an arm around me.

Tilting her head back, she sniffed my breath. "Mmph. Not drunk. That's a horrible idea. The other Vampires would ferret out the ruse in a heartbeat, and then you'd be screwed."

"Not if I truly became a Leanan," I clarified and waited for an explosion. Better to get everything out in the open, though, than to pussyfoot around an incendiary topic.

Cait backed up a foot and stared at me, green eyes snapping with anger. "What the fuck, Liam? Have you lost your mind? By your account, Paddy nearly died when the lot of you intervened so he wasn't Leanan any longer."

"Told you," Padhraic said.

I blew out a frustrated breath. "We need a way to get all the Vamps in one place. If we can't find Selene, we need a messenger they'll trust, and—"

"I fail to see what Selene—that half-dressed slut—has to do with anything. But this is a discussion for everyone, not something for you to hatch up by yourself in some dingy basement room." Her voice had risen until she was shouting.

"Fine. We'll see what we can come up with when we're all together," I conceded.

"Now you say that. Fuck! Be a hero on someone else's time." Cait stomped toward the door. "I'm going to clean up."

The door slammed behind her. I stared at where she'd stood, flummoxed. I'd expected a small amount of pushback, but she'd out-and-out called me an idiot.

"Not one of your better ideas, Liam," Padhraic said. "I'm

going to go back to culling through the lore. Maybe I'll come up with something more viable.

I didn't bother to tell him the whole Leanan thing had actually been his idea, and I'd been trying to save him from himself. I rephrased the same question I'd asked earlier. "What's so different between you masquerading as a Leanan and me doing the same thing?"

"First off"—he thumped my chest with an index finger —"we wouldn't be masquerading. We'd have to be the real deal. Second, you're practically engaged to Cait. It means you have to agree if one or the other of you wants to dive into something dangerous."

"It appears you're developing a relationship with Stacia."

He angled his head to one side. "Brother, is that ever evading the issue. We enjoy one another's company. That's as far as it's gone, and it has naught to do with the topic at hand."

He was correct, it didn't. Maybe transitioning to a Leanan hadn't been one of my more enlightened suggestions, but I was sick to death of Vampires. The sooner we finished them off— most of them, anyway—the better I'd like it.

I nodded curtly and left the study. I could teleport to Malin and see if one of the Sidhe lore books yielded a glitzy new idea, or I could go after Cait and apologize. I opted for the latter, and not only because the idea of joining her naked in hot water was tough to resist. Paddy had nailed it when he'd predicted she wouldn't sit still and say, "Yes, dear," while I morphed into a Leanan. I'd figured she'd be mildly unhappy, but I hadn't anticipated how pissed off she'd become.

I followed her unique energy, rich with the scents of heather and wildflowers, to the same bathroom we'd used before. Rather than summoning magic to open the door, I tried the latch. It wasn't locked, so maybe she was more disappointed than furious.

Because she was worried about me.

I let myself inside. The room was warm and steamy, and felt soothing after the perpetual dampness of the rest of the castle. Cait was in the shower, but it was big enough for two.

Taking a chance, I hastily stepped out of my boots and stripped off my garments. It was a relief to get the clothing off. It still reeked of Vampire whenever I moved. Padding across the tile floor, I opened the glass door and stepped into the shower.

Water streamed down Cait's body. She blinked it out of her eyes, regarding me with an unreadable expression. It would have been easy to lose myself gazing at the perfection of her long-limbed body with its high, firm breasts and amazing ass. But I didn't. That could come later. After I'd apologized.

I shelved the excuses crowding the back of my throat, trading them for, "I'm sorry. Padhraic volunteered to revert to Leanan to lure the Earth-bound Vamps. I didn't want him to go through that again. Me taking his place seemed like a solution, but I never meant to upset you."

"Not upset me?" she shrilled. "What if it did something? What if you liked being a Leanan? What if you didn't volunteer for the transformation back? Or what if you did, and it killed you? Christ, Liam. I mean I get the hating Vamps part. I loathe them, but if we lose ourselves fighting them, what was the point?"

I moved toward her and opened my arms. She hesitated before walking into my embrace and folding her wet body against mine. Spray from the shower pelted us both. We stood there for a long time, holding each other before she grabbed the soap and washed first my body, and then my blood-caked hair. Her touch was silk and fire, delighting my senses.

When she turned away from me and splayed her hands on the tile, I took her from behind just like we'd done in Malin. The heat of her closed around my engorged cock sending shivers of lust to every cell. I cupped her breasts and nuzzled her neck, biting the place it joined her shoulder. Her body tightened around me, and I thrust into her with abandon.

Someday, we'd take our time, but we'd lived through so much, this was a celebration of our life, of our pledge to one another. I needed to mark her, brand her, make her mine, and leave her with zero doubt how much she meant to me. A high keening cry told me she was cresting. I moved a hand between her legs and rubbed her clit to heighten her pleasure. Semen jetted from me in hot, rough pulses that pushed her over the top once more.

Panting, we ground our bodies together, using them instead of words to cement our commitment to each other. After a long while, my cock slid from her body, and she turned in my arms. "I love you," she said, low and fierce.

I cradled her wet face in my hands. "I love you too. No more schemes without running them past you first. I promise."

She closed her teeth over her lower lip. "Uh, guess that cuts both ways, huh?"

"Aye, that it would."

She turned off the water. "I can live with that. It's not going to be easy—for either of us. We're used to making decisions and running with them."

I opened the glass door and grabbed two towels. We worked at drying each other, and then got fresh towels and finished the job. "We have time for another meal before we meet up with everyone," I said.

"I need clothes."

"Plenty of them here," I told her. "Let's rustle up something for both of us that doesn't smell like Vampire."

"Did you think about that part?" She took a robe off a hook and wrapped it around herself.

"What part?" I settled for knotting a damp towel around my hips.

"If you'd turned into a Leanan. They smell almost as bad as the other variety."

I held out a hand; she laced her fingers with mine. "It would have been a small price if it handed us victory, but I'm not going to do it. Besides, it would have required cooperation from Dena and Krin and a bunch of other Sidhe. None of it was a foregone conclusion. They'd probably have come up with as much pushback as Paddy did."

"And me."

"Aye, love. And you."

I shouldered the door open and guided us toward the wardrobe room. We'd come up with something to wear. The clothing would be musty, but magic had kept it from moldering to dust.

"What do you want to be?" I teased. "We have garments from many eras."

"What are my choices?"

"Eh, almost anything from the 1500s on up."

"In that case, I want men's clothing. I have to be able to run, and skirts get in the way."

"Shouldn't be a problem. Right this way." Holding open a door, I kindled a mage light so we could see what we were about. Her scythe flew through the air, landing next to her. It glowed brighter than my light.

She picked it up. "Yes. Yes. I didn't forget about you."

I pulled open armoires and chests. We rustled through them, quick and efficient. I'd lost track of time, and I wanted to make sure Cait had more to eat before Hades and Arawn arrived, and we settled down to the critical business of what came next.

CHAPTER NINETEEN, CAIT

Reapers, Sidhe, the gods of the dead, Cathbad, and Cerebrus had been kicking ideas around for over an hour. The dog lay next to me. I had no idea why he'd singled me out, but Hades didn't appear to mind. I'd found thick, woolen trousers in one of many clothing chests in the wardrobe room and layered a handspun shirt over them, topped by a cream-colored sweater with only a few moth holes.

Apparently, the wool had been enticing enough, moths had braved Sidhe enchantment. Liam wore soft leather breeks, a woolen tunic, and a black leather vest. With all the synthetics in use for modern clothing, I sometimes forgot how little people had to work with hundreds of years ago. Cloth had to be made on a loom or spun from wool. It narrowed the possibilities considerably.

The topic at hand was whether or not to take time to drag Hollis out of the *Dreaming*. No one trusted his idea about opening the Leanans' prison.

I wasn't sure whether to raise my hand or just start talking. I opted for the latter. "Death had this thing she did where she kind of sucked what was left of Vampire shades through gateways. Then we burned the bones. It wasn't all that inefficient, and the enhanced spectrum of Reaper magic allows us to do the same thing."

"The problem with that," Hades said, "is by the time we mow through a few more seethes, the rest of them will go to ground. They have time on their side—given they're already dead."

"What exactly do you mean go to ground?" Krin asked.

"What does it usually mean?" Hades speared Krin with his somber blue gaze. "They will vanish from sight for a long while, maybe centuries."

I turned it around in my mind. They could do that. Since they were dead, they could go into a kind of suspended animation where they didn't move around at all—and hence required zero blood. Rather like an extended hibernation.

"Why would that be a bad thing?" I asked. "It's kind of kicking the can down the road, but at least they'd be out of the way."

"Is that what you want?" Arawn turned his eerie gaze on me. His eyes were so black pupil and iris blended, and he looked daunting in a don't-fuck-with-me kind of way.

"Not unless there's no other choice."

Cathbad walked from where he'd been lounging against a wall. "I have a proposal, but 'tisn't without risk." Side conversations quieted as everyone focused on the big Druidic bard.

He clasped his hands behind him and continued. "The only other time I gifted music was to the Sirens. It dinnae go well. Last thing I expected was that merely hearing my song would empower some of the Reapers. I've discussed it with the Celts, and they suspect Reaper magic shares enough wavelengths with my own, 'twas a natural blending."

"Death couldn't have known," I blurted.

"Agreed," Cathbad said. "She and I have never seen eye-to-eye on anything."

He rolled his shoulders back. "On account of the debacle with the Sirens, I assumed my power was dangerous to those with lesser magical ability, particularly if it took the lead. 'Twas why I adopted a conservative tack when I instructed the Reapers who wield music as part of their power."

"I did as you instructed with Cait," Stacia spoke up.

"Aye, lassie. I know," he told her. "Cait ran into difficulties. Her only chance was letting the music loose, and it worked for her. The magic knew when to retreat."

"What kind of difficulties?" Krin asked.

I got to my feet, aware no one except Liam knew what had happened to me. I filled in the details, using as few words as possible. Except no matter how little I divulged, it revealed Death's crazed mental state.

Hisses from the Reapers joined a variety of disapproving sounds from the Sidhe. Hades and Arawn looked stunned—and furious. Cathbad caught my eye and nodded. I understood it was time to cede the floor and took my seat to let him float his ideas.

"I assumed my music corrupted the Sirens," he went on, "but I was wrong. They were devious before they absorbed my gift. My current belief is the music amplifies whatever it finds within the bearer. Because Cait has a pure heart and honorable intentions, the music dinnae push forward and finish Death off.

Cait would have been helpless to stop such a conclusion, but the music intuited she'd carry guilt for the rest of her days.

"And so, the music established a point—that it had won—and retreated."

"You're giving me too much credit," I mumbled under my breath. "About the pure heart thing."

"Nay, he's not." Liam spoke low into my ear; I leaned into him.

"My idea is this," Cathbad said. "Music has always contained a hypnotic aspect. If many of us joined our voices, we could draw all the Vampires to wherever we wanted them. Hell, we could sing them into a pit we'd already prepared."

He paused, shrewd eyes sweeping the group to assess our reaction. What he saw must have passed muster because he went on. "It wouldn't be easy. Not at all. It would take more magic than most of you have ever run through yourselves, and you'd have to keep it up until... Until we were done."

"I like it," Hades said. "Where would we do this?"

"Somewhere far from mortal settlements." Cathbad unclasped his hands, and swung his arms by his sides. "'Twould take planning. We would work in shifts. Those not singing would be eating and sleeping to replenish their magic."

"We could help," Krin said. "Sidhe power marries well with Reaper magic."

Cerebrus raised a head and woofed. I dropped a hand into his fur, scratching behind one set of ears.

"There is a downside," Cathbad said. "A big one. If we try —and fail—we will have lost any opportunity to corral them. They will know we won't rest until they're annihilated, and they will go to ground. They have extensive subterranean networks. Places they hid themselves during the Middle Ages when the Church decreed their destruction. The old ones have long memories, and they will lead their acolytes to the relative safety of obscurity."

He narrowed his eyes. "The other danger is this maneuver will reveal Reaper identities. So far, Vampires and their minions have only targeted Cait and her direct associates, like Stacia. If they slip past our net, they'll know who all of you are, those of you with musical magic. And they will mark you for failure and misfortune. Not immediately, but whenever they surface, you can bet pursuing you will be their first task."

"No avenue will be without risk," I said.

"True enough," Cathbad replied, "but this route puts Reapers in a direct line of fire."

"Why do only some of us carry musical ability?" Pavel asked from where he stood in a corner of the room.

"I have no idea," Cathbad replied. "Perhaps Death altered the formula of how she made you. Seems to me 'tis mostly the younger Reapers who lack that aptitude."

I made a wry face. Reapers had been enough of a management problem, if Death had been able to strip still more of our "aptitude," she'd have done it in a heartbeat.

"All right." Pavel nodded briskly. "Next question. Would it be possible to add that missing bit of potential for the forty or so Reapers who don't possess it?"

"Maybe," Krin answered. "The bigger question is how long would it take?"

Conversation flowed around me on both sides of the fence. In the end, most of us agreed to go with what we had in the interest of expediency. The younger Reapers would take charge of building portals and ensuring Vampire shades were well and truly past the one-way gate and locked on the proper side of the barrier.

"Are all of you sufficiently recovered to launch this project?" Arawn asked.

"Haste is important," Hades said. "Even now, Vampires are augmenting their defenses since they're convinced more of their lairs will be selected for destruction."

"Does it mean the Master Vamps are talking with one another?" Liam asked.

"That's exactly what it means," Hades replied. "The buzz of their conversation reaches me in snatches. Which tells me how serious they perceive the situation to be. Normally the seethe leaders never communicate with one another—unless they're engaged in a dominancy battle."

"Are the three dark gods involved?" Krin asked.

Cathbad shrugged. "No way to know. If someone created a sound shield around this chamber, I'd teach you the incantation to lure Vampires. Hopefully, without drawing every Undead bastard within a fifty league radius."

"How far will the spell reach?" I asked.

"It will build on itself," Cathbad answered me. "Something about its weave seizes those who are nearby. It should reverberate through their minds and reach others telepathically."

"Should?" Krin arched a dark brow.

"Aye, should. I've never used it for quite such a purpose before. In the past, enemies I've sung to their doom were ranged in proximity to one another, not spread throughout the world."

Sidhe magic flickered around the room, effectively sealing it off from the rest of Scourie Castle—and the Highlands.

Cathbad turned in a full circle, hands extended, as he tested the strength of the warding. Seemingly satisfied, he opened his mouth and began to sing.

The melody was poignant, evocative, and in a minor key that conjured a desire to follow its notes, no matter where they led. My scythe hummed along with it. The combination drove me to my feet before I realized I'd become caught up in the music and its commands.

I'd taken a few steps toward the front of the room before Liam grabbed my arm. About that time, Cathbad shut his mouth and the wonderful, enticing song quit flowing.

A few cries of, "No," and "Keep singing," filled the chamber.

Perhaps to cut through the residual pull of his music, Cathbad whistled once, high and shrill. It brought me back into myself.

"For this to work"—he projected his voice—"you must guard against being lured by the magic. 'Tis a powerful casting."

Understanding flared why we had to find a location far from human habitation. They, too, would get sucked into the spell's magnetism. I shook free of Liam's hand and motioned to Stacia, Pavel, and Abby. "Come on. Let's experiment with warding while he sings."

Fifteen minutes later, we'd established an effective ward that inured us to the song's allure. Shuffling through magic and trying one combination after another was hard. "The only problem," I said, working to catch my breath around talking, "is the ward will drain our magic even faster than reproducing the song."

Cathbad narrowed his eyes. "I hadn't counted on that aspect, but you're right."

Liam trotted to the front of the room. "How about if the Sidhe manage the ward? I was watching while you worked, and we can craft something quite similar."

"Let's try and see if it works," Krin said.

After a few adjustments—Sidhe draw power differently than Reapers—we stumbled on a combination that kept Reapers from falling into the spell's snare. One Sidhe could manage two Reapers, but not more than that.

"Only thing left," I said, "is where we do this."

"I've been thinking about that," Arawn said. "A logical spot would be the far reaches of Siberia, but then every single Vampire would have to travel a long way before we got our hands on him."

"I've been considering it too," Liam said. "It shouldn't take too much to extend our warding—since we'd have that type of casting well in hand to protect the Reapers."

"Say more," Arawn urged.

"We could select a spot in central Nevada. About the only things there are deserted mining operations. And then another in one of the North African deserts."

"You're suggesting we split our forces?" Cathbad eyed Liam, who nodded. "Mmph. 'Tis risky since I could only aid one group at a time."

"Risky on some fronts, but more efficient on others. Vampires wouldn't have to travel as far, and we'd be on the lookout for mortals who inadvertently fell prey to the music."

"Once the song gets going," I spoke up, "it has its own energy." An uncomfortable sensation tracked down my spine, but I felt compelled to add, "None of the rest of you have been caught up by the music, but it's not a comfortable spot. It places you squarely into a position all your magical training has warned you about since your very first forays into spellcasting. You won't be in control."

I took a measured breath. "My error was to not titrate the amount of power the song drew from me. The first time it took off running, it sucked me dry and I passed out." Angling a glance at Cathbad, I shrugged. "Balanced against everything, not having you front and center all the time is the least of my worries."

"What's the uppermost one?" he asked.

"Even though the music has the upper hand, I can still moderate the amount of power it uses, and I have to do a better job with that."

Nods ran around the room. After another brief practice session, we formed two groups of forty Reapers each and nearly that number of Sidhe. Cathbad would teleport back and forth.

"I have no idea how long this will take," he said, "or if we'll be successful. Many things could happen, including unwelcome visits from the remaining dark gods."

"Ha! We'll sing them into the pit along with everyone else," Stacia muttered. She and Padhraic were in the bunch going to Northern Africa. I'd drawn Nevada, along with Liam, Krin, and other Sidhe I'd fought with when we'd buried the Leanan. Hades would be with us; Arawn with the other group.

Our plan was simple. We'd teleport to our battle stations and do the spadework to get a pit happening. Once it was deep enough, several Sidhe would manage the liminal space's energy, and we'd begin singing. How things would play out after that was impossible to predict.

"Ready for this?" Liam said near my ear.

I shot a disbelieving look his way. Was anyone ever ready for major battles? "Probably not," I muttered, "but it doesn't make any difference. Nor does it excuse me from participating."

"Courage is grace under pressure," he told me. "I'd love to take credit for that phrase, but Ernest Hemingway came up with it first."

I smiled at him. Would the world ever be simple enough for me to lose myself in a book again? Or behind the yoke of an airplane? I hoped so.

Our contingent broke into smaller groups, and we teleported away from Scourie Castle after we'd gathered a selection of blades—in case the music wasn't enough, and we were relegated to killing Vamps the old-fashioned way. We'd also parceled out what remained of the silver stakes. Dena didn't have enough dead man's blood left to help at all, and there wasn't time to secure more.

I'd worn my sword belt so much lately, it was starting to feel like a part of me. I didn't know whether to feel depressed about it or proud of my shiny new skillset. As the journey spell unfolded, I thought about Kiko. It would be a while before I could check in with her, and I hoped to hell our summoning spell would remedy her Vampire problem forever.

The cold, dry air of central Nevada was welcome after the perpetual damp of Scotland and the Pacific Northwest. Judging from the sun, it was the middle of the day. Even seeing the sun was a nice break. I decided it was a good omen, blessing our endeavors.

We located a high, flat mesa. The ruins of some kind of mine, complete with rusting trucks and assorted equipment, sat off to one side. We were so far from any highway, I couldn't hear the rumble of traffic.

The Sidhe went to work with their Earth-linked magics as they coaxed the liminal space to share power with them. My understanding of the power holding Earth's boundaries intact was fairly primitive, but I recalled what a bitch it had been managing that bit of magic once it was freed.

Not unlike the musical magic, it had a mind of its own and required a firm hand. While the Sidhe prepared the pit we hoped to lure the Vampires into, the rest of us formed teams of four Reapers each. Four teams would sing while the other six rested; we'd rotate as our power dwindled. Four teams active at all times with two in abeyance for emergencies.

Dirt cracked open a few feet away as the beginnings of a chasm took shape. The pit was growing deeper fast. No reason to wait. I motioned to Liam and Griselda, the Sidhe in charge of the warding for my group of Reapers. Once I felt their power enclose us, I planted my scythe in front of me and wrapped both hands around its hilt.

Its connection with the earth seemed to enhance the ward and made it easier to regulate my magic, so the music didn't burn it up too fast. The other Reapers did the same. To my amazement, a swathe of greens and blues jumped from sickle to sickle until they were connected by their own unique enchantment. That hadn't happened back in Scotland. Perhaps it had something to do with the liminal energies being activated.

So many things I didn't yet know.

So much Death could have taught us—if she hadn't been frightened of losing even a smidgeon of her hold over us. I refocused. Death had no place here. I was only thinking about her because I was scared. It made no sense since she'd scarcely been a source of comfort.

My mouth was dry, my heart jumped to double-time rhythm, and my palms slicked with sweat. Showtime.

The music formed, spiraling from my magical center and finding its way out my mouth. Much like the rounds schoolchildren sang, we entered the song at set intervals.

The net effect was touching and beautiful as the music took off and grew wings, soaring through the deserted plateau as if it had been waiting for this opportunity its whole life. Behind me, the noise of earth rending and tearing as the pit deepened was comforting in an odd way.

We'd set the trap.

Our song repeated, and repeated again. I was careful with my magic, but eventually, our group ceded to another. Daylight faded, replaced by early evening and then midnight.

We'd been singing for hours, but not a single Vampire had heeded our call. At first I figured they were waiting for nightfall, but if they didn't hustle, dawn would be here.

I hadn't believed they could resist the summons, but maybe I'd been wrong. I was on my second shift, having dozed for a couple of hours, when a subtle alteration in the enchantment coating the mesa caught my attention.

I couldn't stop singing, so I used telepathy. *"What is that?"*

Liam angled his head to one side and added seeking magic to the flow powering his warding. His expression darkened. "That's the problem with setting traps," he muttered. "They sometimes attract unexpected garbage."

"Tells me less than nothing." Frustration scoured me, and I missed a few notes. The music pushed back hard, rebuking me with a rush of unpleasant prickles.

Liam tried to answer, but Cerebrus began barking from all three mouths, creating a cacophony that drowned out everything else.

Hades had been overseeing the liminal energy. He leapt to the top of a large boulder. "Keep singing," he shouted. "Sing them to their doom."

Were the Vampires finally here? It didn't mesh with Liam's statement, but I trusted Hades, and we upped the ante on our Siren-esque song. Excitement rippled through my scythe, warming my palms. Fuck. Everyone but me knew what was happening.

Whoops and cries brought my head whipping around. Adva and another man—probably Slototh—rode great horned beasts. Light flared around them, illuminating the night. Every bit as gorgeous as Perrikus, Adva, or D'Chel, Slototh had gleaming black hair, dark-blue eyes, prominent cheekbones, and a strong jaw. A cream-colored linen shirt clung to the muscled lines of his chest and shoulders. Crisply pressed black slacks snugged around slender hips.

For some reason, I'd expected the god of filth to wear ripped and stinking rags.

Their steeds reminded me of feral hogs but with rhinoceros heads. Behind them streamed an army of mortals with a few shades mixed in. Not Vampires, but they'd do. Any humans who sided with the dark gods had to be part of Humans Rule. It was the only group where Adva and Slototh could have come up with such numbers on short notice.

A quick scan verified my suspicions. Feeble magic flickered around the mortals. Their souls had begun to shrink from the edges inward, riddled with necrotic, gray places.

Hades and Cerebrus bounded forward flanked by Sidhe

who weren't required to hold the chasm open. Black lightning forked from Hades' upraised hands. Meanwhile, humans stumbled around the dark gods straight for the pit and its incontrovertible draw.

"Stay back!" Adva shrieked. When the humans ignored his commands, he flattened them with magic.

If I hadn't been singing, I'd have laughed. The dark god had just helped us. I wondered if he understood his temper had played right into our hands. Like lemmings throwing themselves off a cliff, the mortals were no match for our enchantment.

Big surprise. It had been designed for Vampires.

A sheet of dark-tinged magic stinking of ozone and sulfur oozed from Adva and Slototh, winding around the remaining humans and freezing them in their places. Guess Adva had wised up that killing his own troops was stupid.

Gateways formed as the Reapers without music made certain the newly dead couldn't be weaponized any further. I felt sorry for the mortals, but not all that sorry. When they'd decided magic was an abomination—unless they were sneaking it on the side—they'd sealed their fate.

My magic was perilously low. Time to quit before I fell on my face. As I called my team back and we traded with a fresh one, Liam and Griselda joined me. "We have an idea," she said, "but it will take all of us."

I nodded and made come-along motions with one hand. She and Liam outlined a bold and drastic proposal in shielded telepathy. It might work, but if it didn't we were likely to end up in the pit right along with the dark gods.

Where the fuck were the Vampires? Their absence worried me. If we shifted gears, deviated from the plan to snare the dark gods, and the Vamps showed up, it could set everything spinning off the rails. The acrid taste of adrenaline coated my tongue. Surprised I had enough energy left to react to anything, I shambled off to spread the word. Liam and Griselda headed for Hades. The god of the dead had to agree with their new strategy, or we couldn't move forward.

$\mathcal{I}$'m not adverse to setting traps for my enemies, but I far prefer it when they snap shut quickly. Waiting around for hours and hours while the Reaper song echoed endlessly was wearing on me. At least it made it easy to keep a close eye on Cait and make certain she didn't repeat burning her power down to a cinder.

When Adva and Slototh came galloping out of nowhere on steeds straight out of a bad remake of *Lord of the Rings*, I was delighted to see them. Everyone always assumes Slototh will be a slob. His actual title is god of all that's been discarded. Because people toss trash, they made a bunch of assumptions that he lorded it over garbage. Nothing could be further from the truth.

People discard a whole lot of things that aren't physical. Hopes and dreams, for instance. Slototh gathers them up and uses people's failures to torment them. In a way, it makes his interference far more destructive than the other dark gods. Nothing like beating a man when he's down.

Still, I've always viewed him as less of a threat than, say, Adva with his portals, or Tokkhots with his poisoned bite.

The ragtag army they'd pulled together had to be volunteers from the Humans Rule ranks. They were helpless in the face of Cathbad's music, and bolted for the pit until the dark gods built a barrier. They were sloppy, and we could take it down.

Looking past the mortals—and there might have been a couple thousand of them—this was our opportunity to trap Adva and Slototh. At least, that was my impression. Hades might shoot me down. He and Arawn were the ones whose power would hold the dark gods in an all-encompassing fog.

Did he require Arawn's presence?

Could the two of them manage four of the dark mages in whatever cell they'd carved out in Hell to hold them?

I joined Hades on the boulder. He clapped me on the back. "Good to finally see some action, eh?" he boomed.

"Aye. Very much so." Switching to telepathy as private as I could make it, I said, *"Adva is out for blood when it comes to Cait and me. We propose to lure him into the pit—by entering it ourselves. He is sure to follow, and probably Slototh and those things they're riding too."*

Hades' smile faded, and he skewered me with an unrelenting gaze. *"Ye'd be trapped too."*

"Not until you shut the pit."

Hades shook his head. *"Not the way it works. Naught that enters the chasm can leave."*

"What about teleporting?"

He shook his head once more. *"The liminal energy will*

dampen your power, make it impossible to do aught but bide in the hole."

"What about the realm of the dead? Could Cait punch through from the chasm?"

I waited, not hoping for much. Meanwhile, mortals were piling atop Reapers, driving them to the ground until they had to stop singing. Adva and Slototh galloped this way and that. Anyone near their twisted steeds got gored and tossed skyward. Other Reapers and Sidhe jumped into the fray, but the net effect was the music wavered. Not gone, but fading. Soon its magnetism would dissolve.

Realization blazed a path through me. "This is the forward guard," I muttered. "Vampires are out there, but they appealed to the dark gods to do something. Unlike the mortals, they're smart enough to know something bad was waiting at the end of the music trail."

Hades narrowed his eyes to slits. Cerebrus took off like a shot, snapping at vulnerable places on Adva's steed. He must have severed a tendon because the hog-thing crumpled back on its haunches. Adva rained curses on the dog, but Cerebrus bared his fangs and growled.

It was the doggie version of, "Come and get me, motherfucker."

"The realm of the dead should work," Hades said.

It took a moment to register because so much time had passed since I'd posed the question.

"But I'm not certain," he went on. *"I've been talking with Arawn. They've had better success drawing Vampires than us. His work in Africa is nearly done. I shall tell him we need him here, and he will go with you and Cait. If anyone can ensure entry to the realm of the dead, 'tis him."*

A long, satisfied baying howl, followed by an outraged squeal, told me Cerebrus had incapacitated the other hog. He strutted around the downed creature, easily avoiding the sweep of its horn as it did its damnedest to gore him.

"I'll let Cait know. She and Griselda are spreading the word that all the Reapers will have to sing to make the pit's draw as irresistible as we can."

"Should be our turn for Cathbad," Hades said thoughtfully. *"We haven't seen him since this began."*

"Might be why the other group had better luck," I muttered.

"I'd wondered the same." Hades shelved telepathy. An expectant expression wreathed his face. He leaned forward, eyes glittering, as he stared at a spot off to my right.

The star-studded night sky formed a hazy spot that shattered inward. Arawn tumbled through, followed by Cathbad. They somersaulted through the air and landed in crouches. The bard picked up the frayed threads of the song even before he dusted himself off and stood. Coming from him, the music's power took off at Mach 10.

I may have complained about things dragging before, but everything blew up around me, courtesy of Cathbad's music. The humans who'd piled on the Reapers shook off the effects of whatever enchantment Adva and Slototh had spun. En masse, they ran for the pit, yelling and screaming as they threw themselves into it. The liminal space wouldn't be kind to those with stolen magic, but the mortals weren't my concern.

Arawn joined me. His low voice buzzed near my ear. "I am certain I can extract the Reaper from the pit." He stopped there, but I absorbed his meaning well enough. He could save Cait. He was less certain about me, but I wasn't about to let it turn into a stumbling block. Immortal is immortal. I'd get out of there somehow.

"I'll figure things out as I go," I told him. "Let's do this."

We found Cait next to a group of Reapers. As we'd marched through the field, all the Reapers were back on their feet, and they'd joined their voices with Cathbad's magical melody. No longer producing the song in stages where Reapers jumped in at intervals, everyone sang the same notes.

The effect was spellbinding, captivating.

Would it be enough?

Adva and Slototh were on their feet. Big surprise since their macabre mounts would never carry anyone again. A quick glance at one suggested the magic that had cobbled it together had been withdrawn; it was fading from the edges inward.

Cait and I danced in front of Adva. "How's winning going for you?" I sneered at the god of portals.

"Where's that hall of mirrors?" Cait tossed out. "I kind of miss the one that makes me look anorexic."

"You miss a lot of things," Slototh said in a silky tone.

I winced. Last thing we needed was a distraction from Dr. Discarded Hopes and Dreams.

"Don't pay attention to him," I hissed at Cait and moved a meter or two nearer the pit.

The gods followed us. Both of them.

At some point on our trip across the field, Arawn had warded himself. I assumed the dark mages knew he was there, but perhaps they didn't. As I'd hoped, the sum total of Adva's concentration was focused on Cait and me. All around us, humans continued pelting into the pit, whooping it up until they jumped, and then their whoops turned to anguished squeals.

By then, it was too late.

Adva and Slototh had gathered this force but didn't appear to give a shit about them.

"Your hardest loss," Slototh went on, his words aimed right at Cait, "was Death. She loved you like a mother, but you failed to value her. She is sad, crying, locked away in her cottage."

We'd edged nearer the swirling fringe of madness. The liminal energy was in full bloom. Thrilled beyond reckoning at all the bodies feeding it, the chasm had developed fiery contrails marking its boundary. Smoke and flames rose high in the night sky.

Cait stopped and turned toward Slototh. "You know nothing," she gritted through clenched teeth.

"Och, and I know far more than you give me credit for... lassie." He'd segued into a Scottish brogue.

"Shut up," I snarled. "You're no more Scottish than I am."

"Shall I list the things you've lost?" he purred. "You've lived a long time, and your misgivings are rich, deep. Surely, your latest love interest might want to know how your last several affairs ended."

"What's he talking about?" Cait demanded.

"Nothing. He's baiting us. It's what he does."

"You've met him before?" She stared at me.

"Aye, more than once." I took her hand, and we moved nearer the pit.

Adva swiped a hand downward. A glittering gateway formed, almost as appealing as Cathbad's music. With a warm, inviting smile, Adva jumped into its center and stood, outlined by a kaleidoscopic mix of color washing over him. "Come on." He gestured. "I have halls you've not yet seen. Grand ones, and I'll gift you with jewels and gold."

We ignored him and backed still nearer the liminal energy. Perhaps twenty meters remained. We were nearly there.

"*Keep moving,*" Arawn's voice rumbled through my head. "*'Tis a ploy. He won't leave without you. He can't leave, anyway. The music won't let him.*"

"Shit!" Cait yanked her hand from mine.

I lunged for her, afraid she was going to leap toward Adva. Instead, she raised her glowing scythe. Vampire stench rained down on me. Harsh and putrid, it burned my nose and mouth.

My forward guard theory about the mortals had been spot on. The Vampires had been waiting, and not that far away. Cathbad's song had proved irresistible—when it came direct from the bard.

The portal Adva was balanced within shattered around him; he sprawled on the ground next to Slototh. The god of filth snorted. "Are you done grandstanding?"

Adva ignored him and shoved in front of the tide of Vampires racing toward the pit. Power spewed from him as he built barrier after barrier. The Vampires mowed through each one.

"Get off your ass and help me," he shouted at Slototh.

"Why?" the other god retorted. "Vampires are your pets, not mine. They gave up caring about anything the moment they were turned."

I felt like cheering as row after row of Vampires pushed around the dark gods and straight on into the pit. The contrails shot a meter above its edge, turning the sky crimson and gold. This was working better than I'd expected since we'd snared both Vamps and a big chunk of the Humans Rule crowd. Word would get out. It would definitely put a damper on new signups.

Krin raced to me. One look at his face dashed my mood. He was panting, bent over, hands on his knees as he fought to get words out. "We're losing control of the liminal energy."

Made sense. We'd fed it so many souls, it was riding high.

"The second the last Vampire dives in, we have to close it off. If we even can. Get back to your post. We'll need every Sidhe."

Switching to telepathy, I sketched out what Cait and I were planning. He straightened, staring at me. "But ye'll be trapped," he said in Gaelic.

"Have a little faith," I countered. "I've never been down for the count before."

He grabbed my arm. "Liam. Ye haven't been next to the pit these past few minutes. Every time I assess it, 'tis doubled in potency.

"It's time," Arawn said. "If we're going to do this, we must go now."

"See you soon," I told Krin. He clamped his mouth shut and bolted for his spot on the perimeter.

Adva was shrieking at Slototh, who yelled right back. I had to get his attention, so I pushed between them. "Last chance," I challenged.

"What the fuck do you mean?" Adva snarled.

"Cait and I are leaving."

I stopped there, turned, and grabbed her hand. Together, we ran hard for the boiling, bubbling mass, powered by liminal energy. I should have been afraid, but I wasn't. Arawn's energy burned on my other side, steady and reassuring, but maybe I was reading more into it than was actually there.

"Ha! They're following us. We have them both. I knew they couldn't resist," Arawn crowed. He didn't need to use telepathy. The pit roared so loud, no one could hear anything over its din.

"I love you," I told Cait.

"Love you too. See you on the other side."

It was a potent reminder she would see the "other side," while I might have to fight to get there. I pushed everything from my mind, and we jumped through the ring of flames surrounding the perimeter. The pull of Cathbad's music paled in comparison to the way the chasm dragged at me, sucking me into its hungry maw.

The thing was alive, powered by Earth energy, and it knew precisely what I was and welcomed me. I could almost hear it smacking its lips over a Sidhe to dismantle and suck dry.

I thought I heard Slototh screaming Adva had been a fool about the time Hades pushed past, intent on rounding up the two dark mages and adding them to his collection.

"Now comes the tricky part," Arawn said into my mind. *"Let the pit take you as deep as it will. Don't fight it."*

Presumably, Cait heard the same set of instructions. They didn't appear to faze her, but they bothered the fuck out of me. As I sank deeper into the magic powering the liminal space, it took everything I had not to pull power like a madman to launch an escape.

Except it wouldn't work. The pit had my number. It understood how I wielded magic, and it would thwart anything I did until I had no magic left. Over the din of Vampires and mortals squealing their terror and misery, I could still detect Cathbad's music.

Pure and vibrant, it had an affinity for the magic that powered the liminal space. I latched onto the promise in the song and let the pit drag me down. I still had Cait's hand, and the god of the dead was next to us.

"We did a good day's work," he said and smiled. Any resemblance Arawn had to a man had departed. Perhaps it was the liminal energy that showed all of us in our true forms. He shone with a dark brilliance that hinted at his wisdom and his age. Cait's scythe glowed, reflecting what little light remained down here on her face.

Gods, she was so beautiful. Her hair shone, and her Reaper scents thickened around us.

Arawn drove a hand downward. A shimmery gateway opened into the realm of the dead, and he stepped through. Cait followed him, but when I lunged forward I ran against something solid. I could see through to where Arawn and Cait stood, concern scribing lines into their foreheads and around their eyes, but I couldn't breach the barrier.

Cait tried to push back through it, but Arawn gripped her arm, holding her in place. I didn't want her to risk crossing another time, either. She was safe, and I needed her to remain so.

Would telepathy work across the portal? *"Go,"* I said. *"I'll find my own way out."*

"Noooooo!" Cait screamed into my mind.

"Work quickly," Arawn cautioned. *"Once they close the pit..."* He didn't say any more. He didn't need to. Cait was fighting against him, kicking and writhing, but he said something that got her attention. I have no idea what it was, but she nodded once, and then the gateway snapped shut.

I've always welcomed challenges, and I shuffled through possibilities. The chasm's hold on me was deepening fast.

Between that and Arawn's warning, I couldn't afford to guess wrong too many times.

"No wrong guesses," I spoke out loud.

Escaping the way I'd entered was remote. I had no idea how deep in the earth I was, but it would take a gargantuan amount of magic to retrace my descent. I could lay my reservations aside and chuck everything I had into a teleport spell. If it bounced back in my face like an unruly boomerang, I wouldn't have enough magic left to do anything but accept my fate.

If it hadn't been for Cait, I might have been less frantic to escape. Vampires wouldn't be a problem for many a long year. I suspected Humans Rule would wither on the vine, and we had five of six dark gods imprisoned in Hell. Majestron Zelia wouldn't poke her nose out to bother anyone.

Sidhe and Reapers had secured a great victory today. One I was proud to have been part of. My third option was the *Dreaming*. It took very little magic, and if it didn't open for me, I could try to teleport.

Carefully, as if I had all the time in the world, I arranged earth and air to provide entry into the *Dreaming*. Much like the liminal energy, the *Dreaming* was sentient in its own right. I did what I could to reach it, let it know one of its native sons was on his way and in need of its healing.

It wasn't an exaggeration. I'd expended so much magic, even breathing took thought and effort. Once I was certain I had all the elements lined up, I ignited my casting.

Nothing happened. I floated in the blankness of the pit, basting in human misery and Vampire outrage. Slowly, carefully, I altered the mixture of earth and air to include more earth and a pinch of fire.

Still nothing.

Sweat slicked my sides, forehead, and rolled into my eyes. Despite the fire rimming the chasm, it was far from hot this far down.

What was I doing wrong? I forced a calm I was far from feeling and retraced my reasoning. "Aha!" I'd have shouted, but I lacked the energy. The word sort of slithered from my lips, and I made a few adjustments. Magic has additive properties. The liminal field is powered by earth, which meant I probably didn't require any at all in my casting.

So I removed it. For long moments, nothing happened. I girded myself for a teleport spell that would probably rebound, slapping me silly. With no warning, the place I hung suspended, power from the liminal space feeding from me, shattered.

Rather than the pit, I floated in blackness so absolute it was disorienting. I'd escaped the pit, but where was I? Breath rattled from my mouth, and I understood this new spot lacked air.

Sluggish neurons in my overtaxed brain connected. I was in the space between Earth and the corridors spanning it. I had to be. It was the only airless void I knew. With almost the last of my magic, I visualized my home in Malin and set a journey spell in motion.

Too tapped out to tell if my gambit had worked, I waited, lungs reflexively sucking for air that wasn't there. Finally, after forever, the familiar walls of my flat snapped around me. I pitched facedown on my familiar carpet, and everything went black.

CHAPTER TWENTY-ONE, CAIT

"Ye cannae help him," Arawn said in Gaelic for maybe the sixth time. It finally penetrated the frenzied energy rushing through me, and I quit fighting his iron grip.

"But I can share Reaper magic. It worked before. You rebuked him for being in the realm of the dead. Remember?"

"Aye, I recall well enough, but the liminal energy will pervert any such attempt." Arawn stopped for a moment, perhaps judging how much truth I could stand.

"What?" I asked dully, never taking my gaze from Liam. He didn't look worried, but then he never did.

"He knew before we did this."

"Knew what?" My tone sharpened.

"That this exit route might be closed to him. Come with me. He will return to Scourie Castle if he can."

"But I can't leave him," I protested, adding, "I won't."

"Ye must. He requires his full and complete concentration.

As long as ye're standing here, he'll be thinking about you, not what he must do to escape."

It made sense, but walking away from Liam ripped a hole in my guts. And my heart. And everything else about me that mattered. Arawn was done offering choices. He swept me up in his magic; fighting him would have been a joke. The next thing that formed around us was Scourie Castle's great room.

It was filled to bursting with Reapers and Sidhe, all celebrating what had truly been an all-encompassing victory. More of us were arriving every few minutes. Cerebrus ran close and jumped on me, almost driving me to the floor as he licked my face with abandon.

Hades offered a hand, and I grabbed it to steady myself. "Doonae abandon hope, lass. Liam is ingenious, and his magic is strong."

"Adva and Slothoth?"

"I left them with the other two. Dinnae take long since the cell was already prepared." He tightened his hold on my hand. "I meant what I said. Give Liam credit. He's gotten himself out of dangerous spots afore."

I nodded and battled the hot prick of tears behind my lids. I couldn't stay in the great room and celebrate with everyone, not with Liam missing and maybe buried forever in the pit with our enemies.

Well, I could have, but my heart wasn't in it, and I couldn't bear a parade of well-wishers reassuring me. It would pound home the harsh reality that we were here.

And Liam wasn't.

"Thank you." I let go of Hades' hand. "I'm sure he'll figure something out, but in the meantime, I need to be by myself."

I felt the full weight of his gaze on me. "No shenanigans,

Reaper. Not until your magic has had a chance to recover." He was back to English after his Gaelic reassurances.

Heat rose from my chest to my face. I had been considering using magic to track Liam, which was a fool's errand considering how little I had at my disposal. Sickle in hand, sword clanging by my side, and ever-present bag wrapped around my body, I faded from the room, covering my egress with small don't-look-here spells.

Very small. If my scythe hadn't pitched in and helped, there'd have been no spells at all.

Once in the corridor, I made my way to Liam's chamber. His sandalwood-and-wet-greenery scent clung to everything, and it undid me. The tears I'd held back earlier spilled over, running down my cheeks as I set the scythe down, unbuckled the sword belt, and untangled my bag from my body.

Because I was too wiped out to do much else, I lay on the bed we'd shared and pulled the coverlet over me. I would go after him, but first I had to marshal enough magic to travel farther than Scourie township.

Thoughts crowded, most of them bleak, until I lectured myself about believing in him. After that, I visualized Liam succeeding, finding a way out of the chasm. He'd been valiant; surely that should earn him consideration from whichever gods were in charge of who triumphed and who ended up in the *Dreaming* forever.

Realization seared me just before I passed out. The *Dreaming* would have the answers I sought. If Liam was no more, his spirit would be in the *Dreaming*. I'd never been there by myself, but Cathbad would show me the way. I was certain of it. First, though, I'd try to get there under my own steam.

~

I JOLTED AWAKE, unsure how long I'd slept, but it didn't matter. I felt groggy, fuzzy headed, not rested at all. Liam hadn't returned. He'd have stopped by his chamber if he had. Power pulsed within me, maybe half-recovered. Ha. I was dreaming. Maybe a third or a quarter of what it should be. I used a tiny bit to scan the castle. Everyone was still in the great room. Maybe they'd laid down to rest, but more likely they were still celebrating, passing mead around and recounting tales of the last day and our conquests.

Everyone's impressions were bound to be a bit different. It was why sharing perceptions was so important.

I tossed the coverlet aside and shivered as the chill of the room settled around me. I'd slept in all my clothes, so it wasn't as if I had an extra jacket to layer over myself. An ewer and basin sat on a stand in the corner. I got my feet under me and walked to them so I could sluice room-temperature water over my face.

As I cleaned grime from my hands and face, I thought about how worried I'd been about *Carrick Sky Sports* and inhaled deep to forestall another bout of crying. I'd been stupid, focused on all the wrong elements. Nothing meant anything without Liam, but I'd have to find a way to keep going.

I fisted a hand and brought it down on the stand. The ewer and basin clattered against each other. Pain sliced through me, sharp as any knife. This was why I'd avoided entanglements with mortals: so I wouldn't have to stand by and watch them die while a piece of me perished with them.

Feeling very sorry for yourself, aren't you? an inner voice snarked.

I stared at my haggard face in the small mirror bolted to the wall. Huge black patches rode beneath my eyes. My hair was an unholy mass of tangles, but the worst was the hopelessness in my eyes.

I gave myself a brisk mental slap, followed by several more.

I didn't know he was gone for certain.

Not yet.

And it wasn't like me to give up.

My clothing carried the ozone-and-sulfur stench of the dark gods, seasoned with Vampire rot. I didn't care. Fresh garments were low on my list.

I picked up my scythe. The blade brightened in anticipation. It had soaked up the feel of the *Dreaming* and must have intuited where we were going. Liam believed I could enter the Sidhe realm on my own. No time like the present to test his theory. My sickle clearly believed it was up for the task.

Clinging to my Reaper tool, I visualized the *Dreaming* and set a teleport spell in motion. The Sidhe sort of waltzed into their alter-realm, but I'd have to travel another way. I was certain Cathbad was upstairs, celebrating with the others, but I didn't want to bother him unless I had to.

I'd run up against compassion and sorrow in Hades' blue-eyed gaze. I couldn't stand too much more of that. He'd encouraged me, but he hadn't been effusive about it. Maybe he didn't truly believe Liam would escape the pit.

Or perhaps he did, and I'd turned into a seething mess of negativity.

With strict instructions to pull my head out of my ass, I returned my full attention to my teleport endeavor. The *Dreaming* obligingly formed around me. So far, so good.

I traversed a cunning path set between ancient tree boles

until I came to a clearing. While I walked, the *Dreaming* wove its particular brand of magic, soothing my worries and replenishing my magic.

I hadn't anticipated that benefit, but I welcomed it.

I settled on a flat rock in the meadow; small white flowers dotted tufts of grass. Balmy breezes wafted around me. I sent power swirling outward, seeking Liam, but didn't find him. Next, I called him, using his full name both out loud and telepathically.

"Liam Warwick is not here," ricocheted back at me.

"Not here. Not here. Not here," echoed from tree to tree.

The third time I heard the *Dreaming's* reassurance, I got to my feet. If Liam wasn't here, it meant he was still alive. Maybe in the pit, but I needed an attitude adjustment.

The pit was the last place I should be thinking about.

No one was going to come striding out of the forest to meet me, as had happened my other trips here. It might be only Sidhe who merited that level of personal service.

I gathered my thoughts. Liam wasn't in Scourie Castle, and he wasn't here. Had he gone to Seattle, hunting me? Much like when I fly airplanes, I plotted out my next moves. I'd return to Scourie. Then I'd go to Malin. If he wasn't either place, I'd teleport to Seattle. It would give me a chance to make certain Kiko was all right.

Carrick Sky Sports was probably deader than dead, but at this point I didn't care. I would, eventually, but I had to find Liam. I wouldn't rest until I did.

A travel spell jolted me back to Liam's chamber at Scourie. My magic had mostly recovered, thanks to the *Dreaming.* The scythe pulsed, turning golden and clearly pleased with itself for opening the *Dreaming's* gates. I patted it and sent power arcing around me, searching castle and grounds.

No Liam.

I pondered letting someone know where I was heading but decided against it. I've always worked better alone.

Until Liam came into my life.

He'd changed a whole lot of things. With a start, I understood I'd changed too. For the first time, I'd opened myself, my hidden places, to someone else. And trusted them with my tender spots.

Before I started crying again—no reason to mourn, not yet— I strung my bag over a shoulder, tightened my grip on my scythe, and summoned a journey spell to Malin.

My castings lack the precision of Liam's, and I came out in the cobblestone alley in front of his flat. The door was locked, but I urged the deadbolt to yield with a shot of magic. The moment I walked inside, the feel of him surrounded me, far more potent that just vestiges of his magic.

I'd been a fool to doubt him. Worse than a fool.

Leaving the door hanging open, I bounded within and saw him lying face down on the living room floor.

My throat thickened, breath clotting around a huge lump that sat dead center. I tossed my scythe and shoulder bag onto a sofa and made a dive for him, cradling him in my arms. "You got out. Oh my fucking god, you got out," I said before I started to sob.

He twisted in my arms, hazel eyes flicking open as he regarded me. "Of course, I got out. How could I not? You were waiting for me."

Crying in earnest, I couldn't manage words. He tucked my head into the hollow between his neck and shoulder and crooned to me in Gaelic until the emotions buffeting me subsided.

"How?" I croaked.

He made a shrugging movement. "Luck married with determination goes quite a way. I tried to get the Dreaming to open to me. Instead, I ended up in the void between Earth and the corridors spanning it. Once I realized where I was, I teleported to the place that took the least expenditure of power. Turned out to be here." He paused long enough to take a breath. "I'd have let you know, but I didn't have enough magic left for telepathy. Or anything else."

"I was at Scourie," I told him. "Everyone is rejoicing."

"As well they should." His rich baritone rumbled near my ear. "Today—or maybe yesterday now—worked out far better than our wildest predictions."

Familiar energy washed over me, and I looked up in time to see Cerebrus—right before he jumped on Liam and me, whuffing and licking us enthusiastically. Hades was right behind him. "Do you always leave the door open?"

"Only on special occasions," I replied.

Hades squatted next to Liam, me, and the dog. "Everyone is worried—about both of you. I was elected to hunt you down."

Interesting. I'd read him all wrong when I'd assumed he'd written Liam off. My own fear and insecurity got in the way, tripping me up.

The dog rolled off us and sat next to Hades. All three heads sported smiles.

"We need to return with you," Liam said. "If it weren't for Cait, I'd still be asleep. Never meant to pass out like that, but—"

"Never apologize for success," Hades spoke over him.

I slithered to a sit and glanced down at myself. Hades intercepted my appraisal; a wave of magic washed first over me and then over Liam. We weren't any cleaner, but we no longer reeked of Vampire or the dark mages.

"Do you have an automatic wash cycle?" I joked.

"Be grateful for what I did, wench." Hades cracked a very rare smile.

I grinned back.

Liam pushed to a sit and then to an unsteady stand, rocking lightly on his feet. "Damn it. I feel like I went ten rounds with a dragon." His mouth rounded into an O. "The pit. Did you get it shut?"

Hades nodded. "We were winning the day, but Cathbad sang it closed. I swear, that bard has quite the unexpected repertoire of tricks at his disposal."

Liam shook himself. "I'm not thinking. Cait already said everyone was celebrating. No one would have left Nevada if the chasm wasn't well and truly secured. And the other group? The one that went to North Africa?"

"Their travails were far less earth-shattering than ours, probably because Cathbad began there. His assistance with the music lured hundreds of Vampires."

"No mortals?" Liam raised a blond brow.

"No mortals, and no dark mages. Five out of six will have to do. Majestron Zelia won't bother anyone all by herself."

"Hope you're right about that," Liam murmured.

Shame bubbled from my guts. I'd assumed they closed the pit, given everyone's jovial mood at Scourie, but I hadn't cared enough to mine for details about that, or about Africa. Everything within me had been focused on Liam.

Hades dropped a hand on my shoulder. "'Tis understandable, lass. You love him."

"We love each other," Liam corrected the god of the dead.

His words ran through me in a slow, sweet tide bound up with everything right and good in the world.

Twisting from beneath Hades' hand, I gripped it and let him haul me upright. I shut the front door and locked it before picking up my scythe and bag. Once I was ready, Hades swept us into a quick transport spell that dropped us into the midst of ongoing festivities at Scourie Castle.

Cheers and whoops rose once everyone realized Liam was among them again. I stood by his side while toasts ran around the room. Sidhe and Reaper alike came close, sharing some special story or memory. Everyone was tipsy from mead and victory.

Their elation was contagious. We'd earned this, goddammit. Every last bit of it.

Stacia hugged me and whispered in my ear, "About that wedding...?"

Any hesitation about spending forever with Liam had dropped away when I stood on the other side of the barrier. The one that held me in the realm of the dead and refused him entry.

I whispered back, "Soon," and meant it.

I DON'T EXACTLY REMEMBER how we got to Seattle—between the mead and a surfeit of good wishes, I fell asleep as soon as we left the castle great room—but we obviously teleported. Liam must have set a spell in motion because it certainly wasn't mine. We woke in my bed, rocking to the gentle motion of water beneath the houseboat's hull.

I'd missed that sensation. The floaty feeling from water beneath me. Geez, I'd missed a whole lot of things: flying, a normal schedule, a life where I wasn't constantly fighting or on the run.

"Finally awake, Sleeping Beauty?" Liam teased.

I turned in his arms. "Been up for a while, have you?"

"Not so long as all that. I was enjoying looking at you."

"I'm glad because I could look at you forever." I stroked hair away from his cheeks and forehead, relishing in the feel of his skin and the way it stretched over the striking bones of his face.

"What would you like to do first?" he asked. A husky, teasing note in his voice left little doubt about his priorities.

"And my choices are?"

"Shower. Breakfast—or actually dinner, given 'tis evening. Lovemaking. Not in any particular order, and just because we select one doesn't mean we can't do it again."

I kissed his forehead and both cheeks before sliding out of bed, surprised to be mostly naked. "You undressed me."

"And me. Any complaints? Despite Hades' effort to make us more presentable, everything needs washing. Didn't want to add your sheets to the list."

A smile began in my heart before making it to my mouth. "No complaints. Not now, or ever. I need to check on Kiko, and then you'll have my undivided attention."

I located my bag and extracted my phone, not surprised to find it dead. I plugged it into a charger to solve that problem and texted Kiko.

All good?

Her response was instant. *Better than good. Are you back?*

Well, was I?

We're here, but we've been through a lot. Your problem is solved. No more watching over your shoulder. How about if I call you in a day or two?

Perfect. Let's go flying.

I laughed. It was so like Kiko, but like me too. *Yes. Let's.*

Dropping the phone on my desk, I shed my panties, took a two-minute shower, and sashayed back into the bedroom, wrapped in a towel.

"How is she?" Liam asked.

"She's fine." Before I fell into his arms, I sat on the edge of the bed. "Is this truly over?"

"If by *this*, you mean Vampires dropping out of your ceiling, I believe the answer is aye. I also trust Humans Rule will wither and eventually die out." He drew his brows together.

"What?" I prodded.

"Evil isn't gone. We vanquished the most recent display, but something will rise up to take its place. Another group of humans who view us as anathema will form at some point. Also, you haven't seen the last of Death. None of the Reapers have, but we can't overplay that hand. She might have had a change of heart and resurface with a whole new attitude."

"Ha! You don't know her as well as I do."

"Being alone changes a person. Let's not count her out until she shows her screaming Harpy persona again."

"That's fair." I nodded.

He folded a hand around mine. "So long as we're talking and not engaged in...other pursuits, say you'll marry me, Cait. 'Twould make me very happy. You'd never want for aught."

My heart did its special little flip-flop; breath caught in my throat. Words burst from me as if they'd been waiting in the wings for just this opportunity. "I don't care about what you can do for me or buy for me. Even if you were poor as a church mouse, my answer would still be yes."

His eyes widened. Clearly, he'd been expecting me to sidestep his offer like I had before. He smiled, the million-watt version that made him movie star gorgeous. "Whoa! No hesitation at all. Fearing I was dead must have had quite the impact. I'll have to remember that."

"For what?"

"Och, the next lassie I want to take to wife."

He started to laugh, and I laughed with him. It felt so good to just be with him, enjoying one another's company and joking back and forth.

"Do you want a big wedding?" I asked, curious what he'd say.

"Aye, well 'twill have to be big enough for all the Sidhe and all the Reapers, with perhaps a few others, like maybe your friend Kiko."

I let go of my towel and lay down next to him. "Can we elope?"

He wrapped his arms around me. The feel of his skin sliding against my body was exquisite. "Nay. That's more a mortal invention for couples running away from disapproving relatives. Too many of our friends will wish to be part of our nuptials for us to run off. Besides, Krin and Dena will want to officiate. Sidhe weddings are elaborate affairs."

I smiled. "If it makes you happy, an extravaganza is fine with me."

"Truly?" He tipped my chin, and I felt the light touch of his magic caressing my mind.

"Truly. We're only doing this once, and it has to be for both of us."

"I wondered if you were aware of that part," he murmured.

"Which part?"

"You said we'd only be doing this once, and 'tis abundantly true. We will share blood as we pledge ourselves, one to the other."

Understanding filled me. Blood bonds were permanent. "No divorce, eh?"

"Nay. None. Are you still willing?"

The old me would have run screaming for the hills. The new me couldn't wait for the ritual that would bind Liam and me together.

"Can't scare me off that easily." I snuggled close, welcoming the insistent press of his mouth as he closed it over mine. We had eons ahead of us, millennia.

And we'd make every single day count.

Three Months Later
I sat in the right seat of the Cessna 152 trainer, offering occasional corrections and liberal praise. I'd picked up the reins of *Carrick Sky Sports* six weeks back. My schedule wasn't full—yet—but it was moving in that direction.

"Another couple of hours, and you'll be ready to take her up by yourself," I told Lisa Greenstone, a student who'd narrowly avoided running into Vampires a few months back.

She flashed a smile my way. "Do you really think so?"

"Absolutely. Shall we plan on it week after next?"

Lisa nodded. "I'd like that."

"Me too. Best compliment of all is when my students fly on their own. You can log your solo hours, and then you'll be ready to do your cross-country and get your license."

"To say I'm thrilled is an understatement." Her smile broadened.

I grinned back. "One more touch and go, and we'll wrap up today."

Half an hour later, I walked her to her car and bid her goodbye. I had a couple of hours of downtime. Maybe I'd use them to get my perpetually sloppy bookkeeping up to date.

When I'd fussed about Liam paying for things, he'd simply added himself to my bank accounts—via magical sleight-of-hand—and chucked cash into them. At first, I'd made a point of building a ledger to keep track of what was his and what was mine. I still kept it up, but not as religiously.

Liam and I had been married two months ago in a ceremony that still brought tears of joy when I thought about it. Somehow, the Sidhe had come up with a bower overflowing with blossoms—a neat trick in February in Scotland—and we'd been surrounded by Reapers and Sidhe and the Scourie villagers. Kiko had flown over, and she and Stacia were my maids of honor.

Cerebrus had been our ringbearer, padding down the aisle after us carrying two baskets, one with my ring and one with Liam's. Because I was thinking about it, I glanced at the star sapphire surrounded by rubies and emeralds set in white gold. Twin to Liam's ring, it was gorgeous and elaborate, crafted by painstaking workmanship that had gone out of fashion long ago. He'd told me the rings had been in his family for eons moldering in a vault in Malin.

Speaking of Malin, the Sidhe were in negotiations with Malin's town council to finesse returning there. The current plan was to leave a rotating skeleton crew at Scourie to keep it from sinking further into ruin.

I hadn't caught a whiff of a Vampire since Nevada.

The cavalcade of shades clamoring for passage had slowed

somewhat as well. Reapers working independently turned out to be just as efficient as when Death was ordering us about.

I still stood next to where Lisa had been parked, leaning against my beat-up SUV. For now, Liam and I were living in Seattle. Our eventual plan was to spend three weeks of every month here and one in Ireland, once the details of the Sidhes' return to Malin were hashed out.

For the moment, Liam was in Scotland. He'd left this morning, and I missed him already. I swallowed a snort. Guess I'd only been wedded to my independence because I hadn't found the right person to share my life with. I rolled my shoulders back and breathed deep. The day was clear, crisp, and chilly, but held a touch of spring.

I resisted an urge to trot back into the hangar and take a plane up, just to feel the rush of wind beneath its wings. My next student would be along in a short while, and it would be soon enough. I might not be destitute any longer, but squandering money would never be part of who I was.

Yeah, I'd gone on plenty of indulgence flights, but today I needed to work. My scythe hummed softly where it was draped across my shoulder blades. The magical accoutrement had followed me into the plane—and everywhere else. Luckily, it had the good sense to only show itself to those who wouldn't fall back a few steps, recoiling in horror at visible proof of what I am.

I patted it. It hummed louder. Cathbad's song knocked around inside me, enticing and seductive. His music was a great addition to my magical base. Dena was still working on how to incorporate linkage to allow the younger Reapers access to his inadvertent gift.

A happy, trilling bark brought my head whipping around in

time to see Cerebrus loping toward me. I ran to him and bent to wrap my arms around his three thick necks. After many effusive licks, he shook me off him and led the way inside the Quonset hut.

I fully expected Hades to be there.

What I hadn't anticipated was Death standing by his side.

Hades wore battle-scared leather trousers, metal-toed boots, and a long black tunic embroidered in green and gold. His silver hair was gathered in its usual queue with a leather thong. Death had retreated to a simple black robe, sashed in blue. Her scythe—black today—was balanced across her shoulder blades. The robe was hooded, and it hid her long hair. The same imagery I remembered rolled across her eyes, scenes of the dead and dying, replaying in perpetuity. Her high-heeled boots peeked from beneath the hem of her robe.

I narrowed my eyes, aware my heartrate had escalated, along with my breathing. I hadn't forgotten our last exchange when she tried to kill me for the second time.

My sickle jumped from my shoulders to my hand, ready for anything. I glanced warily from Death to Hades and back again. Oblivious to the waves of tension thrumming through my office, the dog sat next to me, body pressing against my leg. His presence was warm, comforting. I transferred my scythe to my other hand and buried my fingers in his rough black fur.

No one said anything for so long, I finally got tired of waiting. "Um, my next client will be here soon. What do you want?"

Death quirked a silver brow. "What? No how are you? Or how have you been?"

I'd clamped my teeth together after my last question. I loosened my jaw muscles long enough to say, "Last time I saw you, you dragged me to the Arctic—and tried to kill me. We don't have much to say to one another."

Hades nudged her. Death turned an annoyed expression on him. "I told you this was a waste of everyone's time."

"For once, we agree on something," I mumbled and half-turned toward my desk. "If it's all the same to you, I have work to do. Happy to babysit the dog, though."

"He likes you," Hades noted.

"I like him too." Reluctantly, I gave up on sitting in my chair and ignoring them. "Why are you here?"

"Not much better than 'what do you want?'" Death noted in her patronizing voice. The one that used to make me want to strangle her.

I set the scythe down and folded my arms beneath my breasts. "This is my office. I didn't invite you. If you don't care for my hospitality—or lack thereof—the door is that way." I jerked my chin at it.

"I heard you married the Sidhe," Death said.

My eyes widened. "Surely, you didn't make a special trip here to tell me something I already know."

"Go on," Hades urged in a far gentler voice than I'd have believed him capable of.

Death nodded once and dug into a pocket of her robe, extracting a small, wooden box. Striding forward, she placed it on my desk and then returned to her place next to Hades.

I looked from her to Hades. "What is it?"

"She wanted to give you a wedding gift," Hades said when Death appeared incapable of speech.

Breath whistled from me. "Thanks for the thought, but I don't need anything." I took another breath and blew it out. "In particular, I don't want anything from you. I don't trust you, and it would be very like you to give me something you'd use as a spying tool to keep tabs on me. Either take it with you, or I'll have Liam get rid of it with Sidhe magic."

"I told you—" Death began.

"For the love of Danu," Hades thundered, any pretense of gentleness long gone. "The two of you are impossible." He squared off in front of Death. "You owe her an apology. A big one. Why would she trust aught to come from you."

He turned to me. "And you owe her a few moments to listen."

Hot words formed in my throat, but I didn't utter them. From where I sat, I owed her nothing, but for his sake, I'd be polite.

Death took a wooden step toward me, and then one more. I was about to tell her she was close enough when she focused on me. "Our last interaction went badly. I am sorry for my part in it."

Shock punched me in the guts. Death wasn't the apologizing type. She stared at me, an expectant look on her face. I suppose I should have offered an apology twin to her own, except she'd been the aggressor, and I'd been fighting for my life.

"All right," I said. She had an ulterior motive. I had yet to figure out what it was.

She cleared her throat. "The music."

"Yeah. What about it?"

"I know why some of you can wield it."

I resisted rolling my eyes. "Dena does too. She's working on it."

Hades elbowed Death as if to remind her of something

they'd hatched up before dropping in on me. "I could help her. It would speed things along."

"She's in Scotland."

"I know where she is," Death retorted.

Unfolding my arms, I pinched the bridge of my nose between a thumb and forefinger before dropping my hand to my side. "Then go to Scotland and offer assistance. If you take too long, Dena won't require your help."

Being subtle and dancing around the point weren't getting us anywhere.

"Things have changed," I went on. "A lot. You've done many things to make us hate you. If you want back into our good graces, you have a whole lot of backpedaling to do."

"If things changed, it's because of you," she said.

"That's fair, but we can't go back." I reached deep, wondering how the other Reapers would react to my offer, before I said, "If everyone agrees, we could include you as part of our newly-formed Reaper council. No guarantees, but I'll float the idea."

"Generous of you," Hades boomed, approval laced into his words.

"Part of the council?" Death echoed.

I nodded. "Yeah. Part of it. The council is made up of us all with half a dozen designated representatives. We're self-governing, and we plan to alternate our delegates annually." I hurried on, wanting to make certain she understood nothing was a done deal. "We will vote," I told her.

"Should I be there?"

I shook my head. "I will find you with the results." The wooden box caught my eye. "Um, about the gift—"

"Before you discard it out of hand, open it," Hades ordered.

He wouldn't have told me to do so if the item held malevolent intent toward me. Still, I had to ask, "Do you know what it is?"

After he nodded, I covered the distance between me and the desk and flicked the cover off the box with my index finger. My lack of trust had to be apparent, but being burned has that effect.

Cerebrus woofed softly. He'd walked to the desk with me. Together we stared at a jeweled pendant. The center stone was a clear, soft red and as large as my thumbnail. Pearls and sapphires surrounded it, and a silvery chain ran through a loop at the top.

"It's beautiful," I said, turning to face Death. "But I don't understand. Why would you almost kill me, and then give me a gift worth a queen's ransom?"

Her guarded look dropped away, and a corner of her mouth twisted into a wry expression. "My temper has never been very...controllable. You of all people should know that. The pendant was given to me long ago by Danu as a symbol of my office—"

"Then I can't take it," I cut in. "Reapers are self-governing now, and—"

"You never did listen well, child," she spoke over me. "The rest of what I was about to say was she and I had a long discussion. She understands Reaping has changed, and she charged me with delivering the pendant to you. Not so you could set yourself up to be another me, but as thanks for ensuring the continuation of a needed service to mortals.

"The talisman holds compassionate magic. No surreptitious tracking devices. Have that Sidhe of yours test it, if you don't trust me."

"I wouldn't have allowed her to gift you with aught that might damage you," Hades said. Cerebrus whuffed and nuzzled my hand.

I smothered a whole bunch of words about why the hell should I trust her. Clinging to anger was a dead-end street. Instead, I said, "Thank you. Your good wishes are appreciated."

"We shall take our leave," Death said.

"I'll let you know what the Reapers say about adding you to our council."

Death nodded my way. Magic shimmered around her, and Cerebrus padded to Hades' side. Before she teleported out of my office, she said, "I hope you and I can find a way to start over. I've missed you."

I struggled to come up with something, anything, that didn't sound like, "No way in hell," but she, Hades, and the dog were gone. Streamers of their magic fluttered to the ground, dissipating once they hit the wooden floor.

My chest hurt, my throat was tight, and my eyes burned with unshed tears. I walked to the pendant and prodded it with magic. Nothing jumped out at me. The gems held power, but nothing that smacked of a tracking spell. I held the talisman in my hand; it pulsed warmly.

I read many things in its mix of jewels, ancient power woven into the realm of the dead. Convinced it wouldn't hurt me, I opened the clasp and latched it around my neck.

Death was right about me knowing her. Today had cost her —a lot. But she'd come to me, anyway. Not because Danu made her, or because Hades had insisted. She was more than capable of saying no to both of them. She'd made an effort because she was hoping for a fresh beginning with me and the other Reapers.

I didn't have to dig too deep to understand I'd been devastated by what felt like a betrayal, and that I'd missed her too. My cheeks were wet, and I brushed tears away. Nothing was permanent. She and I could begin anew. It wasn't as if I was without fault. I'd cast the first stone. I'd been who told her to fuck off and walked out of her life.

I'd had no idea the other Reapers would chug after me.

Feeling more at peace than I'd been in a long time, I settled in at my desk and brought my computer out of sleep mode. My two-hour window had shrunk to half that, but I'd make good use of the time to dive into my neglected spreadsheets.

As I worked, I vowed to do my part to resurrect my relationship with Death. I'd meet her halfway, more than halfway. If I trusted her to do the same, she wouldn't disappoint me.

You've reached the end of *Untamed Reaper*, and the Gatekeeper series. I do hope you've enjoyed it. Thanks so much for reading through to the end. Please take a moment to leave a review. They mean so much to authors, and it helps other readers to know what you enjoyed about a book.
There may be a fourth Gatekeeper book. I'm considering a spinoff featuring Padhraic and Stacia. Let me know if you'd be intrigued by their story.
If you fell headlong into this series, you might enjoy my Elemental Witch books. A sample from *Timespell* follows.

A druid's determination…A witch's stormy rite of passage…

Katerina eats, sleeps, and breathes cultural anthropology. The only stain on her success is her worry she'll go mad just like a few other women in her family. That fear rockets to the fore when she's on a lecture tour in the Scottish Highlands and hallucinations grab her, visions rife with horrors straight out of medieval folklore.

Arlen, Arch Druid for all of Great Britain, hasn't called on his magic much in the past hundred years. No need for it in the midst of the twenty-first century. While attending a lecture, he detects fell forces. A closer look reveals the impossible. He'd thought the Roskelly witches long dead. Brutal, feral, violent, they were the force behind Scotland's bloodiest clan wars. Risen from their crypts, they're intent on Katerina. What he can't figure out is why.

Finally! A challenge for his long-neglected powers. Far from being grateful, though, Katerina doesn't trust him. Why should she? A headlong dash to escape his unwanted attention lands her three hundred years in the past with no way out.

TIMESPELL, CHAPTER ONE

Applause swelled around Katerina Roskelly, and she nodded pleasantly at the well-dressed crowd filling the auditorium to standing-room-only capacity. Her presentation on the early history of the clans had been well received, but it didn't surprise her. She was definitely in the right spot for tonight's lecture since Inverness had been a recognized epicenter for clan activity for hundreds of years.

Northern Scotland was cold and damp in the middle of December, and the days painfully short. She'd almost passed on the invitation to guest lecture at the University of Stirling, but the institution's first-rate reputation overshadowed her misgivings. A relatively new school, particularly by U.K. standards, the university's unique approach and creative, mixed degree programs had achieved staunch recognition.

Those in the front rows surged to their feet amid cries of, "Brilliant" and "Brava." Kat continued to smile and felt her face heat from the crowd's unexpected enthusiasm. She'd devoted her academic life to mapping the Scottish clans that had emerged from the dawn of the Christian era onward. Despite many clans claiming linkages to mythological gods, their appearance and subsequent growth actually had far more to do with political turmoil than divine dispensation. She'd cut her teeth on fieldwork in Scotland's Highlands and islands, and something about the misty lands got into her blood.

She may have waffled about Stirling's invitation, but the pull of the Highlands was tough to deny. She could almost believe in magic here. Almost. Her face warmed still more, and she thanked God no one could read her mind. She was being foolish romanticizing magic, no doubt a byproduct of fifteen hours in the air and very little sleep.

The clapping died down.

"Dr. Roskelly, if ye'd indulge me," a clipped male voice with a strong Scottish brogue rang from the back of the room.

She peered into the dimly lit recesses of the tastefully decorated auditorium, but she'd be damned if she could identify the speaker. The architect had captured an old-time flavor in the modern structure, and it felt soothing. "I haven't officially kicked off my Q&A session," she replied, "so if you have a question, please hold onto it." She unhooked the portable mike from its stand and walked down two steps to the auditorium floor.

"Thanks so much for coming, everyone. This next segment is only for faculty and graduate students in cultural anthropology. I'll take a brief break and see you in a few moments."

A collective groan surged around the room, but she ignored it and turned away. Setting the microphone on a table, she slipped out a side door. The crowd could sort themselves out.

Hopefully, when she returned their numbers would have shrunk to twenty or so, rather than the two hundred packed into a room meant for half that number. A restroom was down a short hallway, and she headed toward it.

She'd agreed to a two-hour lecture, followed by an hour Q&A segment. Then she could catch a cab to her hotel. She had a couple of days to roam about before her return flight. Good thing. Maybe it was jet lag, but she didn't feel quite right. A vague headache throbbed behind one eye. No longer smooth or pliable, her muscles felt like unwieldy rocks. Kat located the ladies' room and pushed the door open. It was a single-stall affair, so she locked the door and strode to the sink intent on splashing cold water on her face.

Maybe it would perk her up a little. Cut through the foggy mess that used to be her brain.

A glance in the mirror startled her. Shit! Not only did she feel tired, she looked haggard as hell. Always too thin, her face had developed gaunt edges, and her blue-green eyes appeared decidedly haunted, with smudges beneath them. The mirror's surface first wavered and then clouded, almost as if it had developed a 3-D aspect.

Crap on a cracker. What the unholy fuck was happening?

She jumped back, heart pounding, but the glass grew murkier still, with silver-and-red tones skipping about like streamers in a brisk wind. Kat dipped her head into a hand and rubbed her eyes, trying not to disturb her eye makeup. When she forced herself to stare into the mirror, only her tired face stared back.

No clouds.

No streamers.

No colors.

Not hallucinating was an improvement, but where was her sense of desolation coming from? The feeling something huge and menacing lay in wait for her was almost overwhelming.

A shiver was followed by a shudder. Something with sharp, insistent claws dragged itself up her back, deepening her anxiety.

"Stop it. Right this minute," she hissed at her reflection. The sound of her voice had a stabilizing effect, but the pinpricks up and down her spine didn't abate.

Resolute, she flipped on the cold tap and bent to cup water in her hands. After a few brisk splashes with water chilly enough to steal her breath, she yanked a paper towel from the dispenser. A few blots soaked up most of the water. Her mascara had run—big surprise—and it made the circles beneath her eyes that much worse.

This time, she turned on the hot water, waiting through what felt like forever before it warmed enough to dab under her eyes in an attempt to repair the damage. Her heart still beat too fast; tension thrummed through her, turning her stomach into a knot and her throat into a desert. Thoughts—impossible ones about portals and gateways and other worlds that couldn't possibly exist—clamored for ascendency. They wanted out, but she forced them back to the subterranean hidey hole where she relegated everything that didn't match up with reality.

She squared her shoulders. It made the weirdness in her back recede, so she stood straighter still.

A very old fear gripped her. One she thought she'd moved past.

Her great-great grandmother had been some kind of self-proclaimed witch. Or shaman. From family reports, her "magic" had edged toward the darker side of things with blood sacrifices and summoning spirits and suchlike. Everyone knew there was no such thing as magic or witches, so Grannie Rhea had to have been mentally ill. Probably schizophrenic, or maybe bipolar. Back in her day, no one labeled such things—at least not with any precision.

Mental illness was genetic, though, and Kat had been waiting to lose her mind forever. Turning thirty had felt like a gift since she'd passed the dangerous years, the ones where all the major mental disorders reared their head. With each subsequent year, she'd breathed a little easier. When she'd hit thirty-five last autumn, she truly believed she'd escaped a speeding bullet and was out of the proverbial woods.

A quick, pointed glance in the mirror revealed nothing but reflective glass. She must have imagined it morphing into a vortex, hungry to suck her into its whirling center.

Must have. No other explanation. Not really.

Rhea had been odd, and long-lived. Kat remembered the old woman leaning over her cradle and playing with her when she was a toddler. She'd been maybe ten when her great-great-grandmother died, but the woman's penetrating blue-green eyes—orbs the same color as her own—and long, thick silver hair lived on in her memory—

A sharp knock on the bathroom door jarred her. She wadded the paper towels into a sodden heap and chucked them into a waste bin.

"Doctor, are you quite well?" a man's voice inquired. It might be the same fellow who'd spoken her name at the tail end of her talk. "I can dredge up one of the women if you're in need of assistance."

Kat inhaled sharply, blew it out, and turned toward the door. Opening it, she offered the best smile she could muster.

"Appreciate your concern, but I'm just tired. Jet lag is a bitch."

The man was tall and broad-shouldered. She pegged him somewhere in his mid-forties. Straight, dark hair fell to his shoulders, framing an arresting face with defined bone structure and a strong, square jaw. A tan corduroy jacket was layered over a black shirt. Black jeans hugged his long legs, and he wore a pair of scuffed black boots. The only thing missing to complete the portrait of an academic was a pipe.

He was attractive in a geeky kind of way, the type of man she'd have maybe wanted to get to know if she had time for anything beyond teaching and research. She'd been waiting to catch a break in her schedule for years, but publish or perish was real, and she'd just gotten tenure.

No rest for the weary.

Her mind was wandering, badly; she shook head a couple of times to regain the razor-edged focus that had earned her the respect of her peers.

The man creased his forehead into a welter of concerned lines. "If you're knackered, we could skip the next part." He kept his dark eyes focused on her face. Even though he was clearly trying to project solicitousness, something else, something extra, gleamed in the depths of those eyes. His intense scrutiny sent another chill down her back.

He had her grandmother's eyes. Not the color, but the look, and the same way of stripping you bare until you got a good case of the creepy-crawlies and ran for cover.

I'm being ridiculous. Nothing a decent night's sleep won't set to rights.

Her shoulders had slumped again. Kat rolled them back, taking advantage of her height that allowed her to see almost eye-to-eye with him. "I'm sure I'm good for another hour without pitching facedown into my soup."

The corners of his mouth twitched, and he quirked a brow. "An American expression, I presume? Come on then, Doctor. I'll see you safe to your hotel once we're done here."

Alarm bells tolled, and she drew back. "It won't be necessary, Dr.—" she quested about for his name. They'd been introduced, but she'd be damned if she could locate the synapses in her addled brain where the information was stored.

"MacGregor," he inserted with a slight incline of his head. "Arlen MacGregor at your service. And I wouldn't dream of having you summon a shuttle."

This dim hallway was scarcely the place to get into an argument. She'd deal with transport once this next part of her agreed-upon obligation was done. With a curt smile and a nod, she pushed around him and marched back toward the auditorium.

Someone had turned up the lights, and a couple dozen people sat ranged in the first two rows.

"Sorry I made you wait on me." Kat dragged a chair so it faced the group and settled into it. She spread her hands and said, "I'm all yours. No worries if we don't get to everything. You can reach me at"—she rattled off both email and phone contact information—"and I'm always delighted to entertain questions. I'm open to joint research projects as well."

A youngish woman leaned forward. Her blonde hair was gathered into a queue low on her neck. "Are you feeling quite all right, Dr. Roskelly?"

"Aye," the woman next to blondie chimed in. "You're looking a wee bit pale."

Kat batted irritation aside. Why the hell was everyone so

bloody interested in her health, never mind assuming the worst. "I'm fine." She kept her tone brisk and businesslike. "Just a bit discombobulated from the time change. I've only been here a few hours, probably should have planned to come a day early."

She made come-along motions with both hands. "Questions? Surely you must have some, or you'd not have scheduled me for this Q&A."

"Tell us about the principal differences between the clans claiming Irish roots and those claiming Scottish," a man at the end of the second row asked.

Words flowed from Kat. This was familiar territory, and the hot, tight knot in her chest started to uncoil. The feeling of dread didn't vanish, but it retreated to a spot where she could function. Another hour, and she'd be home free. A nice bath and perhaps some chamomile tea, and she'd sleep whatever this was away in her cozy turn-of-the-century hotel.

Tomorrow will be a brand-new day.

Give it up, Scarlett, she answered herself and smothered a grin. If she didn't watch it, she'd giggle and make a fool of herself in front of all these intense academic types.

NINETY MINUTES LATER, she shooed everyone out of the amphitheater. They'd asked a lot of thorny questions that fed right into her research, so apparently they'd taken the time to educate themselves about her work. It pleased her. A quick glance at her phone showed it was closing on eleven at night, which meant it was nine in the morning back home in California.

No wonder she felt like warmed-over dogmeat. She stood

and stuffed lecture materials into her briefcase. The same sense of disconnection that had assailed her in the bathroom was back in force, and a wave of dizziness swamped her. The room swam in and out of focus; she bit down hard on her lower lip. A few more minutes and she'd be in the back of a cab.

Walk, she commanded herself. For emphasis, she said it again.

Walk.

Determination could have been her middle name. Telling herself she wasn't dizzy, no, not at all, she snatched up her briefcase and shoulder bag, put one foot in front of the other, and crossed the auditorium to the main door. The presumptuous man was nowhere in sight. As she thought about it, he hadn't been there for the second part of her presentation, either.

Good. Last thing she needed was the unctuous Scot hassling her.

Be fair. Maybe he was just being courteous. No need to put such a negative spin on things.

Kat was hanging on by her fingernails. She didn't answer herself because she couldn't focus on anything but essential tasks. Pushing through the outside door, she winced as the chill damp of a Scottish December battered her. Rain mixed with snow pelted down. Damn it. She should have called a cab before leaving the building. Turning, she made a grab for the door, but it had locked behind her.

Fishing her phone out, she told Siri to find a local cab company.

A sleek, silver something-or-other pulled to the curb. The driver door opened, and Arlen stepped out. His hair was plastered against his head as if he'd been standing out in the weather, which made no sense at all. "Come on, Doc. I'll see you to the King's Arms."

She waved her phone his way. "No need," she said brightly. "I'm just hunting down a taxi." Cold water ran down her face and neck. She should have worn a more substantial coat, but too late to fix it now.

The pleasant expression on his face shifted to concern; he hurried to where she stood and hooked a hand beneath her arm. "Don't be ridiculous. I'm here. The cab isn't. You'll be soaked to the skin by the time one shows up. We're quite a way off the normal transit routes, and the busses quit running an hour ago."

"I'll be fine," she insisted through teeth beginning to chatter.

He leaned close, latching onto her gaze. "I will not hurt you, lassie. There are fell things afoot this night, but I'm not one of them."

It took a moment before she realized he'd spoken in Gaelic, a language she both read and spoke. His brogue had thickened, deepened, perhaps as a result of shifting to what must be his mother tongue. "W-what do you mean fell things?" Her Gaelic wasn't as smooth as his, but surely he'd understand her.

He shook his head. "'Tisn't a conversation to hold in this spot." He tugged on her arm.

This time, she gave in and let him guide her to his car and tuck her into the passenger side. He slid behind the wheel and nosed the car into the dark, empty street. "We'll be at your hotel in short order."

Adrenaline shot through her. He'd named her hotel before, but she hadn't considered what it might mean. "How do you know where I'm staying?" she gritted out through teeth that wanted to knock against one another.

"I'm part of the faculty at Stirling. All of us were privy to your travel plans. Lass"—he angled a pointed glance across the console at her—"do what you must to settle yourself." He looked as if he wanted to say more, but clacked his jaw shut instead.

Kat adjusted the flow of heat. Questions bounced around in her mind, but anything that came out of her mouth would make her sound deranged. Fell things and wickedness were the purview of folklore. No one with any kind of smarts believed in that shit. Was the MacGregor chap not quite right in his head?

"Part of the faculty?" she mirrored his words, hoping for additional information.

"Aye, I'm assistant dean of the anthropology department, and I've followed your work for years." He hesitated before continuing. "Your persistence and attention to details others ignore have always impressed the hell out of me."

"Thank you." Pleasure at the unexpected compliment helped allay the worst of her fears but didn't explain why he'd place any credence in urban myths depicting evil as something deeper than a philosophical construct.

"My pleasure."

Before she knew it, he'd pulled under the portico of her hotel. The rain-snow mix had worsened, so the overhang was welcome. The doorman leapt forward and opened her door. Kat rearranged the briefcase and shoulder bag she'd held on her lap and got out of the car.

Arlen exited the other side. "See she gets to her room," he told the doorman. "She's a wee bit under the weather."

The doorman nodded. "Of course, Dr. MacGregor. We'll take the best care possible of Dr. Roskelly."

Arlen reached into an inner pocket and slipped something into the doorman's coat. The gesture horrified her, but this wasn't the place to make a stink about him paying off the hotel —a hotel that was making five hundred bucks a night from her as it was—for anything extra.

She settled for, "You shouldn't have done that."

"Oh but I wanted to. Get a decent night's sleep. I'll be by around noon, and we'll go on a city tour."

Her eyes widened, and she struggled with what to say. Maybe he was only being kind, but this relationship was over and done with. She'd had enough of his innuendos about fell creatures to last a lifetime. "Thanks, but I'll be fine on my own. You've done far too much for me as it is."

He touched his wet hair in the same gesture he might have used had he been wearing a top hat. "As the lassie chooses."

Before she could say anything else, he'd disappeared back inside the car.

"This way, miss." The doorman propelled her inside. "We'll get you all settled with a nice duvet and a hot cuppa."

She rode up the elevator with him but shooed him aside when he wanted to accompany her down the hallway to her room. Ever polite and bred to serve, he acquiesced, told her if she needed anything at all to ring the front desk, and vanished down a staircase.

After a fumble with her keycard, the door finally opened. Her bed was turned down with chocolates on the pillow. A steaming kettle sat on the sideboard. When she walked into the bathroom, an equally steaming bath beckoned.

Questions blasted her, but she shut her mind off. It didn't

matter if the wee folk left their hills and barrows to turn her room into an inviting bower. It didn't matter no one could have known when she'd be here to time the tea and the bath to coincide with her arrival.

Nothing mattered beyond sleep. Surely, she'd have a clearer head come morning.

She dropped her clothes on the bathroom's tile floor and sank into the steaming water, but it took a long time before the chill leached from her bones.

Keep right on reading. Click here for additional information.

ABOUT THE AUTHOR

Ann Gimpel is a USA Today bestselling author. A lifelong aficionado of the unusual, she began writing speculative fiction a few years ago. Since then her short fiction has appeared in many webzines and anthologies. Her longer books run the gamut from urban fantasy to paranormal romance. Once upon a time, she nurtured clients. Now she nurtures dark, gritty fantasy stories that push hard against reality. When she's not writing, she's in the backcountry getting down and dirty with her camera. She's published over 75 books to date, with several more planned for 2020 and beyond. A husband, grown children, grandchildren, and wolf hybrids round out her family.

Keep up with her at www.anngimpel.com or http://anngimpel.blogspot.com

If you enjoyed what you read, get in line for special offers and pre-release special reads. Newsletter Signup!

Dragon's Call

Dragon's Blood

Dragon's Heir

Dragon Lore

Highland Secrets

To Love a Highland Dragon

Dragon Maid

Dragon's Dare

Dragon Fury

Earth Reclaimed

Earth's Requiem

Earth's Blood

Earth's Hope

Elemental Witch

Timespell

Time's Curse

Time's Hostage

Gatekeeper (Winter 2019 and spring 2020)

Shadow Reaper

Rebel Reaper

Untamed Reaper

GenTech Rebellion

Winning Glory

Honor Bound

Claiming Charity

Loving Hope

Keeping Faith

Ice Dragon

Feral Ice

Cursed Ice

Primal Ice

Rubicon International

Garen

Lars

Soul Dance

Tarnished Beginnings

Tarnished Legacy

Tarnished Prophecy

Tarnished Journey

Soul Storm

Dark Prophecy

Dark Pursuit

Dark Promise

Underground Heat

Roman's Gold

Wolf Born

Blood Bond

Wolf Clan Shifters

Alice's Alphas

Megan's Mates

Sophie's Shifters

Wylde Magick

Gemstone

Lion's Lair

Unbalanced

STANDALONE BOOKS

Branded, That Old Black Magic Romance (paranormal romance)

Edge of Night (short story collection, paranormal and horror)

Grit is a 4-Letter Word (nonfiction)

Heart's Flame (post-apocalyptic romance)

Icy Passage (science fiction romance)

Marked by Fortune (post-apocalyptic coming of age story)

Melis's Gambit (historical paranormal romance)

Midnight Magic (paranormal romance)

Red Dawn (post-apocalyptic paranormal romance)

Shadow Play (historical paranormal romance)

Shadows in Time (Highland time travel romance)

Since We Fell (contemporary romance)

Warin's War (paranormal romance)